# THE TEMPLA

First published in November 2003
by Quest Books (NI)

2 Slievenabrock Ave. Newcastle Co. Down BT33 OHZ

Typeset and printed by
Cypher Digital Print
Park Road, Milnthorpe, Cumbria LA7 7AD


A CIP catalogue record of this book is available from
The British Library

ISBN 1 872027 12 1


Front cover and maps by Carousel Design

# THE TEMPLAR MANUSCRIPT

## BERT SLADER

*A Novel*

Two stories

- one set in 1960 and the other in 1300 A.D.
- linked by an ancient, family manuscript.

*Best wishes,*

*Bert.*

QUEST BOOKS (NI)

To
My Family for their patience,
help and encouragement


# ACKNOWLEDGEMENTS

Although the characters and tales of The Templar Manuscript are fictional, the locations in France, Spain and the Pyrenees in 1960 are as true to their time as memory and research have enabled me to make them.

In the story set in 1300 A.D. the fall of Acre castle in 1291, and the arrest of the Knights Templar in France on Friday the Thirteenth of October 1307, are events of historical record.

The link between these two stories, set six hundred and fifty years apart, was suggested by the existence of the Slader family tree compiled by a relation, John M.Slader.

In the early part of the 20th century there were about fifty showmen with Dancing Bears in Ariège. In the village if Ercé there was a school for training the montreurs d'ours, the bear showmen. Now the Pyrenean bear is close to extinction, only six or seven exist in the wild. The idea of the Bear Sanctuary was suggested by a visit to the Wolf Sanctuary near Tarascon in Ariège.

I am indebted to my wife, Eileen for her expert proof reading, to my son, Dion, who has the knack of finding books which are a creative influence and my daughter, Jenifer Campbell, whose research, textual editing, advice and encouragement have been an inspiration.

My friend Ed Kilgore M.B.E. may have made his name as a mountain rescuer but my thanks are due to him for his computer rescue skills when I needed them.

# THE AUTHOR

Bert Slader, a former teacher and Deputy Director of the Sports Council for N.Ireland, is now a writer, lecturer and broadcaster.

He has travelled extensively in Europe and Asia, has mountaineered in Arctic Norway, the Alps and the Himalayas, and has led expeditions to the mountains of Iran and the Hindu Kush in Afghanistan. In 1985 he spent five weeks walking alone on the ancient pilgrim route to Santiago de Compostela. Since then he has continued his journey on foot around Spain and Portugal in three further stages, finishing back in the French Pyrenees.

His first book, Pilgrims' Footsteps, inspired a ten-day walk to Santiago to raise funds for the multiple-sclerosis charity, MS Ireland. Since then he has led 16 walks for MS Ireland, 11 to Santiago, and the others on the Great Wall of China, in the Drakensberg Mountains of South Africa and in Goa, India.

The second of his five travel books, Beyond the Black Mountain, was filmed for BBC Television. A BBC Radio series was based on his MS Santiago walks and stories of his travels have been broadcast on BBC Radio and RTE.

He has been awarded a Waterford Crystal Walker Award in respect of his books on walking and his leadership of the worldwide fund raising walks for multiple-sclerosis.

His first novel, Belshade, is set in the Blue Stack Mountains of Donegal, in Lourdes and the Pyrenees, in the late nineteen-forties.

THE IRISH PILGRIM is a sequel to Belshade, set in 1950 in Donegal, Paris, the South of France, the Pyrenees and along the ancient pilgrim Road to Santiago.

# OTHER BOOKS BY THE SAME AUTHOR

## TRAVEL AND AUTOBIOGRAPHY

### Beyond the Black Mountain
A Journey around the Ulster of yesterday

### Across the Rivers of Portugal
A journey on foot the length of Portugal

### Footsteps in the Hindu Kush
Set in the mountains of Afghanistan before the Russian invasion

### An Echo in Another's Mind
Echoes in the mountains of Ireland, England, Arctic Norway and Iran

### Pilgrims' Footsteps Revisited
This new edition replaces the original Pilgrims' Footsteps (no longer available)
and celebrates the annual walks to Santiago de Compostela for the
M S Society of Ireland.

### Pilgrims' Footsteps Tape
Readings from the original Pilgrims' Footsteps

## NOVELS

### Belshade
Bert Slader's first novel, set in the Blue Stack Mountains of Donegal,
in Lourdes and the Pyrenees, in the late nineteen-forties.

### The Irish Pilgrim
A sequel to Belshade, set in 1950 in Donegal, Paris, the South of France,
the Pyrenees and along the ancient pilgrim Road to Santiago.

**The Templar Manuscript** is the third novel of this trilogy, set in France, Spain
and the Pyrenees when Anamar, the girl from Donegal, is ten years older.

QUEST BOOKS (NI)
2 Slievenabrock Ave. Newcastle Co. Down BT33 OHZ
T/N 028 437 23359  Fax 028 437 25774

# CHAPTERS

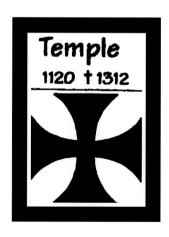

*Two knights sharing one horse -
the Templar symbol of poverty*

# THE PYRENEAN DANCING BEAR

The brown bear lumbered around in small circles. He lifted one huge paw and hopped on a hind leg, all the nobility of uros arctos, the greatest animal of the Pyrenees, long gone. He was dancing to the tune of his master's tin whistle. The crowd cheered in admiration of a man who could make such a massive beast do his bidding. This was the way in Ariège, at the foot of the French Pyrenees, once the foremost centre for bear training in Western Europe, now its last redoubt.

One of the bear's chains was attached to a ring through the muzzle, the other to a neck collar. The muzzle chain was used for tricks, the neck chain to keep him imprisoned. The trainer hauled on one chain and the bear turned around. He pulled the chain again and the bear turned to reverse the circle. The crowd clapped and yelled for more.

There was a roar from the back of the throng and the villagers turned to see their Seigneur, Ramón Barriano Mont L'ours, astride a magnificent black horse. The silver harness jingled, the Spanish saddle gleamed. He was dressed in black, neat jacket and trousers, polished black riding boots and on his head a black broad-brimmed sombrero.

Now he had inherited his mother's family estate in the French Pyrenees it was the only time Don Ramón dressed as a Spanish horseman but it was testimony enough to his early life in Spanish Navarre.

There his Spanish father had taught him to ride. When he was fourteen, he had introduced him to the famous rejoneador, Alvaro de Domenccq y Diez. Don Alvaro was a bull-fighter who fought the bull on horseback. In his quiet, direct way he had explained his training methods to this serious son of his friend - make a friend of the horse - train the horse slowly - never accept a move badly executed - praise as well as correct - teach with a gentle hand on the reins.

His secret was to breed his own horses, half English, one quarter Arab and one quarter Spanish. That would ensure the vital attributes - courage, intelligence and agile speed.

Ramón and his father went to see Don Alvaro perform before the great man left for Mexico for his last bull-fight. When he made the kill, Don

Alvaro dismounted, dropped the reins and walked around the ring. The horse followed him with the reins hanging loose. Each time the rejoneador paused to acknowledge the cheering, the horse stopped beside him, faced the crowd and dropped his head, as if he too appreciated the acclamation.

His father had explained to Ramón that Don Alvaro had made a promise many years before that he would not retire from the bull-ring until he had raised enough money to build and endow a school for boys from poor families, in honour of Saint John Bosco. The school had been built and the visit to Mexico would complete the endowment. Don Alvaro de Domenecq y Diez had kept his promise.

But although Don Alvaro was his boyhood hero, Ramón could never ask him how he could love the one animal so dearly and kill the other so mercilessly.

---

Ramón himself had changed little in the past decade. His hair was a little thinner but he was still the courteous, well-dressed gentleman who had met and married Anamar, a girl from Donegal. She had been making a pilgrimage on foot to Santiago de Compostela and he had advised her on the route. He was a little over medium height but looked shorter because of his strong build. The active life suited him. He enjoyed the hard days travelling on foot or on horseback.

He and Anamar lived in Mont L'ours-les-Cascades, a village in Ariège in the French Pyrenees. The farms, vineyard and forests of the estate were managed by a trusted employee. This arrangement allowed Don Ramón to pursue the working interest of his life - historical research. But his sense of seigneurial duty was accepted in the villages and amongst the mountains of his lands. He was admired and respected for his fairness in disputes and for his thoughtfulness for those enduring hard times.

But this was the one time the villagers would see their Seigneur angry. He hated the spectacle of the dancing bear. In this part of the French Pyrenees there were few enough bears left in the wild. They were not yet a protected species, but this was as bad as extinction. It was human degradation of the animal kingdom at its worst. They all knew that the bears were trained by torture, by starvation, beatings, hot coals to break the spirit and teach the tricks.

Towards the end of the war the occupying German soldiers wanted to be entertained by the dancing bears. They were apparently unaware of the irony of witnessing this domination of the bear by man at the same time as the Great Bear of the Russian Army was inflicting horrendous defeat on their finest divisions in the snows of the Winter of 1943.

But that was seventeen years ago and now the audience was French, all aware of their seigneur's hatred of this droll scene acted out for their amusement.

They began to disperse, some annoyed that their squire had spoiled the fun but all unwilling to risk his rage. In every other aspect of village life they found Monsieur Barriano the ideal squire, but captive bears performing for their entertainment was forbidden on his manor.

Ramón rode across the square as the crowd thinned but the trainer and his bear were gone. He called some of the men by name and reminded them of their duty. Next time they heard of an impending visit of the montreur d'ours, the showman and his dancing bear, they were to telephone him immediately.

---

Anamar awakened from a doze and smiled before she opened her eyes. There were three places, in three different countries, which she could call home but every time she emerged from sleep she knew immediately which one she would see with her first glance.

It was the same on her travels. No matter where she roamed, between the ending of sleep and before her first conscious look, she knew exactly where she was. Some people had a perfect sense of musical pitch - Anamar had a perfect sense of place.

Winter or Summer, good weather or bad, she could always be sure.

Her cottage in the Irish mountains of Donegal was the connection to her roots. Her Granny Mac, the storyteller, had left it to her and it was her haven every time she returned from her travels. It was there, below the Blue Stack Mountains, that she had made the discovery of the spirit of place.

But on this warm Spring afternoon she was not in Donegal.

When she had married Ramón Barriano Mont L'ours ten years before she had gained a second home. His father, Don Henriques Barriano, was a Spanish nobleman and Ramón had been born and raised on the Barriano hacienda in Navarre in Northern Spain.

But as Anamar's eyelids fluttered, ready to open, she knew she was not in Spanish Navarre.

As a young student, Ramón had been sent to England for the duration of the Spanish Civil War. He had enjoyed his stay in County Durham. At university there he had joined a group concerned for the welfare of animals. When he returned home his mother had passed on to him her family estate in the French Pyrenees and with it, its vineyard, farmland and mountains.

On this warm and untroubled afternoon, as Anamar at last allowed her eyes to open, she knew she was in her easy chair, in the shade of a giant oak near their house in the village of Mont L'ours-les-Cascades. The twins, Marie and Henriques and her elder daughter, Deirdre, were playing on a swing and a rope ladder Ramón had slung from stout branches of a tree. From a perch above the rope ladder Henriques whooped like Tarzan. The girls were squashed together on the swing shrieking at the top of every upward arc. They were just far enough away not to spoil Anamar's tranquil moment.

The house was over a hundred and fifty years old, built of cut stone and wood in the chalet tradition of the French Pyrenees. The roof was tiled with large, thin slabs of rock in the particular style of the village. It was two-storied with wooden balconies on two sides under the huge eaves. Since their marriage, Ramón and Anamar had modernised the facilities and extended the building. Now, it was a spacious, comfortable home.

Anamar could be sure where Ramón was at this time of the day. He had been out riding in the morning and now would be in his study working on his research. The study opened out on to the balcony on the other side of the house and at this time of the year he liked to work in the open air.

Nearly ten years of marriage and the bearing of three children had been kind to Anamar. She was no longer the slim girl she had been when first she came to France. Her hair was a slightly darker shade of fair and she wore it longer now.

She had the figure of a woman and was stronger and fitter than ever she had been in her life. Although Ramón employed a housekeeper and a maid and another local girl during the school holiday to look after the children, Anamar insisted, to the embarrassment of the staff, in being involved with the work in and around the house. She spent a great deal of her time with the three children, exploring the estate on nature walks, telling them stories of Granny Mac and Donegal, listening to them reading aloud.

As they spoke French at school, Anamar and Ramón had agreed that the family would usually speak Spanish at meal-times and use English for conversations around the house and in the garden.

Her own passion was walking. Her pilgrimage on foot to Santiago de Compostela ten years before had ensured she would never settle for the sedentary life. She liked to go alone, exploring the countryside, taking off on a long day in the big hills. Now she knew their extensive estate as well as her husband. Sometimes Ramón came too but he was delighted to see his wife so happy amongst these mountains. He encouraged her to take notes on her travels and had offered to have her walking guide published when she was ready.

Somewhere behind Anamar, as if he needed to have both her and the children in sight, Raoul, Ramón's researcher, was sitting in the shade, reading. Unless he was away, his work was done in the mornings and early evenings. The afternoon was his own but he always seemed to spend it here as if part of his job was to watch over Anamar and the children.

Anamar liked Raoul because he seemed to work so well with her husband and the children loved him but it was an irritation to know he was always there, able to see her but out of her view. She had mentioned it to Ramón but he had simply looked at her in blank incomprehension.

Raoul felt himself deeply grateful to be here. He had met Anamar ten years before in Paris when he and a fellow-student, Paul, had been introduced to her by an eccentric Irish Priest. She had been preparing for the pilgrimage to Santiago and he and Paul had offered to accompany her on the difficult and dangerous stage over the Pyrenees.

Before Anamar set out on her journey she had been introduced to Ramón who had walked to Santiago at the end of the Spanish Civil War. She had stayed with him for a short time here in Mont L'ours while he told her about the route and the history of the pilgrimage and taught her some Spanish.

Unknown to her, Ramón had followed at a discreet distance when she set out for Santiago, hoping to be able to help her if required.

Raoul and his friend Paul had met Anamar by arrangement in Lourdes for the stage across the Pyrenees and, climbing into the mountains, had noticed that she was being followed. They had ambushed the stalker but were losing the battle when Anamar realised it was Ramón and stopped the fight.

Once peace had been restored, she had agreed that the three men could stay with her until they reached the foothills on the Spanish side.

Raoul was tall with fair, wavy hair worn shoulder length. He had large feet and hands and moved well, but with the grace of a ballet dancer not the agility of an athlete. When Anamar had first met them, he and his friend Paul had been very close. At home in Donegal the sight of two young men so enamoured of each other would have scandalised the locals but when she had met them in Paris such a liaison seemed unremarkable.

But that was ten years ago. Raoul was now a handsome man when before he had been a good-looking boy. He was heavier, more solidly built but still moved elegantly and affected the gestures of an actor. The neat, pointed beard which he was cultivating was exactly as he imagined a Spanish nobleman like Ramón should wear in his manhood.

He had worked as a part-time lecturer at the Sorbonne and keeping in touch with Anamar after her pilgrimage had led to Ramón recruiting him to help with his current research.

Raoul was impressed by Ramón's interest in medieval history and his writings on the ill-used Cagot people once found in the Pyrenean valleys on either side of the range. He admired, too, the way his employer had sought an understanding of the faith of the Cathars, exterminated in the 14th Century by a Crusade mounted on behalf of the Church.

But as he sat each afternoon pretending to read, it was not his work which was making Raoul so confused and unhappy. He was in love with Anamar. As yet, he had made no advances, given no indication of his feelings but this was beyond admiration and respect. They had known each other for ten years and from the beginning he had cherished their friendship. Now, and perhaps for the first time, he had discovered what it was like to love a woman

His confusion was not because she was married to a man whom he revered and who had befriended him. When first he had met Anamar, he and his fellow-student, Paul, were much more than good friends. They had become lovers when they were nineteen and, although they were no longer a couple, his feelings of love and desire had been for men, until now. Since he had come to live with Ramón and his family he had discovered that he was capable of a passion for a woman far greater than ever he had had for a man.

He and Anamar had often considered the nature of friendship. They had discussed the Buddhist principle of the 'right' conversation with the 'right' people, the North American Indian belief that white people do not listen, even to their friends. They had agreed that friendship should allow each party to develop the good in themselves and discover the good in the other, that true friends gave each other the best of themselves.

Since they had first met, Raoul had been delighted to be a friend of Anamar's, now it was galling to be treated only as a friend.

He brought his chair over and sat down beside her. Gently, he laid a hand on her arm and spoke quietly. She was unhappy, unsettled, he told her. He was certain she was no longer at ease here with little to do now the children were at school. Someone like her needed to have a purpose in her life. She should have excitement and fun, and romance.

He was speaking in English, in a whisper, squeezing her arm with his hand. A few moments before he had thought he would never have been able to talk to her like this but passion was making the words flow. He began to speak of friendship and love and suddenly stopped as if unsure of himself.

Anamar turned to look at him but said nothing. She kept him in her sight as she rose from her seat. He made an attempt to stop her from leaving but she appeared not to have heard, not even to have noticed.

Ramón looked up from his papers when he heard Anamar come out on to the balcony behind him. He pulled a chair over towards his work table so that she could sit down beside him. The balcony was in the traditional style of the French Pyrenean mountain house. It was sheltered by the extension of the steep chalet roof and meant to be used for the storage of garlic and onions and for wood ready-cut for winter fuel.

He had cleared the logs to leave more room but had left the aromatic garlic and onions. With her tongue in her cheek Anamar would confide to their friends that he hoped the pungent bulbs would keep the evil spirits at bay and Ramón would smile and let her have her little joke.

He could tell Anamar wanted to talk to him and was waiting for her to speak when the telephone rang downstairs and he had to excuse himself.

Anamar sat down and waited for him to return. She had never met a man like her husband. He was kind and loving, understanding of her need to have a life of her own. She admired his research and the way he ran his estate. But he was more than a spouse. He was her best friend and her closest companion. If he had a fault, it was his need to have time on his own. Even though she had the same need for solitude, she felt excluded from parts of his life. But how could she criticise him for enjoying his own company when she, too, appreciated time on her own?

She needed to tell someone about Raoul's outburst but was unwilling to burden Ramón with it. Maybe Raoul was right about her needing a new challenge. When she had married Ramón and had come to live here, she had set herself the task of researching the walks of the area. It had taken years of painstaking exploration on pleasant rambles and hard days climbing amongst the high peaks.

But now the walking guide was finished. She loved this village and its people and the mountains of the Pyrenees. She adored her husband and her children. But the urge to travel was on her. Her mother always said that somewhere in her breeding there had to be Gypsy blood.

Before she was married, she had travelled in France. She had been to Lourdes twice on Pilgrimage and had first met her husband-to-be when she was preparing to set out on her long walk to Santiago. Raoul was right, at least about her need for a new challenge.

Ramón came back up the stairs two at a time. The telephone call had been from a man in Bordun, the village where he had stopped the dancing bear entertainment. The man had heard that the showman and his bear were due to return the next day. The show would begin at noon.

---

Jules Laurent would often say that training bears was in his blood. His father and grandfather had been famous as bear trainers. They had travelled to fairs on foot from Perpignan in the East to Bayonne in the West and, as soon as Jules was old enough to walk the distances, he came too. His grandfather, Joseph Laurent had told him tales of the show men of Ariège at the turn of the century sixty years ago, the wrestlers, the acrobats, the jugglers, the celebrated D'Jelmako in his Indian costume who could shoot with bow and arrow or rifle, hitting the mark every time, who could walk the tight-rope and jump through a burning hoop held metres off the ground.

But best of all were Joseph's stories of 'les montreurs d'ours', the show men of the dancing bears who wore wide brimmed hats if they were gypsies or large berets if they were from Ariège. On a fair day they paraded through the village, 'le montreur d'ours' beating a rhythm on a tambourine for the dance of his bear. When the crowd assembled he would shout to the bear,

'Come on Martin, present yourself to these fine people, show them how your parents taught you to steal the little lambs from the mountain slopes.'

Joseph had told him how the bears were taken from the wild when they were very young and reared in a cow-shed. When the cubs were one year old they would be securely tied and staked out on the ground. A ring was inserted through a hole gouged in the upper lip which would remain there until the end of its life.

When Jules was a boy there was a famous group of 'montreurs d'ours' called 'les Oussaillès' who travelled the world with their dancing bears. In the village of Ercé there was a school for the training of 'montreurs d'ours' and about fifty show men with bears in Ariège. One group led by the famous Baptiste Faur-Croustet, whose nick-name was Tatai, toured France, Switzerland, Germany and England before leaving for Canada and the United States. Tatai's bear had died there and was sold to be stuffed in a most life-like pose and exhibited in the Museum of New York

But since the nineteen thirties it had become much more difficult to find young bears to train. Before the war there had been two hundred or more wild bears in the mountain. Then, a hunter could shoot a female so that he could sell her cubs to trainers.

The Government had been concerned that farmers were killing bears because of damage to their livestock and berry patches. An official Plan D'ours had been produced which enabled indemnity payments to be made for livestock killed or berry patches stripped. But it had no affect on the falling numbers. By 1960 it was reckoned that there were only forty bears left in the whole of the Pyrenees and the Government was preparing a new law which would prohibit bear hunting.

Jules had never attended school except for a few days in Winter and had successfully avoided learning to read or write. Counting was different. Cash had to be reckoned and Jules had a way with money. His father would have said it stuck to his fingers like fir tree sap.

Jules had become a dealer by accident. The nomadic life, travelling on foot from village to village, trying to make money by showing his dancing bear, was a hard existence. However, his contacts allowed him to see where goods and animals could be bought cheaply and sold for a profit. It was trade which made his money but being a 'montreur d'ours' was his life.

His travels were physically exhausting, even dangerous. Although many of the villagers enjoyed the spectacle, there were others, like the seigneur of this valley, who despised what he did with the bear. Monsieur Barriano might be determined to prevent him earning his living but there were no police here. The seigneur would have to take the law into his own hands.

His contacts had told him the seigneur would be coming, but on this day he would stand his ground. He waited under a tree with the bear's chains in his hand. The villagers gathered behind the trees which bordered the square.

Ramón arrived in Bordun with four of his men, all on horseback. They dismounted at the edge of the square and Ramón walked across to the showman. He spoke loudly so that everyone could hear, offering to buy the bear. The showman laughed.

'And what would you do with a dancing bear, Seigneur?' he said, 'Do you want me to teach you how to be a montreur d'ours?'

'How much?' Ramón was not in the mood for small talk, 'Name your price.'

He turned his back on the villagers so that they were not able to see what he was doing. Without another word he held out a sum of money in front of the showman's face. Jules Laurent startled back a step and bumped against the bear. He looked puzzled, glancing at the money, then staring back at Ramón.

The Seigneur had never done a deal like this before. What would he do if the montreur refused the money? What would he do with the bear if he accepted? There was no prospect of a rescued dancing bear being returned to the wild. Its new owner would have to make arrangements for its care to the natural end of its days. But there had to be a better life for the bear than the one it had led since capture as a cub.

The montreur said nothing but took the money without counting it. He nodded his head in agreement when Ramón told him that the bear must be delivered to his home in the village of Mont L'ours before noon on the following day. He nodded again, in resignation, when Ramón stipulated that the muzzle chain must now be removed, its ring could be detached later. Until then the neck chain could remain in place to allow the animal to be controlled.

Without the slightest idea of what he would do next, Ramón was ecstatic. For once in his life he had acted impetuously, with no thought for the consequences.

As he rode back home he realised that on this day he had enhanced his own heritage. In traditional Spanish there are three parts to the name; the Christian name, the father's surname and the mother's maiden name - in his case Ramón Barriano Mont L'ours. His mother and her ancestors had been born in the village of Mont L'ours, Bear Mountain. She had passed it on to him and he hoped she would be pleased by the symbolism of the act.

How his father, Don Henriques, would react when he heard the news was less certain. Ramón smiled. His father would shrug his shoulders, laugh quietly and blame this sympathy for animals on the time his son had spent in England as a young man.

Next morning Ramón was seated at his desk on the balcony of his study when he saw Jules Laurent and the bear trudge over the bridge into the village. He waited until they had reached the square in front of his house and came down to claim the bear.

Ramón's estate agent, Guy le Blanc, and his assistant, Maurice Cabanes, had also been waiting. Maurice had prepared a stable for the bear. The Seigneur had told him that the animal would be his responsibility and he would do his best but what did he know about bears? People said that he had a way with animals. He knew about horses, cows, sheep, goats and dogs but he had no experience of wild animals, except as a hunter.

Jules Laurent handed the bear's chain to Maurice Cabanes and turned away. He hadn't told them that his bear had a name. Why should he? They had bought the animal, not the name. He had nothing to say to these men who had taken his bear for money.

He had enough cash now to keep himself for a year without working but he had sold his occupation along with the bear. There were other ways he could make a living, much easier ways than tramping from village to village in all weathers with a dancing bear. But now it was gone. He was a showman without anything to show. It was only now he realised that being a 'montreur d'ours' had been the best part of his life.

The showman seemed so dejected that Ramón offered him something to eat and a glass of wine but the man was away before he could stop him.

Ramón went with Guy and Maurice to see the bear established in his new quarters and then back to his study to discuss what he would do. The ring through the animal's muzzle would need to be removed. Guy would arrange for a visit by the veterinary surgeon to have the job done properly. Ramón and Anamar talked later that afternoon. Neither felt that a zoo would be the right home for an animal which had spent a lifetime entertaining people.

They looked out from the balcony. Jules Laurent was still in the village, sitting on the river bank beside the bridge like a man with nowhere to go and no one to go with.

'What about a sanctuary for bears?' Anamar said as if she had just thought of it, 'You could build a stockade in the Val Sauvage. It's only three kilometres away and it's within your lands. You could take in injured or old bears, or cubs left when a mother is shot, you might even be able to buy another dancing bear, you could ................'

Ramón laughed. When this young Irish wife of his had an idea the words flowed like a mountain stream. At dinner that evening Anamar convinced him that the sanctuary was a practical project.

To her amazement he agreed. He talked about the Val Sauvage as the ideal location. It was a narrow wooded valley with steep cliffs at its head. A stream flowed through the woods. A track led to the base of the woods but there were no dwellings, no summer pastures, no reason for the local people to go there except for hunting. They decided that they would visit the valley in the morning and discuss the idea with Guy and Maurice in the afternoon.

Jules Laurent stayed in the village. He was sitting on the parapet of the bridge when they left for the Val Sauvage next day and he was still there when they returned. Ramón stopped the truck and got out to speak to him.

'Monsieur Laurent, I have a job for you, if you want to work. How would you like to look after your bear?' he said quietly.

Jules looked confused. This man has bought my bear so that it will not have to dance. Now he wants to employ me. Does he want me to show them how to make the bear dance? Does he want me to teach his man how to be a montreur d'ours?

'Have something to eat, monsieur. We will meet this afternoon and I will tell you what we will do with the bear.'

They met around the table in the Seigneur's house, Ramón at one end, Anamar at the other and in between Guy le Blanc and Maurice Cabane on one side and Jules Laurent on the other. Madame Mons served wine and stood back, observing the proceedings. She had received Jules into the house with the minimum of good grace and was keeping an eye on him. In her own kitchen she frightened Jules and he kept glancing towards her to check that it was still all right for him to be here.

Ramón explained that he and his wife had decided to found a sanctuary on his estate for bears who could not survive in the wild. The first inmate would be Jules's former dancing bear. They would take in old or injured bears, cubs left abandoned when their mother was shot. They would also be willing to buy dancing bears to give them a good life in retirement. Animal experts interested in bears would be encouraged to use the sanctuary to study bears, groups of students and school children would be allowed to visit.

Ramón encouraged no discussion of the project. He and Anamar had decided and the meeting was simply to tell those present how they would be involved.

He asked Anamar to describe the location they had chosen. Guy and Maurice knew the Val Sauvage but Anamar described it for the benefit of Jules. The valley was narrow, about half a kilometre wide and the site they had in mind was about one kilometre long. The head of the valley was enclosed by inaccessible cliffs so there was no through route.

There were no dwellings, not even a refuge used by shepherds or hunters. The nature of the terrain would make the stockade relatively easy to build. The forest with its dense thickets at an altitude of between 1200 to 1500m would be ideal. River pools and rock shelters would be constructed, caves excavated, berry patches planted, bee colonies established.

Wooden huts to service the sanctuary would be built outside the main gate. They would take advice from zoologists about the height and construction of the fence. Viewing hides on platforms four metres high would be erected outside the stockade.

When Anamar had finished, Ramón offered Jules the job of warden of the sanctuary once it was built. The showman's face paled and he stood up as if to say something but no words would come. This was a possibility he

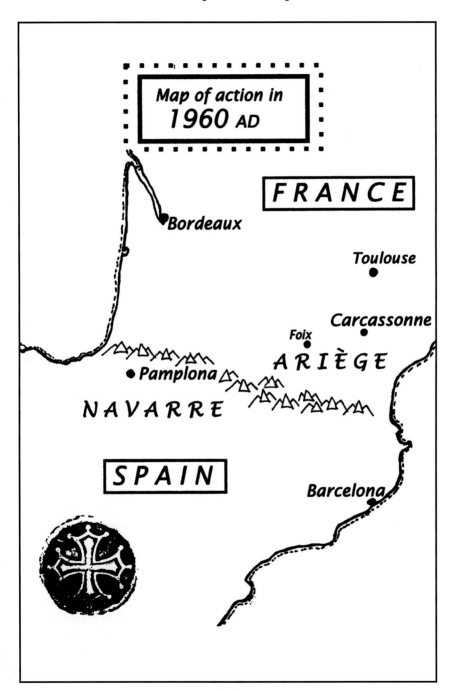

Map of action in
**1960** AD

FRANCE

●Bordeaux

Toulouse
●

Carcassonne
●

Foix
●

ARIÈGE

●Pamplona

NAVARRE

SPAIN

Barcelona
●

could never have envisaged. He had never worked for anyone since he was a boy helping his father. As a montreur d'ours he had been his own boss, but working with bears had been his life. This was an opportunity not to be missed. Ramón rose and shook hands with him, taking his silence as consent. Maurice would be in charge of the construction. Guy would supervise the project and Maurice and Jules would report to him.

They went off to visit the site in the small truck like children on a school outing. The track leading up the valley would need to be improved, Maurice made a note. He and Jules paced out the width of the valley at the level which would be the lower limit of the sanctuary. They followed a faint track beside the river to the semi-circle of cliffs which were the impassable buttresses at the valley's head.

Jules had said barely a word since they had sat around the table in Ramón's house. Now he began to talk to Maurice and Guy, joining their excited chatter as they uncovered new possibilities and speculated about where they would find more bears in need of a home.

When Anamar and Ramón were on their own, she teased about the job for Jules.

'I see you're following the traditional English principle,' she said mischievously, 'When you need a game keeper, employ a poacher.'

Ramón laughed. He was enjoying himself. Since he had taken over his mother's family estate he had developed the vineyard, the farms and the forests. All were now well run. Guy was an excellent land agent and that had allowed him to pursue his research. But this was a new project. He and Anamar, the children, Guy, Maurice and Jules, the villagers of Mont L'ours, they would all be involved.

Within a few days the materials began to arrive and the work was underway. All Jules's energy was directed towards the building of the sanctuary. He appeared to have forgotten his bear, still in the stable but Maurice saw that the animal was fed and watered and allowed out within a secure paddock.

Ten local men were engaged to help with the building work. Ramón and Anamar visited the site each day. If they were going in the late afternoon the children came too. Jules always had time to talk to them. He was at home with the children, telling them stories of his life when he was their age, tramping the roads with his father and their dancing bears.

Deirdre was nine and old enough to talk to her mother about the bear. She understood that her father had bought it to save it from a life of pain. Jules was surprised that this child should be so concerned for the bear. He tried to describe how young cubs were caught and trained and how the adult bear became his partner. But the more he tried to explain, the more questions Deirdre asked. If Anamar heard their discussion she did not interfere. She knew her child well enough not to offer her help when she didn't need it. But Jules's patience seemed limitless. He never became annoyed, never tired of the queries about bears and his life as a montreur d'ours.

After ten days Guy came to Ramón's study in the early evening to discuss progress. The work was going particularly well but Ramón wanted to see it finished as soon as possible. They were interrupted by Madam Mons who had come upstairs to tell him that his mother was on the telephone from Navarre and wanted to speak to him.

Ramón knew immediately that something was wrong. His mother never asked for him when she rang. It was always Anamar she wanted to speak to. The two women were close friends, closer than daughter-in-law and mother-in-law would have expected. Their bond was the children. Doña Marie approved of the way Anamar was bringing up her grandchildren with firmness and love, encouraging their curiosity, developing their confidence.

She came to Mont L'ours four times a year and stayed at least three weeks each time. Her son and his family came to her each Christmas - for a magical two weeks over the Feast of the Nativity and beyond to the turn of the year.

As Ramón lifted the telephone he took a deep breath. His father was seriously ill. Violent chest pains while out riding had brought him back to the hacienda slumped forward over the pommel of his saddle. It was diagnosed as a heart attack. He was confined to bed and the doctor was visiting him every day.

Ramón prepared for an early start the next morning. Raoul would come with him to share the driving. Madam Mons prepared a wicker hamper of food for the journey. Anamar would bring the children a few days later but only if Ramón felt it would help his father.

As soon as he had gone, Anamar realised that she would have to see that the three men charged with building the sanctuary worked together. At their first meeting she was surprised to hear her own voice so calm and directive when they were arguing instead of agreeing work schedules.

When Ramón rang the next morning, the news was not good. His father was very weak. She tried to cheer him by telling him of the work in progress for the sanctuary but his mind was in Navarre not Mont L'ours. Two days later Don Henriques died of another attack.

Anamar drove the children to Navarre for the funeral and Doña Marie came back with them to Mont L'ours two days later. Ramón decided to stay to put his father's affairs in order and to make arrangements for the running of the estate in his absence.

On the way back Anamar told the children that she had walked these roads on her pilgrimage to Santiago ten years ago. She showed them where she had stayed. She pointed to the exact spot near Jaca where she had fainted in the blazing heat and how their father had steered her to a small bar for the shade and a cool drink. Crossing the Pyrenees in a car by a surfaced road was so different from her climb on foot over the frontier ridge.

Deirdre asked the questions. She was the eldest and it was her job. How did she find a place to stay? Was she not lonely when she was on her own? What did she have to eat? Were the people good to her? Was she not afraid of being attacked?

She told them how she had been assaulted by a drunken inn keeper, called Poudri, when she was alone with him at his inn on a mountain pass. It had happened a long time ago but was still fresh in her mind as she described her flight that night down the mountain to the nearest village. But not wishing to make her story too frightening, she made Poudri a figure of fun, explaining how she had outwitted him by going up the mountain instead of down, hiding amongst the rocks to watch him when he was not able to see her.

The children loved the story and wanted to hear it again but they were tired and she encouraged them to sleep. She drove in silence and allowed herself to follow her own thoughts. Those adventures on the road to Santiago seemed to have happened in a different life. Then she had been a stranger in these lands. Now, by marriage and the birth of her children, she had loyalty to three nationalities. She was happy here but had not the slightest doubt that her roots were in Ireland.

## THE TEMPLAR CULT

The next morning Ramón cleared all the current research from his working tables and took Raoul into his confidence. They arranged a work station for him at one side of the room and placed a desk and a table for Ramón and Anamar against the window which looked out over the balcony. Raoul would record and catalogue all the items from the main part of the trunk and they would deal with the material in the top tray.

There were hand-written scripts, on vellum and parchment, on yellowing paper, some with elaborate coloured lettering and the first of the capitals worked in the shape of animals or birds in the style of ancient manuscripts. There were tables of dates, lists of titles, bills, deeds, personal and formal letters, family trees, insignia, geometric designs, maps, drawings of artifacts, varieties of crosses, church silver.

There were plans of villages and sketches of mountain terrain, some in rolls, others carefully bound to prevent damage. The documents were in Latin, French, Spanish, English and the langue d'Oc, similar to the Romany tongue.

In Raoul's part of the chest there were twelve silver drinking vessels, strings of semi-precious stones, jewels in flat boxes lined with red velvet. Near the bottom he discovered ten soft leather bags each containing a medallion on a silver chain. The medallions were identical, each depicting a soaring bird worked in gold on a silver disc enamelled in blue.

Most of the items were on parchment, songs, poems in the old troubadour style, lists of instructions and rules. There were scripts, obviously in code, some in the style of ancient Egyptian hieroglyphics. There were documents in French and English so explicit Anamar gasped in astonishment. The largest document was a book in Latin written by a scribe. It was without a binding and untitled.

Ramón found a leather bag of silver crosses on fine silver chains at the bottom of the trunk. There was another bag of splayed Templar crosses and Cathar crosses with twelve tiny rings at the ends of its arms.

After an hour all the material in the chest had been briefly examined and spread out on the desk, table and floor. They pushed their chairs back.

Raoul looked up and he and Anamar waited for Ramón to speak. He lifted one of the documents in French.

Even after such a brief study, Ramón said quietly, there could be no doubt. His father, Don Henriques had been the Master of a secret cult. It was clear, too, that as his son, he should succeed him. It was not a matter of choice. He read out the title of the document, 'Le Culte du Colombe du Saint-Esprit', the Cult of the Dove of the Holy Spirit and, like it or not, he was now the Master.

They arranged the papers from the tray in order. Although both Ramón and Raoul had a fair understanding of the langue d'Oc, Doña Marie would have to be involved to ensure an accurate translation.

The next morning they began work on the documents again at seven-thirty. Doña Marie was delighted to be asked to join them. Initially, the death of her husband had left her shocked and confused. Ramón's composure in dealing with the funeral and his father's affairs had helped. When she had come back to Mont L'ours with Anamar, her involvement with her grandchildren had lifted her spirits and given her a new sense of purpose.

Ramón's founding of a sanctuary for bears had affected her deeply. The Mont L'ours, the Mountain of the Bears, of her heritage was becoming a reality and she felt herself totally involved. Never before had she been so busy. She felt physically younger and mentally brighter. Now Ramón wanted her to translate some papers. It was very good to feel needed.

From the documents Ramón and Anamar had examined it was not clear what the origins of the Cult were or when it first had been founded. They thought that the answers to these questions might well be amongst the records Raoul was cataloguing. But it was going to take him weeks to record and place in order all the contents of his part of the chest.

The first document was in French and Ramón read it aloud.

## THIS IS THE CODE OF LE CULTE DE LA COLOMBE DU SAINT-ESPRIT

## THE CULT OF THE DOVE OF THE HOLY SPIRIT

*The Cult shall exist to protect and preserve its Catholic Faith, its Treasure and its Cathedral.*

*The Cult's Master shall be the head of the Barriano family of Navarre, the Marqués de Barra.*

## THE RULES OF THE CULT

*The Cult shall comprise twelve or more members.*

*New members shall be appointed by the Master at his absolute discretion.*

*The Cult's membership shall be chosen from such professions as troubadour, physician, builder, nobleman, historian, muleteer, alchemist, moneylender, cleric, pilgrim or any other calling approved by the Master.*

*Members shall not reveal the secrets of the Cult.*

*Members shall help any other member in need of assistance.*

*Members shall defend any other member hounded by the law, dunned by moneylenders or hunted by enemies.*

*The Master shall preside when a member faces trial by the court of the Cult.*

*The Court of the Cult shall comprise not less than five members chosen by the Master.*

*If a member is found guilty by the Court of the Cult, the Master shall decide upon appropriate punishment.*

*Disputes between members shall be settled within the Cult.*

*Members shall treat each other of whatever rank, with the greatest courtesy and shall address each other by title and Christian name.*

*Members shall assist the Cult financially when required.*

## MEMBERSHIP OF THE CULT AT 10TH APRIL 1945 .

| | | | |
|---|---|---|---|
| *Master* | *Don Henriques, Marqués de Barra* | *Nobleman* | *Navarre* |
| *Teller* | *Don Carlos Conde Parrado* | *Transport Company Owner* | *Pamplona* |
| *Treasurer* | *Monsieur Marc Decuré* | *Banker* | *Bordeaux* |
| *Member* | *Monsieur Paul Huguet* | *Hotelier* | *Aulus-les-Bains* |
| *Member* | *Monsieur Jean-Pierre Bernard* | *Silver and Gold Smith* | *Perpignan* |

| Member | Doctor Salvador Vincente Valverde | Physician | Peniscola, Catalonia |
|---|---|---|---|
| Member | Monsieur Raymond Bodelot | Public Official | Mirepoix Nr Carcassonne |

The list gave details of only six members in addition to the Master and it began to look as if the Cult had been in decline. There were intriguing questions and no sign of answers in any of the other documents they had examined.

While the others continued placing the documents in chronological order, Ramón went downstairs and contacted the exchange for a telephone call to Carlos Conde Parrado, the Teller. It was as if Don Carlos had been waiting to hear from him. He knew of the death of Don Henriques and had been to the funeral but had not introduced himself, feeling that it was best to leave it to Ramón to make the first contact.

He could come at once, he said. It was important that Ramón and he discuss the situation as soon as possible. No direct mention was made of the Cult. Telephones were not a private means of conversation. They arranged to meet the following afternoon at an hotel in Lourdes. It was not exactly half way but it would save Don Carlos making the full journey to Mont L'ours.

The hotel was beside the railway station in Lourdes and by four in the afternoon the two men had met, introduced themselves and were conversing as if they had known each other for years.

Don Carlos treated Ramón with the greatest respect as Master of the Cult. He was relieved to hear that Ramón had accepted the position and intended to fulfil both the letter and spirit of his legacy.

Ramón felt instinctively that he could trust this man. He leaned forward and spoke quietly.

'Tell me about our society, Don Carlos. I must hear everything you know about the Cult and its members.'

'I wish I could tell you all the secrets,' Don Carlos said, 'But we know so little. The Cult has been dying of neglect. Twenty-five years ago the Civil War created divisions between us and members began to lose interest. At the end of World War 2, seventeen years ago, we agreed to meet once a year but that lapsed and we have not had a meeting for six years. Your father was reluctant to appoint new members to fill vacancies caused by death or resignation. He felt we should allow the Cult to slip quietly into oblivion.'

Don Carlos was as tall as Ramón, neatly-dressed, dark haired and with black hair on the back of his hands. He moved quickly and his mind was sharp, his body lean and wiry.

'When I attended your father's funeral and, although we did not meet, I knew for certain that you would rejuvenate the Cult. Before you telephoned me I had a dream that you would bring the Cult back to life. I prayed to the Holy Virgin in the Cathedral in Pamplona, certain that my prayers would be answered.' He spoke in a slightly embarrassed way in case Don Ramón felt he was being too familiar.

'Only six members have survived your father.' His sallow, serious features allowed a gentle smile. 'I am sixty-four. I was born in 1896 and am the oldest. But you have the power and energy of a young man. You must appoint young men to fill the vacancies. But this old man will not fail you by default.'

The two men agreed to stay overnight in the hotel and walked the streets of the town in the early evening. They met again at dinner.

Although both were aware that this was an important business meeting, they were in France and the hotel had a well deserved reputation for its food and wine. Ramón ordered Rosé de Bourgogne as an aperitif, cured ham and grilled mullet for the meal and a bottle of Chablis.

While they were waiting for the first course Ramón could contain his curiosity no longer. He asked about the Cult's Cathedral and Treasure.

'We have found a manuscript which seems to locate the Cathedral in the Pyrenees but there is nothing about the Treasure. I'm sure there is a page missing from the document'

Don Carlos nodded.

'Twenty years ago four of us studied every Cathedral on both the French and Spanish sides of the Pyrenees without uncovering any indication that one of them was our Cathedral. And we know even less about the Treasure. There have been rumours that it might have been part of the lost treasure of the Knights Templar. We could make no sense of the documents.'

They decided to arrange a meeting of the Cult in one month's time and it was Don Carlos's suggestion that they hold it at an hotel in Ariège owned by one of the members, Monsieur Paul Huguet.

When they parted Don Carlos stepped out to his car like a young man. Don Ramón would have his full support, he said. His eldest son could take over the transport business which he had built up over the years. That would allow him to retire and give him the free time to work for the Cult. This could be the most exciting moment of his life.

Without having any evidence that the Cult was anything more than a moribund secret society, Ramón was certain that this was more than his heritage, like the Sanctuary for bears, it was his destiny.

When he arrived home that afternoon he told Anamar every detail of his discussions with Don Carlos. He asked her to suggest names of possible new members to bring the membership of the Cult to full strength. He invited her to become the first woman member. To his relief she was delighted to be asked. Examining the contents of the chest had already made her feel involved. But this would not be easy. Ramón had always treated her as a partner but all-male societies were usually conservative and often implacably opposed to the involvement of women.

Next day at breakfast she had a name for him, Father Brian de Courcy, an Irish Priest based in Paris. When she had been searching for a pilgrim road to travel ten years before he had been recommended to her as an authority on pilgrimage and had become a friend and advisor.

Father Brian was small and rotund, as light on his feet as a dancer. He was capable of including a serious thought and an hilarious joke in the same sentence. Anamar's dear friend Deirdre, for whom her first child was called, had told her that the dancing priest was supposed to be in Paris to research a book he was writing on medieval pilgrimage. Father Brian had helped Anamar choose the Camino de Santiago as her pilgrimage journey and had introduced her to his Parisian friends, including Raoul.

She had heard from Raoul that Father Brian was still in Paris, still living at the Irish College, still researching the same book ten years later, still enjoying the café life rather more than his calling should have accommodated.

Ramón wrote to Father Brian inviting him to become a member of the Cult.

Two days later he was working with Raoul on the papers when it suddenly occurred to him that his researcher was privy to the documents in the chest and should also be invited to become a member. Raoul accepted willingly, as did Father Brian by return post and now Ramón had three new members to introduce at the meeting of the Cult.

For many years Monsieur Paul Huguet had been a reluctant member, never showing any real interest in the Cult or his fellow members. However, when Ramón made a special journey to book his hotel for the meeting, with a gourmet meal and accommodation for all the members at his own expense, his attitude changed dramatically. He smiled broadly. He would facilitate the entire proceedings. They would have the very best of the cuisine of Ariège. And he would personally ensure total secrecy.

If this new Master revitalised the Cult there would be more meetings. If Don Ramón was impressed by the hotel, he would look no further for a future venue. This could be business worth having.

Raoul's work on the documents was proceeding slowly. He was taking the greatest care, translating each one into modern French, seeking help from Doña Marie when they were in Spanish or langue d'Oc, His method was to type out a fair copy from his hand-written notes, arranging every item in chronological order.

The work was fascinating. This was the most exciting research with which he had ever been involved and he was delighted that Ramón had recognised his efforts by asking him to be a member of the Cult.

But he was no closer to Anamar than ever he had been. He could find no opportunity to speak to her privately. Although she was never unpleasant to him, she spoke to him like a stranger and sometimes ignored his presence entirely. The frustration was unbearable. It was making him ill. After meals he would feel physically sick. When he went to bed, he fell asleep immediately but woke three or four times during the night and found it almost impossible to go back to sleep,

---

The Sanctuary for Bears was becoming better known and it had become a popular day out for local people. Ramón had made it clear that he wanted everyone who lived on his lands to feel that the Sanctuary was theirs.

Ramón noticed that the three men, Maurice, Guy and Jules found it hard to work together. His solution was to direct Guy back to his estate management duties, leaving Maurice and Jules to be involved with the Sanctuary.

Jules now had three responsibilities, the welfare of the bears, the maintenance of the facilities and the enlightenment of visitors to the

Sanctuary. Maurice was happy to be left with the administrative work, paying for materials and supplies, sending out information, taking bookings for groups. To others it might have seemed that he and Jules were now friends but work was their only common ground. Each found the other completely unfathomable.

Maurice tried to teach Jules to drive and although he could not claim to have succeeded, Jules could now dance the truck at speed across the unsurfaced roads as if he had been driving all his life.

Through his old contacts Jules heard of another dancing bear in a village to the East and was staggered when Ramón gave him the money in cash and sent him off in the truck to buy it. When he returned with the bear, Jules found it hard to refund the balance of the cash advance which had not been needed to close the sale. However, it proved even harder to hold on to this money which belonged to the only man who had ever truly trusted him. Even his father had made him account for every sou. He gave the balance back to Ramón and failed to see the smile on his employer's face because his head was down as he concentrated on counting out the money.

The bear was old and suffering from a serious infection of the hole through which the muzzle ring had been inserted. The veterinary surgeon was called and although the removal of the ring was a difficult operation it was completed satisfactorily and the bear installed in his new quarters.

In the early afternoon of the meeting of the Cult, Ramón sent Raoul to collect Father Brian from the Paris train to Tarascon-sur-Ariège. Ramón was reassured when he met the cheerful cleric who immediately told him he had agreed to become a member, not because he felt any affinity with the Cult, but for two reasons only. One, any friend of Anamar the pilgrim, was a friend of his, and two, he believed that a half-open door was an invitation which must always be accepted.

On the way to the meeting Anamar drove with Father Brian beside her and Ramón and Raoul in the back. They arrived in Aulus-les-Bains at five to find that Don Carlos Conde was already installed. While the others settled into their rooms, Ramón invited Carlos to inspect the arrangements in the dining room.

The menu for the banquet to precede the meeting was already in place on a wooden stand in the hallway.

# Les Trois Seigneurs

## Hôtel *** Restaurant

AULUS-LES-BAINS • ARIÈGE • PYRÉNÉES

### Diner - Huit Heures ce Soir

Poireaux à la vinaigrette

Sole aux Champignons

Filet de Boeuf Rôti

Fonds d'Artichauts et Choufleur au gratin

Soufflé au Gran Marnier

Fromage du Pays

⁂

| | |
|---|---|
| *Le Vin Blanc* | Entre-deux-Mers Sec |
| *Les Vin Rouges* | Côte-de-Beaune |
| | Mont L'ours-les-Cascades |
| *Les Liqueurs* | Bénédictine |
| | Anisette de Marie Brizard |
| | Izarra jaune |

⁂

*Propriétaire*   Paul Huguet

Ramón and Don Carlos were waiting in the reception hall to meet the other five existing members as they arrived.

At eight o'clock everyone was in the dining room waiting to be allocated a place. The long table was laid for ten people and Ramón sat at the head with the Teller, Don Carlos Conde, on his right and the Treasurer, Marc Decuré, on his left. Each of the existing members wore a medallion on a silver chain depicting a soaring dove in gold on a silver disc enamelled in blue.

When the members were seated there were three empty chairs as Anamar, Father Brian and Raoul sat on a bench at the back of the room awaiting their invitation to the table.

Before the first course was served, Ramón thanked the members for their welcome to him as the new Master.

'I accept this legacy,' he said, 'And I intend to fulfil it in both the letter and the spirit.'

He announced that he had appointed three new members - Raoul Robert who was helping him to research the family archive he had inherited - Father Brian de Courcy who was also an historian - and his wife, the most adventurous person he had ever met.

She would be patient, he said, while they adjusted to the innovation of a woman as a member. She wished to be known simply as Anamar. Ramón then produced four medallions from the chest and presented one each to the new members and accepted his own from Don Carlos.

Carlos showed Anamar, Father Brian and Raoul to their seats and there were welcoming handshakes from the members. Paul left the table to arrange the serving of the first course and the wine and when that was done Father Brian was invited to say the Grace.

The dining room had a high ceiling with ancient beams and a decor which had changed little since the beginning of the century. The acoustics were excellent for conversation. Paul was nervous. He had scarcely sat down when he was on his feet again, checking the staff, visiting the kitchen to see that all was in order, making sure that wine glasses, water jugs and bread baskets were replenished.

For the rest of them it might be an important meeting but for Monsieur Paul this was important business.

In his more irreverent moments, Father Brian would often say that food and wine were the two loves of his life and as soon as he had tasted the leeks in their vinaigrette dressing he knew that this would be a memorable meal. He admired the French for their elevation of humble vegetables to celebrity status by good cooking, while in Ireland they would have been regarded as mere fillers destined for death by boiling.

By the soufflé course the conversation, the food and the wine seemed to have convinced everyone present that they were dining in the very best of good company. Even Monsieur Paul was beginning to enjoy the evening. When the cheese was served, he told the staff there were to be no interruptions and ceremoniously closed the door.

Ramón rose to begin the meeting by asking the members to introduce themselves.

'I am Ramón Barriano Mont L'ours, born in Navarre, now living in Mont L'ours-les-Cascades, custodian of my mother's family estate. My interests are historical research, bears and now the Cult of the Dove of the Holy Spirit.'

Don Carlos rose to his feet.

'I am Carlos Conde Parrado, the Teller of the Brotherhood. My home town is Pamplona. I am sixty-four years old and have retired from my transport company. The Cult has been asleep for too long and I believe that our new Master will waken the dove and let it soar. I wish to thank Don Ramón for hosting this meeting for all of us.'

Wheezing audibly Marc Decuré struggled to his feet, determined to speak next. He was a large man with an immense paunch. He leant forward with his small hands on the table to steady himself.

'I am a banker and the Treasurer of the Cult. We have funds in my bank and that is all you need to know until there is good reason for spending money.'

There was a pause before the next member rose. He was so nervous his hand shook and he had to set his wine glass on the table.

'My name is Jean-Pierre Bernard of Perpignan. I am a silver and gold smith.'

Paul Huguet introduced himself with his professional maître d'hotel smile, managing to be both shy and sly at the same time.

Doctor Salvador Vincente Valverde said he was a physician from Peniscola in the old Kingdom of Catalan.

The last of the existing members spoke without rising to his feet.

'I am Bodelot from Mirepoix near Carcassonne and I don't know why I came,' he said dismissively, 'I've never felt part of this Cult.'

Now it was the turn of the three new members. Anamar nodded to Father Brian.

The priest rose and skipped around behind his chair. Although of the same build as Monsieur Decuré, Father Brian was constructed on a much smaller scale. While Decuré was ponderous, he was as nimble as a dancer.

'I am Father Brian de Courcy born, reared and ordained in Ireland, domiciled in Paris where the Church may feel I can do least damage to its cause. To dine and wine as we have done this evening can only be good omens of the best of times to come. I will do my utmost to safeguard your souls.'

It was Anamar's turn. She smiled.

'I am Anamar Barriano Cassidy from Donegal in Ireland, now living in Mont L'ours-les-Cascades with my husband and three children. Ten years ago I made a pilgrimage to Santiago de Compostela. Being a member of the Cult will be, for me, another great journey of discovery.'

Raoul slowly drew himself up to his full height. He was the tallest of the company and also the youngest. Most of the others were a generation older. Why was he here? He reminded himself that there were two compelling reasons. He was Ramón's employee and Anamar was now a member too.

'My name is Raoul Robert. I am twenty-eight years of age and work as a researcher for Don Ramón. I am an artist and a poet and believe that love is the greatest adventure of all.'

Ramón spoke for a few moments about his family archive and the research work on the Cult being done by Raoul, Anamar and himself. He mentioned the Cult's Treasure and its Cathedral and suggested that they were not yet ready to discuss these two mysteries. In the meantime he wanted members to write to him with any information they thought would be helpful.

Almost before Ramón had finished speaking Monsieur Jean-Pierre was on his feet.

'Don Ramón, I have a confession to make,' he said nervously, 'I have a paper from the archive which may help. Many years ago Don Henriques and I were examining the documents and when I arrived home one of the pages was with my papers. I should have returned it immediately but hesitated. The longer I held it, the harder it was to send it back.'

He looked at Ramón apprehensively.

'When I heard of your father's death I decided to return the document. It is in French but it makes no sense. The words and sentences are not in order. It must be a form of code.'

There were gasps of astonishment as he handed the document to Ramón. The members were angry. Monsieur Marc rolled in his chair and pointed an accusing finger but could find no words to make an allegation. Don Carlos stood up as if he was readying himself for action. Monsieur Jean-Pierre held out the missing page and it was passed to Ramón. Some of the members called for a reprimand but the face of the new Master showed no emotion.

'Thank you Monsieur Jean-Pierre for the document.' he said quietly, 'This offence was outside my tenure and no action will be taken against you.'

Anamar had insisted on bringing the silver drinking vessels found in the chest and they were used now for the liqueurs. The Master closed the formal part of the evening and the conversation continued into the night.

Anamar and Ramón excused themselves after midnight and sat up in bed trying to read the document returned by Monsieur Jean-Pierre. It was in French but seemed to be a translation from another language. Although the lines were arranged like a poem or the lyric of a song there was neither rhyme, rhythm nor metre, nor was there any apparent sense within every line, nor connection between the lines.

The word 'nave' appeared a number of times in the script and Anamar was sure that it referred to the Cathedral.

She wrote the translation of one line on her pad,

'Where the Evil One stands above the Cavern of the Bull,'

If the document was indeed about the location of the Cathedral she knew the whereabouts of the 'Evil One' and 'the Cavern of the bull'.

There was a light tap on the door and Ramón rose to answer it. Monsieur Raymond Bodelot, the one member who had lacked any enthusiasm at the meeting, was standing in the corridor. He beckoned Ramón to his room and closed the door quietly.

'Forgive me Don Ramón,' he said quietly, 'I am as excited for the future of the Cult as you or Don Carlos. But you have an enemy within the camp.

He feels the Spanish have held the post of Master of the Cult for too long. He believes it is now the turn of the French. He has already been in contact with me asking for my support.'

'I will visit you in Mont L'ours on my way home today and tell you all.'

Ramón shook hands with this new ally and went back to his room to tell Anamar. However, she had already decided not to mention 'the Evil One' or 'the Cavern of the Bull'. She needed to consult a map first. And, each with his or her own thoughts, she and Ramón lay awake until dawn.

## FRIDAY THE THIRTEENTH

Next morning the members dispersed after breakfast. Monsieur Raymond was one of the last to come down and appeared disinterested. It was as if the conversation with Ramón during the night had never taken place.

Anamar insisted that she should drive back. She enjoyed being behind the steering wheel. Ramón always had a good car and had taught her to drive soon after they were married. Now they had a beautiful dark blue Citroen saloon of the Light Fifteen series. Ramón appreciated the advanced engineering and the front-wheel drive which made this car special. Anamar loved driving on the mountain roads around Mont L'ours. It had been the very best of practice when she had been researching her walking guide book as some of the start and finishing points had been over forty kilometres away,

Monsieur Raymond was waiting for them when they arrived back at their home in Mont L'ours and Ramón took him up to his study at once. Father Brian willingly accepted Anamar's invitation to stay on for a few days and he and Raoul went out for a walk. Raoul wanted to hear the news of their friends in Paris and had suddenly become aware that he missed Paris and his friends there far more than he had realised.

Anamar did not want to interrupt the conversation in the study but she needed a map. She excused herself, found the one she wanted in the cupboard and left them to it. Ramón wondered what was happening. Why did Anamar need a map so urgently? She had been preoccupied since the end of last night's banquet. But he had urgent business himself. Monsieur Raymond had not yet told him the name of the enemy within the camp.

'Marc Decuré is the man you must watch, Don Ramón,' he said evenly. At the meeting of the Cult Raymond had been detached. Now he was a different man, so intense he could hardly remain in his chair.

'I have known for some years that Monsieur Decuré wished to succeed your father. He made no secret of his ambition amongst the French members. But a short time ago I discovered irregularities in the Cult's accounts. When I went to Navarre to tell your father he had already been taken ill and I could not burden him. When he died I decided to wait until you were confirmed as Master.'

He produced a sheaf of papers.

'Before I retired I was an accountant within the administration of the Département, Don Ramón. Someone has tampered with these accounts. Our balance sheets have been altered. Bills for services are clearly bogus. Five of these companies to which we have paid sums do not exist, neither does the last Charity to which we sent money. I can prove that most of the expenses incurred by Monsieur Decuré are fraudulent. While he has been our treasurer our funds have been plundered. Your father knew nothing of this. He trusted Monsieur Decuré as a reputable banker.'

Ramón was feeling the lack of sleep but he willed himself to concentrate. He studied the papers closely and sat back in his chair.

'I am deeply grateful for your vigilance, Monsieur Raymond, but we must proceed carefully. I trust our Teller, Don Carlos and will ask him to contact you to verify your findings. If you both agree that there is a case to answer I will call a meeting of the Cult and demand that Monsieur Marc Decuré present himself to face the charge of fraud.'

By the time the two men came out into the garden Anamar had finished her study of the map and Monsieur Raymond was anxious to be on his way. The previous evening he had sounded disagreeable and looked old. Now he appeared cheerful, younger. Before he drove off he shook hands with Anamar and smiled. She found herself thinking he must have been a handsome man when he was younger. Ramón now had another ally he could trust but being Master was not going to be easy.

While the two men had been upstairs Anamar had been relating the information in Hilaire Belloc's book on the Pyrenees to the map. She was certain the document which Monsieur Jean-Pierre had returned the previous evening was concerned with the location of the Cathedral because it mentioned the word 'nave' a number of times.

She found oblique references in Belloc's book to each of the landmarks mentioned in the document. Was 'The Evil One' the peak 'Maladetta' and 'The Cavern of the Bull', 'The Trou de Toro'? They were both features in the Esera Valley above the village of Benasque on the Spanish side of the Pyrenees.

But this valley was surely far too high in the mountains and remote from habitations to be the location of a Cathedral.

She wandered away from the house up the track towards the forest, wondering why she was so reluctant to reveal her thoughts to Ramón. She tried to persuade herself that, if she did so, he would tell Raoul and she was determined to keep it from him.

But that was only part of her dilemma. She was hearing, in her inner ear, her own call to adventure. She wanted to find the Cathedral herself. It would mean an expedition on her own to the Esera Valley. But keeping her findings secret, setting off alone, that was just what she needed. When the time came she would pass off the journey as wanderlust and tell Ramón and the others her findings when she was ready.

Ramón found himself busier than he had been for years. The Sanctuary seemed to be working well but Jules and Maurice needed him to be available for decisions every few days. Raoul's research was enabling him to make more sense of individual papers. But he needed to work with Raoul every day to keep up with developments.

There was also the problem of Monsieur Raymond's allegations. Now he had involved Don Carlos he could leave it to him and Raymond to complete the investigation. But it was still a worry.

Over the next week he was vaguely aware that Anamar was behaving oddly, then he remembered the map and smiled to himself. She was preparing for another journey. He pretended not to notice and feigned surprise when she mentioned it one afternoon when they were visiting the Bear Sanctuary.

'I hope it won't make things awkward for you,' she said, 'But I'd like to go off for a few days to do a walk on the Spanish side of the mountains. I'll need a lift to Benasque, where I intend to start and I would appreciate a ride home from Bagnères de Luchon when I cross the range into France.'

Ramón admired his wife's adventurous spirit. He worried for her safety when she went off on her own but he knew that she saw these trips as much more than an achievement of kilometres walked or peaks climbed. He kissed her on both cheeks and offered to drive her to Benasque himself.

That evening Anamar showed him the maps and discussed the walk. It would take her past the ancient building which housed the hot baths of the spa above Benasque. She would visit the ruins of the old inn, the Hospital de Benasque and climb high into the Esera valley. She would search for routes to the North and East and finish by crossing the Col de Benasque to the elegant town of Bagnères de Luchon on the French side of the mountains.

Anamar decided to make no mention of her discovery of the place names mentioned in, what she now called to herself, 'the missing document'. Ramón was unfamiliar with that part of the Pyrenees and the Spanish maps would call the features by their Spanish names rather than the French names used on her map. For the moment these would remain her secret and a leaving date for her journey was arranged in early August to suit Ramón's commitments.

In the meantime Anamar decided to make her own study of 'the missing document' returned by Jean-Pierre to see if she could link it with any of the other documents.

A week later Ramón seemed to have forgotten about 'the missing document'. He was preoccupied with the vast number of research papers yet to be studied closely. Then Raoul gave him a sheaf of typed and numbered pages he had translated from the book without binding or title. They had been written in Latin on the finest calf-skin vellum. Raoul was familiar with such ancient books. Occasionally a binding would have been removed, presumably because it was so ornately worked by the scribe it was more valuable than the text and could be sold. He had provisionally dated it as of the 14th century.

To a student of ancient manuscripts this was treasure trove. For three years he had worked at the Sorbonne, in Paris, cleaning and preserving old documents and paintings, translating texts into French. But this was an exceptional opportunity to demonstrate his skills. His particular experience was in translating from the original Latin and Ramón encouraged him to use a degree of licence in the interpretation to make the document readable in modern French. He was now delighted with the results.

As Ramón scanned the first translated page it was obvious that this was the story of one of his ancestors, Alfonso de Codés. Alfonso had been a nobleman born in 1273 and reared in Navarre, as had Ramón himself, their births separated by six hundred and fifty years. Raoul had written an identifying name for the book on the first translated page and Ramón settled himself to read it word by word.

### THE TEMPLAR MANUSCRIPT

*Alfonso de Codés took the vows of a monk and joined the Military
Order of the Knights Templar when he was seventeen. A year later*

*he found himself fighting with the Crusaders at the battle for Acre Castle in 1291. The Saracens won a great victory and finally succeeded in driving the Christians from the Holy Land.*

*Most of the garrison's Templar Knights were killed in the battle. The Saracens usually spared the lives of knights taken prisoner who could be ransomed for large sums of money but, such was the reputation of the Templars as fierce and fearless fighters, they were beheaded, so that they would not live to fight another day.*

*During the battle Alfonso's Commander, Gilbert de Nantes, ordered him to escape and entrusted him with a leather satchel. closed and sealed. He was told only that it contained a vital part of the Sacred Templar Treasure and he was instructed to deliver it to a French Templar, Bernard de Troyes, at the Order's Commanderie at Bordeaux in Aquitaine. His Commander's last words were that the satchel was not to be opened except by Bernard de Troyes. Before he left an aide gave Alfonso a leather purse containing a sum in gold coin to expedite his safe passage back to France. When the battle was lost Alfonso was one of a small remnant of Christian knights who evaded capture by escaping through a secret tunnel which led from the castle to Acre port.*

Ramón shook his head in admiration. Raoul had surpassed himself. His translation had caught him in its spell but it was late in the evening and he sent Raoul off to bed. Madam Mons was still in the kitchen and she made him coffee. Ramón took the Manuscript up to his study, checked that Anamar was asleep and settled down to read on into the night.

*As Alfonso fled from Acre with a small group of knights, of which he was the only Templar, they were attacked by a much larger party of Saracens. In man-to-man combat he wounded a young Saracen warrior but spared his life. The light was fading quickly and Alfonso's horse was killed. As darkness fell he became separated from his companions. Rather than flee from the skirmish on foot, Alfonso decided to hide in a nearby hole. It was well concealed, hidden in a small clump of fig trees behind a pile of rocks.*

*The battle won, the Saracens made camp for the night nearby and moved away at dawn. When Alfonso emerged from his hole in the rocks he found, amongst the corpses, the young warrior whose life he had spared. The Saracen was not badly wounded. He spoke a little French and explained that his companions had left him as he lay. They had wrongly accused him of theft and he had feigned death to escape detention.*

*He, too, had lost his horse, but amongst the dead bodies and abandoned equipment were cloaks and blankets, water bottles, bags of fruit and almond paste wrapped in fresh leaves. Alfonso still had his sealed satchel slung over his shoulder and his small bag of gold coins.*

*The Saracen was called Hassan and he and Alfonso agreed to make their escape together. With drawings in the sand and the names of a few places they both recognised, they made a plan. Their route would take them to Cyprus and on through the Mediterranean by boat to Western Europe. Alfonso stripped himself of his Templar cloak, shield, sword and helmet and left them in the hole. They hid in the rocks by the fig tree grove until the evening. Under cover of darkness they travelled North towards Tyre, posing as merchants.*

*Four nights later they arrived at the port of Tyre. Alfonso hid amongst the fishing boats and Hassan went to negotiate passages to Cyprus. He was not sure that he could trust the fisherman who agreed to take them but the boat looked strong and seaworthy and a small gold piece settled the transaction.*

*They sailed at night, trekked across Cyprus to the harbour at Kyrenia and arranged a passage to Rhodes. This time Alfonso drove a hard bargain. He felt that they had paid too much from Tyre. It would never do to give the impression that they had money. He insisted that they land at night at the fishing port of Lindos rather than the city of Rhodes. The island was a Crusader citadel defended by the Hospitallers, the Knights of St. John. There would be Templar Knights here, too, but Alfonso had no intention of making contact with his brother monks.*

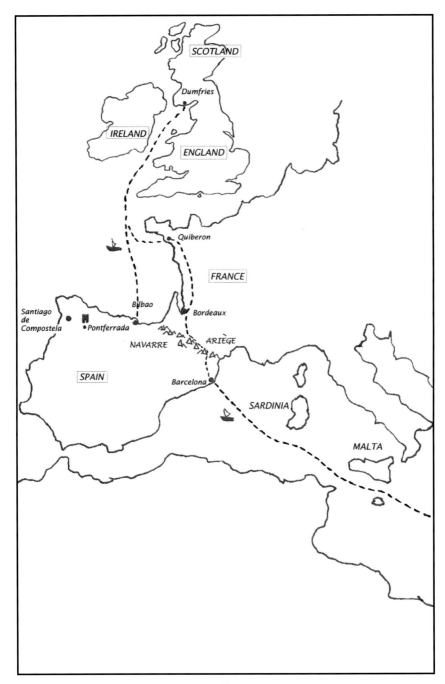

Map of action in
Europe in 1300 AD
~
ALPHONSO'S JOURNEYS

GREECE

RHODES
Lindos

HOLY
LAND

CYPRUS

Acre
castle

MESOPOTAMIA

MEDITERRANEAN SEA

*His orders from his Commander at Acre had been to deliver the satchel to Bernard de Troyes at Bordeaux and no one else. Had he made his mission known to the Templars in Rhodes, it was certain that he would have had to hand over the satchel to the Commander there.*

*Lindos was a tight clump of sturdily built white houses and taverns above a safe harbour and a sheltered bay. On the sky-line above were the ruins of what must have been a glorious temple. While they waited for news of a passage to the West they lodged with the widow of a fisherman and Alfonso began to teach Hassan the Spanish language. They paid their way for food and board by repairing boats and nets and this allowed them to keep Alfonso's money secret.*

*Arranging the passage to Spain proved difficult but after two weeks one of their fisherman friends brought a merchant to meet them. Manuel Diego Bin-Rahman was a small, bulky man, completely bald, his face tanned and his hands surprisingly large and strong. He was from Aragon, the neighbouring kingdom in Iberia to Navarre where Alfonso had been born.*

*Manuel's father had been a Spanish soldier, injured and taken prisoner by the Moors. When his wounds healed he had remained with his captors and married the daughter of a Moorish merchant. In Christian countries he called himself Manuel Diego, spoke Castillian Spanish and worshipped as a Christian. In the East, or in Moorish Spain he retained his mother's maiden name, Bin-Rahman, spoke Arabic and conducted his business as a Moslem.*

*Before the meeting, Manuel had spent a number of small sums of money finding out about Alfonso and Hassan. They were young and strong, not attached to the Crusader Army, not in anyone else's pay and, he guessed, reliable.*

*He told them that he was returning from the East with a consignment of spices. He had ginger, nutmeg from Far Eastern islands, cloves, all small in bulk but highly prized in the West. In port or at sea a cargo like this was easily pilfered and his two guards had been killed in Egypt. Alfonso was amazed at how*

much Manuel knew about Hassan and himself but it was
reassuring that he was prepared to trust them.

They accepted Manuel's offer to guard his precious cargo for small
wages and free passage to Barcelona. Alfonso's little hoard of coins
would not be depleted.

Manuel Diego was reassured that he had chosen well when they
hired a mule and transferred the cargo to their lodgings. They
turned a room into a cell by blocking the window and having the
locksmith make and install a good lock with a key.

It was another three weeks before a passage could be arranged but
once the voyage was underway the three men became firm friends.
They were all sea-sick in a fierce storm near Sardinia but Manuel
could see that neither of his guards relaxed their vigilance even at
the height of the tempest.

When they reached Barcelona it was agreed that, as Alfonso was
now going back to his life as a Templar, Hassan should stay with
Manuel and help him with his business. Manuel paid Alfonso his
due and he used the money to buy a good horse for the trek over
the Pyrenees to Bordeaux. Before they parted they swore an oath
to meet again.

Alfonso arrived at the Templar house in Bordeaux at a bad time.
The Commander, Bernard de Troyes, had died. His successor was
a sour, elderly, drunken monk who doubted Alfonso had ever been
to the Holy Land. When the satchel was presented to him, he
threw it in a corner amongst the rubbish and fell asleep.

Next day he ordered Alfonso to go immediately to the Templar
castle at Ponferrada in Northern Spain to protect the pilgrims on
the Road to Santiago de Compostela. That night Alfonso made his
way into the old monk's quarters and found the satchel amongst
the rubble. It was still securely fastened and sealed. Although he
was unsure what he would do with it, he was certain that this
house was the wrong place to leave it.

Alfonso left on horseback next morning with the satchel slung over
his shoulder under his white Templar cloak and his own small
treasure of gold coins sewn into a secret pocket under his tunic.

*When he reached Ponferrada he felt unwelcome. The Commander was young and unfriendly. As his brother knights saw it, Alfonso had been involved in the Templars' greatest defeat and he had fled the battle for Acre like a coward. There were times when Alfonso was tempted to tell them about the treasure in his satchel. But he said nothing. He quarried a deep hole behind a block of stone in the wall of his cell and concealed the satchel and his gold coins.*

*The years passed slowly and it was a relief when Alfonso was posted to an important Templar Commanderie at Pluviguer in Troisième Lyonnaise, known in English as Brittany. Alfonso opened up his secret hiding place and retrieved the leather satchel and the gold. He rode alone, back along el Camino de Santiago, the Road of St James. In Navarre he was distressed to find his family lands devastated by poverty and sickness. He had heard of the death of his father and mother after short illnesses but was amazed to find the extent of the havoc wrought by disease. Four weeks later, when he arrived at the Templar house at Pluviguer on the 12th of October, he was still depressed. It was late in the evening, he was a stranger to the other knights, and not yet on the official strength of the Commanderie.*

-------------------------------------------------

It was the darkest hour before dawn but Ramón could hardly restrain himself. He knew what was coming. This was the story of the infamous Friday the Thirteenth of October,1307, when all the Templar Knights in France were arrested on the orders of Philip the Fair, a date still regarded throughout Europe as the unluckiest combination of day and date of all.

Ramón's primary research interest was medieval history and the story of the Knights Templar was the most intriguing of that era. He knew that the Order had been formed in Jerusalem in 1119 to protect pilgrims travelling to the Holy Land. They were pious knights, willing to face martyrdom. Although they took religious vows, they were regarded as a religious order of knights trained to fight, not as monks of the old tradition for whom killing was forbidden.

The Templars wore their hair short and their beards long. Their tunics and caps were of dark material and their mantles white with a red cross.

Their sergeants dressed in black with a white cross on the mantle.

These knights were men of action, often illiterate. The Rule of the Order was expressed in Latin but they kept few records. They developed extensive commercial activities using fleets of cargo ships and mule caravans. One such route brought cloth from England to La Rochelle, the foremost port on the Atlantic and across Southern France to Collioure on the Mediterranean. They transported salt in the Holy Land, wool in the West. They rented farms, forges and mills. They acted as couriers, carrying money, precious stones and expensive cargo. They served as almoners and treasurers to the rich and powerful.

They had great skill in mounted warfare which required training and considerable investment in good horses and reliable weapons. The Templars had such wealth. They inspired a reputation as formidable warriors, based on their expertise and courage, and the ferocity of their onslaughts in battle. They learned from the fast, agile, lightly-armoured Moslem cavalry and developed their ability to conduct devastating raids, known as 'chevauchees', on enemy territory and property.

Ramón was aware that when Pope Innocent the Second confirmed the Rule of the Order in the 12th century, the Templars had been given great privileges. They were excused the payment of tithes to the Church on the produce of their lands. They could retain booty captured from the Moslems. They could build private chapels to hear divine office. They need not give oaths of loyalty to anyone outside the Order, which meant, in effect, that they were directly responsible only to the Pope.

Ramón was familiar with the works of Matthew Paris, the chronicler of St. Alban's Abbey in England in the 13th century and he admired the detailed descriptions of Acre Castle written by the Secretary of Master William de Beaujeu in the same era.

And Ramón, himself, had written about the defeat at Acre in 1291. The Crusader castles were regarded as the last bastion of Christianity in the Holy Land. One was reputed to have a garrison of three hundred knights, four thousand men and enough food, water and armaments to last for five years. When Acre was captured by the Sultan of Egypt, it was the last castle to fall and the defeat allowed the Saracens to drive the Christians out of the Holy Land.

The Templars had withdrawn to the West and centred their operations in Western Europe. Over the years they had become so rich and powerful that they were the envy of every ruler within whose domain their Commanderies were situated.

Philip 1V of France had been particularly jealous of their power and wealth but he had to claim the support of the Church before he could move against them. Then events conspired to assist him. The Pope was kidnapped and disappeared, presumed dead. Soon after, the new Pontiff's successor died mysteriously and Philip was able to ensure that his ally, the Archbishop of Bordeaux, became Pope Clement V.

On that one fatal day in 1307 the soldiers of Philip 1V had conducted a highly secret operation to imprison all the Templars in France and to confiscate their properties. The knights were arrested and interrogated. They were charged with heresy but, when they were tried in 1312, Pope Clement V did not find them guilty. The verdict was not proven. However, the damage had been done and, later in the same year, the Order was disbanded.

Ramón was deeply impressed by Raoul's translation. This document clearly linked his forebear to the events of Friday the Thirteenth of October 1307.

He trimmed the oil lamps and read on.

### ............THE TEMPLAR MANUSCRIPT CONTINUES

*Having arrived between Vespers and Compline, Alfonso was allocated a room on the top floor of the Commanderie. It was small and sparsely furnished as befitted a monk's cell. There was one circular window under the eaves, partly shaded by an ancient creeper which climbed beyond it on to the roof. The window was the only ventilation and was open, pivoted on a horizontal bar across its diameter.*

*He had been too late to record his name on the register or to eat with the brother monks and was given a plate of food and a carafe of wine to take to his room. He found it impossible to sleep. Although it was Autumn it had been a sunny day and the room under the eaves was hot and uncomfortable. In the early hours he was drawn to the window for a breath of night air. There was no moon and not even the slightest breeze.*

*An owl hooted from a near-by tree. Alfonso poked his head out of the bottom half of the window. Everything else was still and quiet.*

*The night air was cool on his face. There was a village at the front of the house but here at the back there were no dwellings, only the forest, a deeper black than the darkness of the night. He could hear nothing and could see no one. But Alfonso's warrior instinct sensed that there were people within the trees.*

*Then he heard a low metallic rustle that might have been chain mail on a moving figure. He strained to hear, hardly daring to draw breath. There was a dull clank of arms against armour. The owl hooted loudly, eerily. Its call was so sharp and clear it must have been perched in the nearest tree, the branches of which touched the Templar house.*

*Alfonso felt a shiver of apprehension across the back of his neck. The years as a soldier monk had honed his sense of danger to a fine edge. The Commanderie was only lightly defended. Templar houses in a friendly country were not built for defence in contrast to the Order's formidable castles.*

*It was still an hour to first light and, although he could see neither shapes nor movement, Alfonso was sure there were soldiers gathering in the darkness. He felt for the thick arm of the creeper and eased himself out of the window as far as he dared but, although the faint sounds confirmed his suspicions, he could see nothing. Gradually his eyes became accustomed to the starlight. He heard the rasp of a sword being drawn from its scabbard. There was a flash of light on armour and he saw moving figures creeping quietly towards the Commanderie.*

*When they emerged in the first glimmer of light before dawn there must have been forty soldiers, moving silently, hands on scabbards to prevent the rattle. Alfonso remained still, any movement might have caught the attention of one vigilant soldier. They disappeared around the end of the house and seconds later they were hammering on the main door.*

*Alfonso drew himself back into the room, dressed quickly and opened his door a crack to hear what was happening.*

*The soldiers were the King's men, their captain read a proclamation in a voice which carried throughout the house. The orders were from Philip the Fair himself. All Templars were to be arrested at dawn on this day, Friday the thirteenth of October. They were to be held captive, interrogated, charged with heresy and if guilty, burnt at the stake. There was no point resisting, the captain said. He had forty-five armed soldiers and he knew that there were only eight Templars in the house.*

*For the second time in his life Alfonso left behind his helmet, sword, shield and white Templar robe with its red splayed cross. He took only his secret purse of gold and the leather satchel, still unopened. He squeezed through the bottom half of the window and used the thick creeper and the branches of the tree to climb up onto the roof. The Commanderie had been extended and, where the ridges of the two buildings met, there was a valley between the roofs where he could hide, unseen from ground level.*

*It was a long day without food or water but, like the skirmish after the battle for Acre, it was better to hide than run. Alfonso crawled along the valley between the roofs to watch the soldiers leave with their eight Templar prisoners under close guard. No one had told them of the new arrival. No doubt the information might be revealed later under torture but not now.*

*After dark Alfonso climbed back into his room. The servants had fled. The Commanderie was empty. Having taken possession of the building some of the soldiers should have remained there but they all wanted to go back with the prisoners. Alfonso took a little food and some clothing and walked out through the open front door dressed as a villager.*

*He headed south towards the sea and reached the fishing port of Quiberon shortly after dawn. It was a good time to arrive. The boats had just come in from a night's fishing. The families of the fishermen were there, anxious to see the size of the catch. There were fish merchants determined to pay as little as possible. Women had brought their baskets hoping for a bargain. It was easy for Alfonso to become part of the crowd.*

*Later, when the the town came to life, he bought a good cloak at a street stall which would help him pass himself off as a merchant. As usual he paid in silver coin. He had long since decided to keep the gold hidden in public. When he needed to change gold coin for silver, he found a money lender and did a private deal with him away from prying eyes.*

*The town was on the end of a small peninsula with a sheltered harbour on the lee side. The village inn was the biggest and best building in the town. There was a steady trade of travellers sailing to and from England, Ireland and Les Isles Normandes, called by the English, The Channel Islands.*

*Alfonso took one of the four rooms at the inn and paid in advance for five nights. The innkeeper introduced himself as Le Poing, The Fist. Le Poing was pleased to have a customer he could talk to man-to-man and treated Alfonso as an honoured guest. His interest deepened when Alfonso told him he was seeking a passage to Ireland. Le Poing was an imposing man, not by his height but by his burly physical shape. It gave him the look of a powerful fighting man. By the second day he had guessed that Alfonso had money. It was his business to know such things. And his new guest carried himself in a way which plainly showed, to a man of his perception, that he had a warrior staying at his inn.*

*The inn was the best business in this part of Brittany. Le Poing took a pride in being the first with the news, good or bad. The villagers said that he had men in his pay from whom he bought information. He was welcome at the castle and the monastery. He had often been to the Commanderie to which Alfonso had been posted. His own method of collecting information was to share the news with everyone he met in the course of business or pleasure, hoping they would do the same. He revelled in intrigue. He knew that if he offered confidences he would receive secrets in return.*

*Over a few glasses of wine the next night he told Alfonso about the arrest of the Templars.*

*'There are four other Commanderies in the area, all raided at dawn on the thirteenth. The King and the Pope are in it together,' he said with his eyebrows raised. 'They are jealous of the Order's great wealth and influence. Some might say that the Templars are too interested in business and making money to be good monks but the charges the King brings against them are ludicrous.'*

*Alfonso listened and asked a few casual questions, doing his best not to show too much interest. But Le Poing needed no encouragement.*

*'The Templars are being charged with denying Christ, spitting on the cross, worshipping the preserved head of a bearded man, kissing each other obscenely, adoring a cat.'*

*He began to chuckle. He held his arms across his massive chest and his whole body shook gently with laughter.*

*'Would you believe it - adoring a cat! The King must think we are all imbeciles. There could be reasons for charging the Templars but this is a farce. The King wants their money and now he has the Pope in his pocket all he has to do is convict them of heresy.'*

*Although he had heard the captain of the King's soldiers announce his orders, Alfonso was still bewildered by the arrest of his fellow knights. He had taken his vows willingly, had been proud of the Templar's reputation for valour, for protecting pilgrims. True, a few of his brother monks had been drunken, lazy, dishonest but there were many, like his commander at Acre, whom he admired. Le Poing, the innkeeper was right, these charges were absurd.*

*It was five days before a vessel was due from the South, bound for Waterford in Ireland. Alfonso roamed the bays and headlands of the rocky coast. He had time to think and the more he thought the more certain he was that his days as a Templar Knight were over.*

*He had already broken his vows.*

*His vow of Poverty had gone when he had held on to the gold given him by his commander at Acre to expedite his return to France with the sealed satchel containing the Sacred Templar Treasure. He had also kept the money earned by guarding the merchant Manuel Diego Bin-Rahman's cargo of spices on the voyage.*

*His vow of Obedience had gone by default when he retrieved and held on to the sealed satchel containing the treasure when it had been tossed aside by the drunken commander at Bordeaux .*

*But the easiest of all the vows to break had been Chastity. When he and Hassan had escaped by boat from the Holy Land, they had spent four weeks at Lindos, a fishing village on the island of Rhodes. They had stayed in the house of the young widow of a fisherman. She had looked after them well and shared her bed with Alfonso. He had prayed to the Lord for strength to resist his urges but when night came he had always gone back to her bed.*

*And now the Pope was to dissolve the Order of the Temple. He was no longer a religious. He was now a free man. It must be possible for him to build a new life. But not in France. This time he would not hide, he would run.*

*On the day the boat sailed, making passage first to Waterford in Ireland, Alfonso felt a tug of his sleeve as he waited to go on board. Le Poing was standing behind him.*

*'Now you are leaving, my secretive friend,' the innkeeper said confidentially, 'You can tell me who you are.'*

*Alfonso laughed and gently punched the Fist's shoulder, the gesture of the friend who wishes to say nothing. The Fist leaned forward to whisper in his ear.*

*'I think you could be a Templar,' he said, 'You have the shoulders of a warrior and the gait of a monk.'*

*Alfonso laughed again but Le Poing was concerned for him.*

*'If you are a Templar don't land in Ireland. The Norman spies are everywhere. Stay on the boat. She will sail on to Dublin, then to Scotland. The King there is Robert The Bruce and he has no love for King Philip of France or Pope Clement. You will be safe there and both the lords and the warrior caste speak French.'*

*He stayed at the quay-side as the boat sailed.*

*'You know where to find me if you ever need a friend,' he yelled into the wind and shook his fist with the fingers showing forward.*

*Alfonso had already decided to take Le Poing's advice before the coast disappeared behind the horizon.*

---

Raoul had pinned a hand written note to the next typewritten page. It explained that a section of the manuscript had been defaced. He had repaired the damage and collated the information rather than translating it directly. The next typewritten page was entitled -

### SURMISED FACTS FROM A DAMAGED SECTION OF
### THE TEMPLAR MANUSCRIPT.

*The voyage was uneventful with fair winds and a calm sea. Listening to the conversation of the crew Alfonso heard that there was a steady trade between France and Scotland and the men enjoyed their time ashore there. They disliked the weather and the passage through the Channel between the North of Ireland and Scotland although it was calm on this voyage. He learned, too, that although Gaelic was spoken in the North of the country, in the south Northern English was the common language. Norman French was spoken by the aristocracy, the warrior class, the educated and the merchants.*

*With the language very much in his mind, Alfonso decided to keep to the South and disembarked at the first port of call in Scotland, the Port of Dumfries. He installed himself at an inn in the centre of the town and decided to remain there for a time to decide on his future.*

Another note from Raoul indicated that the narrative could now be continued without him having to surmise the facts.

### ............THE TEMPLAR MANUSCRIPT CONTINUES

*After three weeks Alfonso found himself enjoying the life of the town. He met merchants, had become friendly with the captain of the guard at the castle and had visited the monastery. There, the monks treated him without suspicion, as a gentleman of leisure who was more devout than most of the local men of means.*

*Early one evening the captain of the guard came to the inn to see him. Like Alfonso, he was in his thirties but looked older. He was a quiet man, born and bred locally, unmarried, a soldier all his working life. It was hard for a man in his position to have friends. Friends might want special treatment. They might betray a trust. There were times when the job had to be done, regardless of who might suffer.*

*James Lamont had risen through the ranks to be made a captain. He had only known this foreign gentleman for less than a month but they were now friends, making no demands on each other. He suspected that Alfonso had been a soldier. It was the way he held himself, calm, watchful, unafraid.*

*One evening they were alone before the hearth.*

*'I need to be sure you have been a soldier,' James said as if no answer was needed to this first question. 'I think you have been a Crusader.'*

*Alfonso smiled and nodded. In this country and to this man whom he trusted he felt no need to hide his past.*

*'Why do you ask?'*

*'One of the guardians of Dumfries, John Comyn, otherwise known as the Red Comyn, was killed by Edward 1 two years ago and lawlessness is now the rule. The Earl of Killhaven's fiefdom is within three day's march and he needs the help of two experienced captains. He has good soldiers but they do not know how to find and punish the outlaw bands. He needs two men to train his soldiers like Saracen raiders or Crusader Knights.'*

*James Lamont sat back and waited.*

*Alfonso allowed himself a smile. This was a task to stir the blood of a warrior.*

*'I'll need a good horse and the best sword money can buy here in Dumfries. We can leave for Killhaven Castle tomorrow.'*

*The Earl of Killhaven was no leader of fighting men nor had he the slightest desire to succeed as such but he was clever, astute, some said the most cunning man in the country. He knew James Lamont, captain of the guard at Dumfries and was certain he would not recommend a partner unless he felt the man was worthy.*

*In a month James and Alfonso had reorganised the soldiers into companies of ten. Each unit trained on its own. They wore light armour. Their horses were fast and agile. The men were taught to skirmish, to engage the enemy fiercely, to retreat if the move did not immediately succeed, then to attack again ferociously as the enemy regrouped. Unless they were in action they were expected to practice every day, hand-to-hand combat, archery, quarter-staff combat, horsemanship, tracking, searching at night.*

*From the first day the lord Killhaven was certain his new captains could defeat the brigands but he was unsure that they would administer the kind of hard punishment which would eradicate this plague of violence from his lands.*

*One evening after they had eaten at the castle he told them that the English had set an example. He describe the punishment by slow death of the Scot William Wallace only a few years before. A horseman had dragged him for four miles around London. Wallace was then publicly castrated, hanged by his neck, cut down while still alive, disembowelled and decapitated. Parts of his body were then exhibited around the city.*

*He told them about the English treatment of the ladies of the vanquished when King Edward had defeated Robert the Bruce at the Battle of Methven. Bruce's male supporters had been executed and the women had not been spared. Lady Isabel, Countess of Buchan, had been imprisoned in a cage hanging on the walls of Berwick Castle. Robert's sister, Mary had been incarcerated in a cage on the tower of Roxburg Castle. Neither lady had yet been released.*

*Alfonso and James roamed the lands of Killhaven, attacking the robber bands on their own ground, rooting out their hideaways, burning their shelters, administering summary justice by hanging the leaders, imprisoning their followers in the dungeons of the castle, terrorising the outlaws. By the Summer of 1308 the thieves and brigands were dead or had fled the Killhaven lands.*

*'My captains,' as Lord Killhaven called Alfonso and James, 'Are the finest in the land. They have rid me of the brigands who infested my domain. Before, we were prisoners on our own lands. Now, it is the felons who know the meaning of fear.'*

---

It was almost dawn when Ramón came to the end of the last of the type-written pages. Raoul had assured him that, within a week, he would have completed the translation. Ramón was exhausted, not in the physical sense of needing rest or sleep. His body felt tired but his mind was excited beyond imagination.

Alfonso was his ancestor, that was obvious. But there was more to come. He paced his study to let his mind come to rest. When he went into the bedroom, Anamar was asleep. He would tell her the story to-morrow.

## ANAMAR'S EXPEDITION

The sun was shining when Ramón awoke. It was ten-thirty and he had never slept so late since he was a boy. He was mentally refreshed, revitalised. After a few quiet years since his marriage, his life had changed dramatically. His wife and children were thriving in Ariège. He was now the patron of a sanctuary for bears. His father's death had not only given him an estate in Navarre but an archive which was revealing family secrets back to the 14th century. It had also given him the duty of master of an ancient cult. He felt younger. He was ready for anything.

Over breakfast he told Anamar the story in the Manuscript. She was delighted to see him so exhilarated and wanted to hear the next part of the tale.

But she made no mention of her own study of 'the missing document' produced by Monsieur Jean-Pierre at the meeting. And it had revealed another clue.

'**Flows the secret river, born in the hidden depths of the sacred nave.**'

Put that line below the previous clue and it read -

**'Where the evil one stands above the cavern of the bull**
**Flows the secret river, born in the hidden depths of the sacred nave'**

Hilaire Belloc's book on the Pyrenees was again helping to unravel the mystery. Belloc loved the Pyrenees. Like the voyages he had made on his boat, the Nona, his wanderings in the Pyrenees had been a refuge from the hard graft of writing and lecturing for a living. Knowing of Anamar's appreciation of Belloc's poetry and mountain stories, Ramón had searched for a copy of his book, 'The Pyrenees', published over fifty years before in 1909 and now out-of-print. After months of searching he had found it on an outdoor book stall in Toulouse. Anamar treasured it as one of the best presents she had ever received.

She had studied what Belloc had to say about the Esera valley above Benasque and he had solved the first clue for her. 'The Evil One' must be the mountain massif of Maladetta and 'the Cavern of the Bull' was certainly the Trou de Toro. Belloc had described the torrent which tumbled down into the huge hole and disappeared underground on the Spanish side of the mountains. He maintained that this was the same river which emerged on the French side, 2000 feet lower down, the head-waters of the mighty Garonne.

This river which poured over the waterfall into the cavern must be 'the secret river'. If she could follow it back up the valley below Maladetta where it flowed above ground, would it lead her to the spring which fed 'the sacred river'? Its source must be underground. Could this be where 'the sacred river' was 'born in the hidden depths of the sacred nave'? If so, 'the sacred nave' surely must be the Cult's Cathedral!

It suddenly seemed obvious to Anamar that the Cathedral was not a building above ground but an underground cave. And that would not be unique in the Pyrenees. On their honey-moon she and Ramón had visited the Caves of Lombrives near Tarascon, reputed to be one of the largest cave systems in Europe. Deep underground they had visited the highlight of the tour, a vast cavern, called by the guide, 'la Cathédrale'.

Although she was excited Anamar still found herself unwilling to share her discovery with anyone, even Ramón. But it was reason enough for her to visit the Benasque Valley. If she was right and was able to find the cave, the discovery would be a special gift to him. At least that was how she rationalised her secrecy. In the back of her mind she had a guilty feeling that she was deceiving her husband. However, she felt sure that the moment of revelation would be more than enough to appease him.

She had kept possession of 'the missing document' but only to keep it away from Raoul. He was the last person she wanted to be involved in solving the mystery. Anyway he and Ramón were far too busy unravelling Alfonso's story to bother about the location of the Cathedral just yet.

---

Interest in the Bear Sanctuary was growing. Le Sud, the newspaper with the largest circulation in the South of France, sent a reporter and a photographer. There were more visitors who now paid a small entrance fee to support the work of the Sanctuary. A veterinary surgeon brought in a new inmate, a younger female, badly injured by hunters and found unconscious by the roadside.

The vet had treated the bear and now she was partly recovered but she needed to be in a safe pen where he could keep a check on her progress.

The newspaper wanted the two cubs to become its mascots. A sum of money was offered as a gift to the Sanctuary's costs and a competition arranged to name the young bears. It was restricted to children under fourteen and there were hundreds of entrants. Anamar and the children, Deirdre, Henriques and Marie were invited by Le Sud to act as judges. They chose the names Fi-Fi and Rudi for the cubs. The Editor of Le Sud was delighted and published another illustrated article about the Sanctuary with photographs of Fi-Fi and Rudi and the two children who had won the competition.

The afternoon before Anamar left on her expedition to the Esera Valley above Benasque she was returning from a walk when she met Raoul. He seemed to have been waiting for her.

'I need to talk to you,' he said nervously, 'When we spoke before I said too much. But I felt so strongly. I needed to tell you about my feelings.'

Anamar raised a hand to stop him.

'It doesn't matter,' she said evenly, 'I've said nothing to Ramón. Let's forget it happened'.

Raoul took hold of her elbow.

'Please Anamar, please listen to me. I need your friendship. You are the reason I came here. You mean everything to me. I will do anything for you.'

Anamar pulled her arm free and shook her head.

'Can you not understand? This is ridiculous. There's nothing more to be said.'

'Can we not be friends?' Raoul said anxiously, 'You will hardly speak to me. If we can't be lovers, can we not be friends?'

Anamar left him and walked on so quickly it was almost at a run. Raoul stood, head in his hands, hiding the sight of her fleeing.

That evening at dinner they were discussing the journey to Benasque when Raoul turned his attention to Anamar.

'I would like to ask a great favour of you,' he said, smiling. His composure now returned. He was a different man from the pathetic, love-sick swain of the afternoon. He raised his hands in a theatrical gesture of good-will.

'I've completed the translation of the Manuscript and Ramón has kindly given me some leave. If he is agreeable, would it be all right for me to accompany you on your walk? The Esera is a wild part of the mountains and two would be safer than ...........'

Anamar pushed back her plate and stopped him with a look so baleful he cringed back in his seat. Ramón was startled. He had never seen his wife so angry. He was immediately sorry he had allowed Raoul to raise the question. When they had talked privately before dinner it had seemed a sensible idea. Anamar suddenly realised that the two men must have discussed the suggestion beforehand and Ramón was now included in her wrath.

'I can hardly believe my ears,' she said loudly, 'The pair of you have been deciding what I should do and who should go with me.'

She was almost shouting. Doña Marie sat impassively, behind an enigmatic smile. Madame Mons had been putting the finishing touches to the cheese-board and she turned to face the wall so that no one could see that she was smiling. They both disliked Raoul. He had made himself too much a part of the family. He was too familiar with his employers. And, fond as they were of Ramón, in an argument like this they were both on Anamar's side.

In spite of her rage, Anamar was suddenly aware that she was not nearly as angry as she appeared. She almost laughed. But this was too good an opportunity to miss. She was sorry for Ramón. He was white-faced with worry. But this was the time to make a mark on Raoul.

'The answer is No!. Do both of you understand that?'

Her voice was piercing, uncomfortably loud even in this big room. 'This is a journey I want to make on my own. I need to go alone. You can help by leaving me off at the start and collecting me at the end but make no mistake about it, I intend to do this journey by myself.'

The two men were silent, trying to think of a way to mollify her. But she would allow neither to speak. They looked so pitiful, all dignity gone, struggling for some word of appeasement. They were so absurdly pathetic she began to laugh.

'Do you remember a time in the Pyrenees when, unknown to each other, you were trying to protect me. One of you laid an ambush and the other walked into it. It was left to me to stop the fight. There you were, two grown men spraghling about in the snow like drunken snowmen?'

Ramón risked a smile and Raoul looked in vain for a sign that would allow him to smile too.

'Finish your dinner,' she said, ' And let's hear no more about it.'

Madame Mons served the cheese, still trying desperately not to laugh aloud. This young Irish woman had a temper. She was more than a match for Don Ramón and, as for the Parisian, he would need to watch his step or he would find himself out of a job,

They left next morning at eight, Anamar happy for Ramón to take the wheel. She owed him the opportunity to earn her approval. At first he was wary, doing his best to apologise without making it worse. Then she felt closer to him and placed her hand lightly on his arm to let him see all might be forgiven.

They drove on through St-Girons and Montrejeau and turned South to climb towards the Spanish frontier. The new tunnel near Viella took them under the main range of the mountains. Their route led through magnificent mountain terrain on the Spanish side and they looped around tight bends on rugged, narrow, unsurfaced roads to the small town of Benasque. It was well over two hundred and fifty kilometres and took all day.

They had dinner at nine and stayed the night at a road-side inn on the edge of the town. Before the meal they discussed Anamar's plans and arranged for Ramón to meet her at the end of the trek. The rendezvous would be at Bagnères de Luchon on the French side of the Pyrenees at noon in six days time. Anamar felt her emotions confused. She could hardly contain her excitement to be on her way but she was so sorry to be leaving Ramón, he looked so miserable.

She knew he was proud of her spirit of adventure but if he was worried for her he said nothing. It was easy to cheer him up. She smiled and all was forgiven. They were so elated during the meal she hardly noticed what she was eating. And, such was the delight in each other's company, Anamar wondered why they did not spend more time travelling together.

They left the inn early next morning to drive to the road head. She planned to have a breakfast stop on the open mountain after an hour or so and he could eat when he arrived back in Benasque before the long journey home. The dirt road climbed into the narrow mouth of the Esera valley on a ledge above the river. To the left, great cliffs concealed the Posets Massif. Across the river to the right, forests and rock walls rose steeply towards the Western flank of Maladetta.

High on that slope Anamar's eye followed a track as it zig-zagged up to an impressive stone structure like a mountain monastery. On the lower side, the building looked to be all of four storeys high but she guessed that, such was the steepness of the slope, on the upper side there would be only a single storey. Ramón had seen it too.

'That's the famous Baños de Benasque,' he said, ' It may not be as grand as the great spas of Europe but the curistas have been coming to bathe in these waters for hundreds of years.'

The dirt road dipped towards the river and crossed over a bridge. On the other side it became a rough track and Anamar insisted that Ramón should not try to take the car further.

She felt herself confused again as they parted. He was trying to be cheerful but all he could manage was a wan smile and a bear-hug. She kissed him, keeping back the tears, shouldered her rucksack and headed up the track. He waited, waving every time she turned, exactly as he had seen her off at the beginning of her pilgrimage to Santiago de Compostela ten years before, when he had known her for only a few weeks.

Ramón had never climbed in this part of the Pyrenees but he had found her a good map. He was very much in her mind when she reached the ruins of the Hospital de Benasque. The Hospital had once been a huge mountain inn and it was sad to see what must have been an impressive building, in such a dramatic mountain setting, now tumbled down. The door and windows had collapsed, the roof caved in, the huge slates and beams scattered as if part of a gigantic children's game wantonly destroyed. Some of the beams were a metre thick like those which had held the stone chimney above the inglenook.

The map showed that this was on the old mule track across the Pyrenees, through to Luchon in France. Ramón had told her that there had been a building here for almost a thousand years. Old documents he had seen showed that the Knights Templar had a Commanderie on this site in the 12th century.

She sat down on a rock in front of the ruin and, without an appetite but because it was important to eat, she faced a breakfast of bread, jam and fruit juice. She felt herself reluctant to leave this ruin for the solitary journey in the mountain wilderness ahead. This was the last trace of the world of roads and dwellings and the comfort of husband and family.

When she willed herself to pack her rucksack there seemed to be more food and equipment than before but there had to be sufficient provisions and camping gear for a five-night stay. She smiled ruefully, shouldered the pack and, as she moved on, her mood changed.

The valley was narrow here, a massive cliff on one side above a river and steep wooded slopes on the other, like an Irish glen on a vast scale. It was as if she had shed years from her age, back to her childhood. Anamar, the little girl of ten, wandered up the valley in child-like awe. The track led through trees and wound around rocky knolls, a scary, thrilling, bewitching world for a wee girl from Ireland.

Back in those days, her Granny Mac had lived in a cottage a field away from the family farmhouse. Her stories had brought to life the mountains of Donegal, peopled by fairies and leprechauns, guided by wizards and wise-women called 'conjurers'. In Celtic mythology the 'conjurer' had a special affinity with nature. She could use plants and herbs to cure ills and tell the future. She would have possessed stones or bottles given to her by the fairies which could work magic.

After school Anamar and her friends Maureen and Eamon McGinley would go to Granny Mac for a story. Half-an-hour later they would be up in the great glen of the Blue Stack Mountains collecting pebbles. The stones from below the Doonan Waterfall were the most highly prized and always looked more beautiful when they were wet.

In a secret place, marked with a cairn of stones, they would bury a green bottle filled with secret charms and written notes as presents for the wee people. Maureen and Eamon would always ask Anamar if her Granny Mac was a 'conjurer' and she would smile and never answer. But all three of them understood that knowing Granny Mac was all the protection any of them would ever need from witches and wizards and even Demon Kings.

Anamar came out of the trees on top of a hillock. The valley was wider here. A little stream flowed through a flat meadow and she could see from the map that this was the Plan d'Estan. It was a perfect day for the mountains, a few small fluffy white clouds riding a wind above the peaks, the air fresh, the ideal temperature for walking.

Suddenly a shrill cry split the silence and startled Anamar.

'Peep! .... Peep! .... Peep-Peep! .... Peep-Peep!' It was a high-pitched piping call like the distress signal of a bird but louder, much louder. Then she spotted a marmot sitting up on a prominent rock, warning the family of an intruder in their domain. He looked like a gigantic squirrel, as big as a full-grown hare and Anamar smiled in recognition and waved.

She was no longer the child in Ireland. Now she was eighteen, the year she had first come to France with a parish pilgrimage to Lourdes. She had found a job and stayed when her fellow-pilgrims had returned home. She had met Hank, an American ex-GI, mentally scarred by the war. When Anamar had helped him to face his demons by letting him take her climbing in the Pyrenees, she had given him hope. And he had taught her about the marmots and the mountains.

A year later she had thought it possible that they might have married but she had married Ramón, whose inspiration had enabled her to make her pilgrimage to Santiago. Hank had become the partner of her friend Deirdre Ryan. Ten years later Deirdre and Hank were still her best friends. They would both have loved an expedition like this but then, so too would Ramón.

She crossed a log bridge over the stream. The valley narrowed here and the track climbed around a rock buttress. It crossed a shoulder below the Maladetta glacier to reveal another plan where the valley opened out again. This one was called the Plan de Aiguallut. These plans were meadows which had been used for summer grazing for centuries. But there were no cows here, neither were there sheep nor goats. It was as if Anamar had the whole territory to herself.

The path led through the plan and the stream was a mere trickle here flowing from a single spring. A rocky hillock obscured the way ahead but the path climbed and she realised she was walking too quickly. She slowed down as she heard in her head Hank's voice softly saying, 'Doucement! Doucement ma brave!'.

At the crest, a new view was dramatically revealed. A huge waterfall surged over a cliff and fell into a chasm. This was the place which had brought Anamar to the Esera, the 'Trou de Toro'. The Spanish map called it by a different name but this was certainly the Cavern of the Bull.

Here, a river, fed by snow-melt from the glacier of Maladetta, plunged into the cavern and disappeared underground. Anamar sat down on the rim of the chasm, opened her rucksack and took out her notes. Her day dreams of the past were gone. She was back in the present, a married woman with a loving husband and three children and with her freedom for wandering still intact.

When Anamar had first discovered the clues at home, she had been hopeful that this was where she must look for the Cult's Cathedral. Now she was sitting where 'the evil one' stood above 'the cavern of the bull' and she was certain that this was the very place. She read aloud the clues from her notes on 'the missing document'.

**'Where the evil one stands above the cavern of the bull.**
**Flows the secret river, born in the hidden depths of the sacred nave'**

Directly above was the massif of Maladetta, 'the evil one'. At her feet was 'the Trou de Toro', 'the Cavern of the Bull'. 'The secret river' must be the one which flowed over the waterfall into the cavern. It was called on the map the Torrente de Barrancs and she traced it back up-stream with her finger. If she was right, she could follow 'the secret river' to where it was 'born in the hidden depths'. That must be underground, in a cave system higher up the mountain.

And if she could find the caves they would surely lead to 'the sacred nave', the cathedral of the Cult.

She shuddered as if from the cold and put on her sweater. It began to bother her again that she had not been able to discuss her discovery of the clues with Ramón. But it was too late now. She was on her own. If she failed in her quest, no one would be the wiser. If she succeeded, Ramón would be overjoyed and he would forgive her without question.

She ate and drank water from the river. Above, the Esera Valley separated in two, a broad cliff-ringed basin and a narrow gorge cut directly into the flank of Maladetta by the Torrente de Barrancs. A single file path climbed steeply up through the ravine, easy to follow but a physical effort at this altitude. Above the gorge there was a small plan, grassy, sheltered, with plenty of dead wood from an age when the tree-line was much higher. There was one large rock and space to pitch her tent in its lee. It was a perfect camp site.

It took over an hour to erect the small green tent, build a stone fireplace and find two large flat-topped rocks, one as a seat, the other as a table. She collected enough dead wood to keep the fire going all evening. The fire was easily lit and ten minutes later the water boiled to make tea. Anamar always liked a brew as soon as camp was pitched. The map showed that the altitude of the camp site was about 2,200 metres, over 7,000 feet. Usually she drank tea with milk and no sugar but at this height she preferred sweet tea without milk. Coffee might be fine lower down but it was much less refreshing than tea at altitude. Anamar smiled to herself. Little things were important at a mountain camp, especially when she was on her own.

She spent a couple of hours exploring the area around her camp. Lower down at the ravine there was a meeting of the waters. Two cascades became one in the depths of the gorge. Fortunately the path climbed beside the stream to the East, the Torrente de Barrancs. She had followed the right cascade.

On her way back up to the camp she felt tired. It was as if her energy had suddenly drained away. It had been a long walk, carrying a heavy pack. Back at the tent her appetite had gone. There was no reason now to cook a dinner. She made herself eat an apple and a bread and jam sandwich and made yet another mug of tea.

The little fire was a comfort. She would go to bed as soon as it was dark, rise early, take some food for lunch and climb to the head of the valley. On the way down she would do a thorough exploration, looking for the entrance to a cave system, checking the origin of each stream, taking photographs, drawing sketches, making notes, collecting information to make a map. But that was the plan for to-morrow. By eight o'clock she was ready for bed. Once the fire was quenched, she crawled into her sleeping bag and fell asleep.

It was still dark when she wakened and an effort to stay in bed until dawn. Outside the tent it was so cold she put on her spare clothes and her waterproof cape over all to keep the heat in. The sun rose over the rim of the cliffs. It was time to take off the cape and start the day's work.

At this altitude she was amongst the high peaks. It was magnificent terrain, great crags and scree slopes below a rim of summits whose huge snow fields draped their slopes right down to the valley. Here and there in the scree single storm battered trees were holding on where others had fallen. Tiny alpine plants grew in cracks in the rock, ferns flourished in damp crevices. Near small streams the Monk's Hood was still in deep-blue bloom. The previous day, near the Hospital de Benasque, they had been faded, turned to seed. But that was 2,000 feet lower down and now in Autumn. Here it was still high Summer.

It was a shock for Anamar when she realised that it was only a little over twenty-four hours since she had left Ramón near Benasque. It felt as if she had been in the mountains for a week.

But there was no sign of any caves, nor was there any feature which might have been helpful in her quest. By four o'clock in the afternoon she had arrived back at camp and lit the fire. The hot tea raised her spirits but it was disappointing not to have anything to show for her efforts. Writing up the notes and making the map had to be done. An hour spent gathering dead wood gave her a pile which would last at least two days. The cooler air began to settle into the valley and it was time to cook dinner.

For the first time since she had arrived Anamar was hungry. She decided to cheer herself up with a special meal. When they had been preparing her provisions for the expedition Madame Mons had mixed flour and a little baking soda and Anamar made soda bread farls using the frying pan as a griddle. A visit to the larder in the snow bank yielded a thick slice of gammon and she grilled it on the cooling tray she had brought to act as a grid. She fried two eggs in the pan and the feast was almost ready.

Amongst her stores was one bottle of red wine and now was the time to open it. The equivalent of one glass full was poured into the enamel mug, the cork replaced and she was ready to begin.

Anamar rose later next morning, about seven o'clock. The air was still cold and she lit the fire. She was in no hurry to begin her exploration again so she made more bread. These mountain farls were best eaten fresh and she took her time over breakfast considering what she should do next. Still undecided, she washed socks and underclothes lower down in the stream. More wood gathering increased the pile and she climbed the scree slope above her camp to the snow bank to check the larder. All was in order.

Without understanding why, she felt she was not alone in this wilderness. It was her Granny Mac again. When she was alive Anamar had always felt much closer to her than her mother. Just before she died, Granny Mac had told Anamar not to grieve for her, she would always be with her in spirit. And that was the way of it now. How could she be lonely with her beloved granny at her side?

She was about to go down the scree to her tent when she heard Granny Mac tell her to look at the bottom of the cliff.

There, a bird on a big boulder caught her eye. It flew off and she saw that the boulder was in a small depression at the foot of the sheer cliff above the scree. A dry channel between the boulder and a spring below gave the impression that the stream had once emanated from underneath the boulder. She had better have a closer look.

The boulder was as big as a small car. It was set against the cliff, solid, immovable.

When she had been studying 'the missing document' at home Anamar had found a third clue but only now did it seem worth considering. She took out her notes and read it aloud.

> **'And at our hallowed sanctuary's door,**
> **It is not enough to kneel and pray.**
> **To lie and writhe is the only way.'**

Could the big boulder hide the entrance to a cave? Granny Mac seemed to be whispering in her ear again. She knelt down beside the boulder and heard Granny Mac whisper the words again.

> **'It is not enough to kneel and pray.**
> **To lie and writhe is the only way.'**

She lay down along the length of the boulder. Hidden by the undergrowth there was a space about a foot and a half high. It allowed her to wriggle under the rock. 'To lie and writhe is the only way,' she said aloud to herself, hardly daring to believe that it was happening.

Leaning on her elbows, Anamar slithered sideways for a few feet and raised an arm. She waved it in different directions and could feel she was past the boulder. It was pitch black, impossible to see the size of the space she had now reached. She wriggled sideways back out from under the big stone and sat up in the sunlight, dazed, disorientated for a few moments.

Her torch was in her rucksack down at the tent. She jumped to her feet and ran down to fetch it. In a few moments she was back wriggling under the boulder again but this time with a light. The beam of the torch filled the cave. It was as big as a small room in a house. The floor was dry but a pebble strewn channel indicated that once a stream had flowed through this cavern. A passageway at the back, high enough to allow Anamar to walk upright, led to a second cave.

It was much bigger than the first, with a pool of water like a well. The water rose from below, over-flowing into a fissure which drained it from the cave. In a niche in the wall of the chamber was a metal drinking vessel.

Anamar was tempted to lift it down but decided that it would be best not to touch anything unusual until she brought Ramón here.

Beyond this cave, a rock fall blocked the way but she could hear water flowing on the other side of the debris. A small gap allowed her to see that the passageway continued. Excitement had overcome anxiety but this was as far as she wanted to go. She turned back, hurried through the caves and wriggled out into the sunshine again. Surely she had found the cave system which would lead to the Cathedral of the Cult.

It was only then that she realised she had been frightened in the cave. She shivered in the sunlight, hugging herself against the cold, like a child, not knowing whether to cry or shout for joy.

There was plenty of tea in her food stores and it was a comfort now. The excitement of the discovery had exhausted her energy and she sat by the river, rising only to tend the fire and make more tea. After the disappointment of the previous day there was also a profound sense of relief. It was only the third day and her work was done. There would be no point crossing the range and walking down into Luchon. It would be three days before Ramón was due to meet her there.

By evening the weather had changed. It was cold and overcast with occasional heavy showers of rain. A plan was forming in her mind. She grilled two small lamb chops for dinner, fried an onion in olive oil and made soda bread. She celebrated the discovery of the cave system with a second ration of wine and sat in the shelter of the doorway of her tent, wrapped in her sleeping bag against the cold night air.

The weather looked worse in the morning. It was time to act on the plan she had made the previous evening. On this, the fourth day of her expedition, she struck camp, packed her gear and headed off down the valley towards the Baños de Benasque.

The heavy, deep grey clouds grew darker by the minute. It seemed to take an age walking back down to the Hospital de Benasque. The heavy rain began to fall in separate drops. She hid her tent and cooking pots in the ruins of the Hospital. Her rucksack was lighter now and it was downhill. But on mountain terrain, even on a path, there is a sensible speed. Go too slowly and it takes forever. Go too fast and good rhythm is lost, and there is always the risk of a stumble.

It was the end of an afternoon, in the back end of summer but the air was cold. Big spits of rain fell on the hood of her cape with an amplified spat. Time to give herself a pat on the back. She had seen this wet evening coming and this was why she was heading down. She'd had her nights alone in the tent, now she wanted a roof above her head, a dry bed and a good meal cooked by someone else.

The rain was heavier now, soaking the hem of her skirt below the cape and stinging her legs. Flashes of lightning at the rim of the sky seemed miles away. And then she saw it. The inn which housed the baths of Baños de Benasque was perched high on the steep slope on the other side of the river. In the mist and rain the building looked massive, like a fortification.

Anamar crossed the bridge as the heavy rain turned torrential. A great flash of lightning hit the ground on the other side of the river. At the same precise moment a crack of thunder shook the stones of the track. The eye of the storm was rushing up from behind, chasing her like the devil's pack of hounds. The dirt road became the bed of a fast flowing stream and she climbed the steep twists as fast as she dared. At the upper side of the Baños there was a car park with one dilapidated bus. The water was streaming off her cape. Her legs were beginning to wobble. Her lungs felt raw as she gasped for breath but she had made it.

The building looked quite different up here. It was only one storey high. There was no shelter on the doorstep. Anamar knocked loudly with her stick. There was no reply.

She tried again, hammering with her stick on the heavy wood and iron-studded door. Then she saw it. A wisp of cord peeped through a tiny hole in the door at shoulder height. A knot at the end allowed her to grip it firmly. She gave the cord a tug and heard the clunk as the latch lifted on the inside. The door swung open as if of its own accord. It was a minor miracle. She whipped off her cape, shook it outside, rolled it in a manageable bundle and closed the door behind her.

As she paused in the hallway to catch her breath, great gusts of wind and rain battered against the door of the Baños building . She made her way down the passage and knocked on a door with a sign which said, 'Privado'. A man about her own age, tall and pale, harassed looking, asked what she wanted. That was easy. All she needed was a bed and a meal. Silently the man led her through a labyrinth of corridors to a room on the other side of the building.

There was no furniture except a big bed with a thick coverlet, a plain upright chair and a wash stand, both unvarnished. An enamel wash bowl on the stand and a chamber-pot below the bed completed the furnishings. To Anamar, this was luxury.

A small square window was set into the thick wall, shutters open. It looked across the storm-swept terrain like the view from the gallery of a theatre. The river was lit by three successive bolts of lightning. The driving rain swept the valley in huge gusts. A few moments before she had been lashed by the deluge, running scared from the fiery flashes and cracks of thunder, now she was sheltered and safe within the walls of the inn. Anamar shuddered with relief and hung her dripping cape on a hook behind the door.

Dinner was at seven thirty the man said and asked her if she wanted a bath. It took a second or two before Anamar twigged that he meant a bath in the naturally heated sulphur waters of the spa. And suddenly it seemed like a great idea.

She followed him back down the corridor and watched as he took a huge white towel from the biggest hot-press in Christendom. Half an hour later two elderly ladies who had just finished their ablutions were showing her how things worked. There was a row of partitioned cubicles each with an immense bath. Half way along one side a spout poured a great stream of warm water into the bath. It was at the perfect temperature. With the plug-hole at the bottom stoppered and the bather in place, there was no way to turn off the inflow, the excess water was simply drained away by an over-flow placed to ensure the correct depth of water.

The tumbling sound of water from the spa's mineral spring, the humid warmth and sheer volume welling up from the hot depths of the earth, even the slightly pungent smell of sulphur, were purest bliss. She lay back and her skin felt as soft and smooth as the finest silk. It was a moment of rapture, one of the most luxurious experiences of Anamar's life.

At seven-thirty she went to the dining room to find a queue waiting for it to open. They were all Spanish and had apparently come together in the 'bus. They were here to take the waters of a spa reputed to cure a range of ailments from arthritis to stomach malaise, respiratory disorders and heart conditions.

There were more women than men, all middle-aged to elderly. When the dining-room door opened, they swooped inside, ladies leading the way at a trot, claiming their own tables. Within seconds they were all seated, spoon in hand. Bring on the soup.

The tureens arrived and they were all served immediately. After what seemed like a few seconds the soup bowls were being cleared away. Chops and green beans followed and they were dispensed, eaten and the plates cleared with similar dispatch. Four girls and the tall, pale man did the work and they had started to collect the empty bowls which had contained the crème caramel dessert before all had been served.

It was over in a matter of minutes and it was all Anamar could do not to laugh aloud. The speedy waiter and waitresses sprinting around the tables, the silence when food was served, the empty plates spirited away, the burst of conversation when dinner was over, it was more like a competition than a meal.

The residents moved to the card tables at the other end of the room and Anamar was invited to join a group as they settled down to their games. She declined with a smile and found an easy chair where she could write up the notes of her expedition.

After the deluge of the night, the morning sky was clear. A waist-deep mist ascended from the ground as the sun dried the mountainside. Anamar walked back up the valley to the ruins of the Hospital, delighted that she had chosen not to stay and fight the storm at her camp. She collected her hidden gear and kept to the path as it zig-zagged up the northern flank of the valley, skirting the White Peak, La Peña Blanca.

At the very crest of the rocky ridge which separated France from Spain, a narrow cleft, the famous Port de Benasque, led the way through the cliffs. The map showed that it had been an eight hundred metre climb from the Baños and it was a wonderful place to stop for a rest. The peaks crowded around the pass. Anamar remembered Hilaire Belloc calling it 'the turning point' of the Pyrenees.

She planned to camp out one last night as she was not due to meet Ramón at Bagnères de Luchon until noon on the next day. Two hundred metres below her feet, three beautiful lakes sparkled in the sunshine.

It was a very steep descent, made much easier as parts of the path had been constructed of flat stone steps with one side built up, where necessary, to allow the passage of mules as well as people. She pitched her tent between the lakes and it was a splendid afternoon to sit and rest with nothing to do but enjoy the sunshine. She was longing to tell Ramón what she had discovered but first there would be one last night in the wilderness.

Her camp was above the tree-line and there was no wood for a fire. She fried bacon and a small onion on her tiny methylated spirit stove and served them with a tomato and the last of the Spanish bread. There was still some wine left in the bottle, enough to fill the mug half-full. She sat on a soft bank, back against a rock. The wine had a strangely flat taste as if it had once been effervescent but was now well shaken up by its journey through the mountains. Anamar smiled. The wine connoisseurs could have their talk of premier crus but what she had on this evening was fine by her.

The view was across the lakes and the foot-hills, looking out of the mountains, down to civilisation. But she was still in the wilderness, not yet returned to the world of habitation and cultivation.

# THE TEMPLAR'S RETURN

On the sixth day Anamar walked the last leg down to Luchon as if there were springs in her heels and feathers in her rucksack. She passed another ancient inn, the Hospice de France, the French counterpart of the Hospital de Benasque in Spain. Bagnères-de-Luchon was one of Anamar's favourite towns in the whole of the Pyrenees. It had been a spa since the Roman emperor Tiberius built thermal baths. In the 19th century it became a charming, sophisticated resort with Parisian architecture and elegant pavement cafés on impressive boulevards.

Anamar saw Ramón's dark blue Citroen parked beside a café before she spotted him. He was at a pavement table and rushed across to welcome her back. He kissed her on both cheeks, with a third one for good measure and she took hold of him in an Irish hug.

He looked so young and smart and so pleased to see her. The little break from each other would restore their relationship. On her walk, she had thought of him every day but there had been danger before she left. Her mother used to say that it took less than a year to cool the ardour in a marriage and after ten years the choice for a woman was - put up with it or run away.

Ramón took her rucksack and ordered her an ice-cold Grenadine and lemonade.

'I've exciting news for you,' he said as calmly as he could manage, 'Raoul has translated the next part of the Manuscript. It's an extraordinary story, leading from the Middle East to France and Scotland and back to my family home in Navarre. But it will keep. Tell me about your adventures in the wilds of the Pyrenees.'

Anamar began to laugh. If they were not careful, each would be insisting that the other's tale be told first. She decided to tell him about the expedition but keep her discovery until later. And smiling a wicked smile to herself, she thought that the best time might be just before they arrived back home in Mont L'ours!

'I had a wonderful trip.' she said, 'The tent kept me warm and dry at night. I visited the Trou de Toro and the Valle de Barrancs and its beautiful tarn. The young isards playing slides on the snow entertained me every evening before dark. Belloc was right, the view from the Col de Benasque is magnificent. I camped at the lakes on the French side last night and here I am in Luchon, right on time.'

The drive home was only fifty kilometres and they had lunch in Luchon before leaving. Ramón had brought the translation of the Manuscript and, as they sat in the Autumn sunshine, he began the story.

###### ............THE MANUSCRIPT CONTINUES

*Alfonso and James Lamont were well rewarded by Lord Killhaven. He encouraged merchants to use the captains for the protection of their goods in transit through his lands. 'My captains', as Lord Killhaven called Alfonso and James, had cleared his lands of lawlessness and now he was pleased to allow his noble friends to use their services, insisting that they too were generous.*

*One particular achievement of Alfonso's earned him the admiration of rich and poor. In almost every village there were warlocks and carlines, as witches were called in this border region. They lived by fear and used their black arts to terrorise the people. In a remote mountain valley, at the edge of Lord Killhaven's domain, a carline held sway. She dressed like a nun in black robes and wimple and was called the Devil's Bride. For what seemed like a life-time the villagers had been enslaved by her sorcery.*

*One morning Alfonso rode to her remote valley without an escort and called on the carline to come out and face him. He dismounted and when the villagers assembled, he challenged her to do her worst. The Devil's Bride screamed her curses but Alfonso stood erect and silent. She roared her incantations and cast every evil spell she could conjure with all her black arts.*

*But it was clear that, to the Devil's Bride, Alfonso was untouchable. He commandeered a horse and cart and supervised the men while they packed it with her clothes and belongings. Together they torched her hovel with its store of potions, plants and dead animals. As the villagers stood in silent awe, Alfonso banished the Devil's Bride from the Earl's lands on pain of death should she ever return. As the hated carline disappeared over the hill there were shouts of joy and Alfonso joined them for the singing and dancing before he returned to the castle.*

*Although the Church had been involved in the destruction of the Templar Order to which Alfonso had belonged and he had forsaken his own vows, Alfonso's training and religious observance as a warrior monk had left him with an unquestioning belief in Christianity. He knew that it was the power of his faith which had enabled him to challenge the force of the black arts of the devil and prevail.*

*Lord Killhaven's sister was particularly impressed. Lady Margaret had never married. She was too tall for most men. 'Too long, too lean, too fond of her own way,' a friend of his had confided to his lairdship when they were in their cups. Her face was of a form rarely admired as beautiful. A nose on the large side, almost hooked, with thin cheeks and a receding chin gave her a fearsome look when angry. However, that was a rare occurrence in one of such a happy disposition and in repose, or caught in the act of smiling, she was radiantly handsome.*

*Lady Margaret was well aware that it was now unlikely she would wed and she was not unhappy about that prospect. All the eligible men she had met in her youth seemed to be dull, feeble or small. She liked to ride, to walk the glens. She took an interest in the every day life of her brother's domain. She was educated, well-read, fond of good conversation, music and travel.*

*Now there was a man about the castle who was tall enough, interesting and unattached. He might be a few years younger than she was but he seemed to appreciate her company. There were times when he was too intense, too serious, too dedicated to his work of finding and killing villains. He seemed to avoid the social life of the castle except when involved by the call of duty.*

*Lady Margaret decided to encourage Captain Alfonso de Codés. She knew her brother, the Earl, would notice, but he would raise no difficulties, of that she was certain. He admired this Spanish soldier who had established the rule of law in his domain. Don Alfonso was a formidable leader, even his brother captain, James Lamont was happy to defer to him on important matters. His greatest triumph had been to recruit and train a company of soldiers who were the envy of every nobleman from Stirling Castle to the English border.*

*Soldiering made Captain Alfonso wealthy and the Earl of Killhaven saw to it that his captain participated in commercial ventures which were likely to succeed. This man was suitable.*

*Within a month Lady Margaret and captain Alfonso were companions. Two months later they rode and walked together over the whole extent of the Killhaven lands. Within six months they were lovers. They travelled to Edinburgh, to the English border. They sailed to the Mull of Kintyre and the Isles, often on the Earl's business.*

--------------------------------------------

Ramón paused and ordered more coffee. Anamar was mesmerised and asked no questions. He was obviously relishing the role of the storyteller and she smiled to herself remembering her Granny Mac, the seanscealai, the Irish storyteller from Donegal. Her granny dared the listener to join them in the tale. And Alfonso was not only Ramón's forebear, his story was the history of the family to which Anamar now belonged as wife and mother.

Ramón lifted the document and began again............

............THE MANUSCRIPT CONTINUES

*One evening, when Alfonso and James Lamont were returning from Stirling, they reached Dumfries late in the evening and decided to stay the night at an inn in the town. After they had eaten Alfonso became bored with the company and climbed the open stairway to his room, while James sat on at the fire talking to a young man of means whose two servants were playing cards.*

*Alfonso was about to undress when he heard the roar of a violent commotion. He rushed down the stairway which led directly into the room below. James had his back to him and was held fast by two men. A third man was about to run him through with his sword.*

*Alfonso appeared unarmed. But he carried a throwing knife*

*hidden in a sheath underneath the collar at the back of his jerkin. His right hand reached behind his neck and grasped the knife by the handle. In one movement he drew the blade and flung it at the young swordsman as he lunged forward. The knife hit and entered the man's chest with such force it swung him sideways. His sword slashed through James's jerkin but missed his stomach.*

*The two men holding James released him and fled and when Alfonso reached the young swordsman he was dead. Years of practice of a knife-throwing skill taught him by the young Saracen, Hassan, had saved the life of his friend and comrade-in-arms.*

*By his clothes and the quality of his weapon, the young swordsman was a nobleman. Later it transpired that he and James had been talking around the fire as his servants watched. The wine had been flowing and a derogatory remark from him about the Clan Lamont had brought a riposte from James. In seconds insults had led to blows. Swords had been drawn and James had been grabbed from behind by the servants. Now the nobleman was dead.*

*Alfonso and James settled their bill and left immediately for Killhaven Castle. They rode hard, arrived an hour after dawn and sought a meeting with the Earl as soon as he had risen. Lady Margaret joined them. James left it to Alfonso to relate the story. The Earl asked questions but there were no recriminations. He was sure he knew the young nobleman.*

*'A peevish wretch, always spoiling for a fight.' The Earl was furious, not with Alfonso and James but at the prospect of bad blood between the young earl's family and his own.*

*'They will want vengeance,' he said slowly as if a plan was forming in his mind. 'We need to act quickly. You must leave here within the hour and flee the country. You must sail to France or Spain.'*

*Alfonso had always believed that there was a time to stand and fight and a time to run. He and James accepted the plan.*

*Lady Margaret stood up to speak.*

*'I will go too,' she said firmly and Alfonso smiled.*

*For the first time the Earl looked shaken. He and his sister were close. Her lack of suitable suitors when she was young had ensured that they had played and worked together. He had always asked for her advice in the management of the estate. Her judgement of character was unerring. But he knew she had never known the happiness she now had with Alfonso.*

*'If that is your wish, so be it.' he said, close to tears. 'But remember this is your home. When the heat for vengeance cools we will be united here.'*

*As if the time for emotion had passed, the Earl went back to the plan.*

*'I have a good ship berthed at Maryport across the border in Cumbria. She is due to sail for La Rochelle in a week's time with a cargo of fine wool. Take her and her cargo as my sister's dowry. It is two days ride to Maryport. I will give you deed of ownership to show to the captain. Set sail at once and you can fly to safety on the wind.'*

*A little more than an hour later a small mounted band rode quietly away from the castle. There were six soldiers from the Earl's company, Lady Margaret's maid and two men servants. Six pack horses were led by grooms.*

*They rode hard and long on the first day, started more slowly on the second and arrived at noon. The captain of the ship was known to James and he was quickly taken into their confidence. They sailed at dawn the next morning and, with the exception of two volunteers, the soldiers, grooms and men servants returned to Killhaven Castle. The volunteers would act as messengers to bring back news to the Earl when the party had found somewhere to settle. Lady Margaret's maid insisted on remaining with her mistress and set about making comfortable quarters for her on board.*

*Alfonso knew exactly where they should go.*

*'I was born in Navarre in Northern Spain,' he said as they dined with the captain that night. 'I left home when I was eighteen and*

*when I went back my parents were dead and the castle and lands, derelict. It is time I claimed my inheritance.'*

*Margaret and James clapped, it was so good to have a destination. They were no longer fleeing from their foes, they were sailing to a new life. They drank a toast to the Earl of Killhaven and another to their new life in Navarre.*

*That night Lady Margaret saw, for the first time, the sealed satchel Alfonso had kept with him since the Battle of Acre. He sat on the bed and told her his story. Margaret tried every playful, loving art to have him break the seal but Alfonso withstood all her pleadings and promises.*

*'When we are settled in Navarre,' he said, laughing. 'I've had this satchel so long I've lost the will to open it. But once we're settled in Navarre, we'll break the seal on our wedding night.'*

---

Ramón paid the bills and he and Anamar drove on to St-Girons. They stopped to stretch their legs and Anamar was sorely tempted to tell Ramón her news as they walked through the town. Now it was too late. It would spoil his tale. They sat down on a bench near the river and she persuaded him to start again.

---

*The sea was calm for the voyage and the captain hugged the coasts of Ireland, France and Spain. He sold the cargo of wool in La Rochelle and picked up a shipment of oak barrels for wine. Within a month of leaving Cumbria they arrived in Bilbao on the North Coast of Spain. Alfonso made arrangements for the ship to be based there to enable her captain to ply his trade to Atlantic ports.*

*He and James purchased horses and pack mules, hired grooms and servants, bought arms for the whole party and set out for Navarre. The roads were poor but there was safety in numbers. They travelled without hindrance, climbing through the formidable mountains of Cantabrica. After three hard days they crossed a high ridge and the great lands of Codés de Barra lay at their feet. It was the perfect viewpoint. Alfonso could have led them into the lands of the hacienda by an easier route. But this was the place for a first sight of their new home.*

*They dismounted and he showed them the haunts of his youth. Three valleys led down from the mountains to the plains in the far distance. The valleys were rocky above, forested in their middle reaches and fertile below. There were three villages, one in each valley. Dorca was the largest and situated in the main valley. Zaruzza was a thin straggle of dwellings beside a stream.*

*The furthest away was Codés del Camino at a bridge across a road which marked the southern boundary of the Codés lands. Alfonso explained that the words 'del Camino' meant that this village was on the pilgrim road to the West, el Camino de Santiago, the Road of St James.*

--------------------------------

This was as far as Raoul had translated and they drove on towards Mont L'ours talking about Alfonso's story. Ramón slowed the car and stopped on a wide verge. He turned to look at Anamar and thought he had never seen her so happy since the birth of their children.

When first he had met her she had been preparing to walk the Camino de Santiago. He had been a Santiago pilgrim himself before the war and had helped her plan her route. Fearing for her safety as a woman alone, he had walked with her across the Pyrenees and as far as Codés del Camino. Now Alfonso had arrived at the place of his birth and Ramón's too, six hundred and fifty years later.

He took Anamar's hand and they sat in silence. To Ramón the legacy of his family hacienda and his role as master of the Cult were of the greatest significance. Alfonso's story was Ramón's heritage. It would connect him to his ancestors, allow him to be a part of their ancient family.

They drove around a corner and their home village, Mont L'ours, came into view. Ramón turned right to cross the river. It was as if there was an impish spirit within Anamar holding back her secrets. They reached the bridge and she could restrain herself no longer.

'Is that it?' she said, pretending she had been waiting impatiently for this lull in Ramón's story. 'Is it all right now for me to say my piece?'

'I think I've found the entrance to the Cult's Cathedral.'

Ramón's mouth dropped open. He stopped the car and they sat, parked in the middle of the bridge. Anamar quietly told him about finding the clues in 'the missing document'. They had led her to the Esera valley above Benasque. She explained how she had followed the underground river clue back to its source in the Valle de Barrancs.

Ramón sat motionless, his face pale and fixed in a look of sheer incredulity. But Anamar's investigation was logical. Of course he knew the Trou de Toro and Maladetta. Years before, when he had first bought her Hilaire Belloc's book, they had laughed together when Belloc made fun of the scientists. The experts had poured dye into the river and had watched it disappear into the Trou de Toro on one side of the Pyrenees. Meanwhile, their colleagues had waited in vain on the other side of the mountain for the coloured water to issue from a spring and so prove it had become the great river Gironde.

But it was the deduction that the Cathedral must be underground which changed doubts to certainty.

He would organise an expedition to the Esera Valley right away, he said. They would bring lanterns and digging equipment to the cave entrance which she had located. It was as if he was speaking in a dream. They would set up a camp nearby and stay as long as it took to explore the cave system.

He restarted the car and drove through the village. Doña Marie and Madam Mons were waiting for them, wondering why they had stopped on the bridge. They gave Anamar the warmest of welcomes, both proud of this young woman. She was a good mother, the hub of her family. But she was also independent at a time when most married women were totally dependent on their husbands. She was her own woman and both could see glimpses of their youth in her.

Doña Marie was worried about Ramón. He looked so pale and preoccupied.

'Are you feeling ill? You look as if you've seen a ghost.'

Ramón's faint smile was meant to be reassuring.

'No! No! I've seen no ghosts,' he said quietly, 'But now I know where to find them.'

That night at dinner Anamar described her adventures in the Esera. She took them on a journey to the river which disappeared into the Trou de Toro. She described the magnificent view from the door of her tent in the

Valle de Barrancs and the young isards playing slides on the snow slope a hundred metres above her campsite. But again she held something back. She said nothing about her discovery of the entrance to the cave system until Madam Mons had left for the kitchen. Then Ramón said,

'You'd better tell them how you solved the mystery of the Cult's Cathedral.'

He smiled broadly and watched the faces of his mother and Raoul as Anamar recounted how she had found the cave.

Raoul was sceptical at first but Doña Marie was delighted. Her son deserved a wife like this.

'Just as well there was a woman to do the difficult part,' she said, 'You men glean the facts from dusty books but this young woman has solved your riddle with her brains and her feet.'

Anamar should have been able to let them into her final secret. Buried in the script she called 'the missing document', there were three more apparently unrelated lines. Taken together they had revealed the way into the cave system which must surely lead to the Cathedral.

> **'And at our hallowed sanctuary's door,**
> **It is not enough to kneel and pray.**
> **To lie and writhe is the only way.'**

But the exquisite pleasure of revealing the secrets one by one ensured that she would keep this one until Ramón's expedition reached the actual place on the mountain. Then, 'Abracadabra' or whatever the Christian equivalent might be, and she would divulge the final mystery.

Ramón reminded them all about the need for total secrecy and announced that he would lead an expedition to the Esera in two weeks time. He would be accompanied by Anamar, Raoul, the Cult members, Don Carlos Conde and Monsieur Raymond Bodelot and Jules Laurent whose skill in moving large rocks might well be useful in the cave.

The next morning Ramón telephoned Don Carlos and Monsieur Raymond. They had completed their investigation of the Cult's finances and were satisfied that the Treasurer, Monsieur Marc Decuré had been defrauding the Cult for years. Ramón decreed that when the Cult assembled in six week's time the meeting would be preceded by a meeting of the Court.

He then had amazed the two men by inviting them to join him on a camping expedition to the Pyrenees, 'on the Cult's business'. Both were keen walkers and retired from their former work. They accepted immediately.

Jules Laurent was harder to persuade. He was unhappy at the thought of leaving the bears in the Sanctuary. They knew him. They trusted him. He went without fear into all of the pens. He was the only person allowed to feed them.

But Ramón was insistent. He intended to hire two pack horses to carry the food and equipment and Jules would be a help, but there were other reasons. They would have to clear a rock fall and would be exploring the unknown when they penetrated the cave system. It was essential to have a practical man in the party.

Jules had developed a loyalty to Ramón which overshadowed his doubts. Ramón required him on the expedition and that was enough. It would be possible to train Maurice to prepare and serve the bears' food and keep an eye on their well-being. Once it was agreed, Jules was as excited as any of them. He had been a travelling man all his life until the Sanctuary had stopped him in his tracks. Now he was on the road again.

Two nights before they left Ramón, Anamar, Doña Marie and Raoul met for dinner. It was time to hear the next part of the Manuscript. This was Raoul's moment and he intended to make the most of it. He fetched the type-written translation and stayed on his feet to have room for gestures. He could feel himself a part of Alfonso's adventure. He was back in the past with Don Alfonso and Lady Margaret as their little party arrived at his ancestral home in Navarre.

............THE MANUSCRIPT CONTINUES

*Before Alfonso remounted he gathered his party around him and presented the two volunteer soldiers, who had come with them from Scotland, with their reward in gold coins. They would return to Lord Killhaven to tell him that Alfonso and Margaret had reached their destination. The two men remounted and started back along the way they had come. For Lady Margaret it felt as if the last link with home had been severed. But her place was with Alfonso and this domain was her destiny as well as his.*

*'This is our new home.' Alfonso said with the weariness of the journey in his voice. 'I left here eighteen years ago and in my*

*absence a virulent disease killed all my family. Since then the lands have been looted by robber bands and exploited by nobles. Now we have come to claim my inheritance. You have known me as Alfonso Codés. From now on you will call me Alfonso Barriano.'*

*They rode slowly down towards the village of Dorca. There were fields of stunted crops, beans, turnips, grain. They came upon the ruins of the castle. As they arrived on the outskirts of Dorca they rode past scavenging goats and thin cattle. The houses were in poor condition, the whole village in an impoverished state. A group of men dressed in rags, unarmed, came forward to meet them. Women and children hid in doorways. They were all afraid of the strangers.*

*Alfonso raised his hand with an open palm in a Roman salute. The older villagers whispered together. They knew this man. He was the son of their lord who had died ten years before.*

*'I come in peace.' Alfonso said loudly so that all could hear. 'I have returned to my family lands and with your help we will change poverty to plenty. But now you will call me Alfonso Barriano, Marqués de Barra.'*

*He made camp near the village and within the walls of the ruined castle. Next day he and James rode the length and width of the lands, visiting the other two villages and outlying dwellings, proclaiming the same message. Everywhere there was evidence that the whole estate had been neglected for years. There was clear evidence of the looting and destruction of war, of famine and poverty. The houses were in a ruinous state, the roads unrepaired, the drainage systems eroded away. The forests had been cut down for fuel, without replanting, the fields were unkempt. Only the church was in reasonable repair but there was no sign of the priest.*

*On their return Alfonso was distraught. James and Lady Margaret did their best but he was inconsolable. In his youth this had been a fertile land ruled firmly and fairly by his father. The village houses, roads and drainage canals had all been in good condition. The people had worked the land and in return they had been housed, fed and protected.*

*That night, on a hill behind the camp, he slept alone under the stars. He spent the next day on his own without food, drinking from streams, wandering on foot up the valley into the mountain. In the evening he came down to join the others for the meal. Lady Margaret took him to one side and held his hands.*

*'Amongst all this poverty and destruction there is hope,' she said gravely, 'I am with child.'*

*Alfonso took her gently in his arms. They had both been waiting for this moment, neither daring to think it could happen like this. They held on to each other to make it real. When they stood back, holding hands at arm's length, each saw a different person.*

*Margaret was now in the full flower of her womanhood. Alfonso was a new man, a father-to-be, a leader with a cause. They walked back to James, sitting at the fire and told him the news. James leapt to his feet, caught an arm of each and spun them around in a wild dance. The servants came with goblets of wine. Alfonso sat the other two down on a log. He needed to tell them his thoughts.*

*'When we arrived here I was distressed by the chaos and destruction,' he said calmly. 'These people have been deprived of the protection and enterprise of my family for ten years. We will bring them leadership.'*

*'I have made two decisions. We will make our home here and we will transform this desolation into a land fit for a proud people to live safely and well.'*

*He put more logs on the fire and turned to smile.*

*'I have also decided how we will do it. We three will form a fraternity dedicated to the restoration of this estate. There will be ten or more members, some chosen from the most able people here, others from elsewhere. Each will have a particular responsibility.*

*'I will act as master of the fraternity and will oversee the rebuilding of the castle. James will recruit and train a band of soldiers to protect us and the Santiago pilgrims. Lady Margaret will supervise the improvement of the villages. Our new members will  help us rebuild houses and roads. We will restore the*

*irrigation system, the vineyard, the forests. We will develop trade. We will build a new inn in the village of Codés del Camino for the Santiago pilgrims.*

*The money we have brought with us will be used to buy food from other estates until we can grow our own. We will buy arms and supplies. The people will be expected to work hard but we will transform their lives.'*

There was a sudden scuffling noise behind Alfonso and the sound of footsteps. Out of the darkness beyond the light of the fire, stepped the priest.

*'I am Father Romero and I have been hiding behind a rock, listening to your speech.'* The priest was a tiny man with powerful voice and a presence which demanded attention. This was the first time he had met Alfonso. He spoke loudly so that the servants could hear, *'It is a grand design but how can I trust a man who has changed his name and who may be a renegade Templar.'*

Alfonso's gestures welcomed the priest to a log seat at the fire.

*'The past is dead Father,'* he said quietly, *'Would you sacrifice the future of the people here to obey an order from another country. You and I have no quarrel. We will need a priest to guide us, to care for our immortal souls. Join us in our fraternity and your first duty will be to bind Lady Margaret and me in holy matrimony.'*

The priest began to laugh. He could tell by the surprised look on Lady Margaret's face that she had not yet been asked to be a bride. And, now he could see as well as hear Alfonso, he felt that this man had the strength to turn dreams into reality.

Alfonso covered his confusion by calling for wine for everyone and made a public proposal. Lady Margaret consented with due formality, smiled sweetly at the priest and informed him that she would make arrangements with him for the marriage which would take place as soon as a new dwelling could be built.

Before he left, the priest spoke privately to Alfonso about their bargain. If Alfonso would encourage religious observance and involve him in the development of the estate as a member of the fraternity, he would agree to support Alfonso in all matters *temporal and would pledge his silence on Alfonso's past life as a warrior monk.*

*The next day Alfonso sent for representatives of the three villages to announce his plans. He would supervise the building of a stone and wood house for his entourage within the castle's walls. The restoration of the castle would have to wait.*

*The work began immediately. Alfonso and Father Romero took to meeting early each morning to review the work of the previous day and to plan for the future. On the third morning the priest brought four men to meet Alfonso. Two were from the village of Dorca and one each from Zaruzza and Codés del Camino. Alfonso had asked him to nominate some new members of the Society and he introduced Pedro as a good man to supervise the repairing of houses. Bernardo could re-establish the vineyard, Garcia oversee the replanting of the forests. Father Romero explained that the fourth man, Xavier, had a way with animals and suggested that he would improve the animal stock by breeding.*

*Alfonso was elated. He now had eight working members of the fraternity and all seemed keen to make a success of their jobs. But Father Romero had a surprise for him.*

*'This is a serious business, Don Alfonso,' he said, as if he was addressing the people at Mass, 'Our members should swear an oath before God that they will devote themselves without stint to the work of the fraternity.' He paused to assure himself that Alfonso supported what he was saying.*

*'And I have a new name for the fraternity. I beg to suggest that it be called the Cult of the Holy Spirit.'*

*From that moment Alfonso was certain that they must plan on the grand scale. The priest was right. Bound together in the Cult they would make it happen.*

---

Raoul was reading the story with the passion of an actor, his face drawn, his voice shaking with intensity and Ramón chose this moment to pour a glass of wine and encouraged him to have a drink before continuing.

## THE HOLY ICON

Raoul appreciated the draught of wine. The reading was draining his energy but he was enjoying the performance for this special audience. He began again in case someone suggested a longer break.

............THE MANUSCRIPT CONTINUES

*Alfonso decided that it was time to add to the members of the Cult, this time from outside the region. He considered the friends he had made on his travels. Hassan was an Arab and the expertise of his race in creating water systems was legendary. He could reinstate and develop the irrigation. The half-Christian, half-Arab, Manuel Diego Bin-Rahman could be their trader, acting as the contact with the captain of their ship, organising mule trains to transport goods all over Spain. And if Captain James was Alfonso's right-hand man, Le Poing, the innkeeper in Brittany, could be his left.*

*That same day messengers set out on horseback, two good men travelling to Brittany to find Le Poing and two more to Peniscola on the East coast to find Hassan and Manuel. Alfonso's invitations to the three men were memorised carefully by the messengers. They would explain the exciting challenge of restoring the hacienda without revealing too much.*

*Hassan and Manuel arrived within a month. They had stayed together since the voyage from the East. Manuel had taken Hassan as a partner and they had prospered but Alfonso's invitation was a challenge not to be resisted.*

*They were an odd couple, Alfonso had not seen them for years and both had changed. Hassan was taller, still dark-haired and athletic, but his Arab nose was now like a hawk's beak and his desert-tribesman's features were sharper, the lines etched on his face like the dry wadies of the desert.*

*When he and Alfonso had fled together from the Holy Land, he had the energy and agility of a boy, now he had the strength of a warrior. The difference in Manuel was less obvious. He was still small, rotund and bald but his hands and arms were as strong as Alfonso had ever seen in a man. Before he had seemed to be a cunning dealer, now he had presence, the confidence of a man of business who knows he has been successful.*

*From the moment they arrived it was as if they had never been parted from Alfonso. Hassan now spoke fluent Spanish and the three of them embraced and chattered away in that tongue while Margaret and James smiled at each other and waited to be introduced. Alfonso broke away laughing and presented them to his wife-to-be and his friend from Scotland.*

*'All your message needed to say was,"Come!" and we would have ridden day and night to answer your call.'*

*It was a much longer journey from Brittany and it was another three weeks before Le Poing arrived. He came at night, brought to Alfonso's tent an hour or so before dawn by the camp guards. He was alone. The two messengers sent to find him had been killed by a robber band as they had travelled back through the Basque country. Le Poing had escaped but had travelled the rest of the way at night.*

*He and Alfonso sat outside at the camp fire embers so they would not disturb Margaret. As Alfonso revealed his plans for the restoration of the estate, Le Poing was elated. He understood the role of the fraternity immediately, as if he and Alfonso had designed it together.*

*'I was born and raised in Brittany,' he said, 'But when your message arrived I knew I had to come. A man must seek adventure before time catches him unawares and makes him prisoner in his own home. I have no wife but the woman who has borne my children will run the inn while I am away.'*

*Alfonso now had eleven members of the Cult, one more and it might be enough. He decided that it was time for the first meeting of the Cult of the Holy Spirit and that the last vacancy should be left for the present.*

*Relationships between those chosen as members of the Cult were friendly, with one exception. Although Father Romero and Hassan* seemed to accept each other, there was obvious antagonism between the priest and Manuel.

*Alfonso had to listen to a tirade from Father Romero.*

'Is this man Christian or Moslem, Don Alfonso, or both, or neither when it suits him? He wants to take Mass in church but seems more at home with the ways of the Saracen. The infidels have over-run our country. They now control the Holy Land. The Pilgrimage to Jerusalem is dead. Is this man fish, flesh or fowl? Is he an Arab spy in our camp?'

*Alfonso stopped the onslaught with an irritated wave of his hand,*

'Father, Don Manuel Diego is my friend. I trust him.' It was said firmly, brooking no argument. There was a hint of menace, too, all the more chilling as Alfonso was such an amiable man. Since his ordination this priest had been the temporal as well as spiritual leader of these people. Now he must accept that those days were over.

*Alfonso mentioned the conversation to Manuel and was not surprised to be approached by the trader a few days later.*

'All is well Seigneur. I have made the Church a gift of a barrel of wine and the good priest and I have been sampling it together over the past few evenings. You may take it that we are now friends.'

*Le Poing set about learning Spanish and found Margaret and James being schooled by Manuel.* There was a sense of urgency throughout the lands of the hacienda. Alfonso's stone and wood dwelling was almost finished. The village houses and roads had been repaired. The people now had work to do and food enough to eat for the first time in many years.

*One evening Father Romero brought a Santiago pilgrim to Alfonso.* The man had been attacked and robbed by brigands. His companions had been killed and he had staggered into Codés del Camino on the point of death, Lady Margaret and Morag her maid installed him in a tent and cared for him. James sent out one of his bands of skirmishers to find the culprits and administer rough justice.

*As the patient grew stronger he asked to speak to Alfonso and Lady Margaret privately.*

*'I have a secret which must be kept from your priest,' he said quietly, 'Fifty years ago the Church mounted a crusade to destroy my people, the Cathars. Our villages were subjected to the interrogation of the Inquisitors. Our beliefs were declared to be heretic. Our castles were taken and destroyed. Our followers were tried by the Inquisition and burned at the stake unless they recanted.*

*'A few families of Believers avoided capture but the Church has renewed its efforts to crush us. Two months ago my father, two of my brothers and I fled the Inquisition by joining a Pilgrim band in Saint Jean-Pied-de-Port. Before we reached your village of Codés del Camino we were attacked by brigands and all three of them were killed.'*

*He tried to sit up but the effort still caused him pain.*

*'You have saved my life and I want to repay you. When I am well I will do whatever work you want me to do. But the priest must not find out that I am a Cathar.'*

*Alfonso put a hand on his shoulder to ease him back in the bed.*

*'We all have our secrets, friend, even the priest. Strangely, his secret is my secret. If he divulges it to his lord the Bishop, he will be the first to bear the consequence. You have offered your secret to me and I will honour your trust. When you are well we will find work for you, of that you may be certain.'*

*The young Cathar's name was Pierre Ranisolles. As he recovered his health he talked to Lady Margaret about his life in Languedoc. His home had been near the town of Tarascon in Ariège and he was a scribe, fluent in French, Catalan and Spanish as well as the langue d'Oc.*

*A whisper from a friendly priest had warned his father that the Inquisition was about to investigate his family. His mother had escaped with an older sister and the younger children to her home village near the frontier with Catalonia in the Pyrenees. He and two brothers had slipped away with his father and joined a band of Santiago pilgrims. Now his father and brothers were dead.*

*Lady Margaret was moved by the story but she was delighted to have a new member of the entourage who was so cultivated. Pierre was able to read and write. He was familiar with the fashions of the nobility in Ariège. He described the exotic foods and amusements of the banquets at the great castles. He was conversant with the troubadour traditions. But Lady Margaret insisted that Pierre should rest. When he was fully recovered there would be time for reading and writing, for conversation and music.*

------

Raoul paused, sensing that Ramón wanted to move upstairs to his study to allow Madam Mons and the girls to clear the table. They brought their glasses and another bottle of wine and, when they were all comfortably seated on the balcony, Raoul began again.

------

*With the house nearly finished Alfonso decided to have the first meeting of the Cult. Father Romero suggested that it be held in the church and proposed an elaborate form for the inauguration but Alfonso had already decided on simplicity.*

*The members met by candlelight in the late evening and sat around a long table improvised for the event with planks of wood across barrels. Alfonso rose and proclaimed the formation of the Cult of the Holy Spirit. He stated that its purpose was to restore and develop the hacienda lands of Codés. He welcomed each member by name and invited Father Romero to administer the oath.*

*In spite of a twinge of conscience because he could never reveal this rite to his Bishop, the priest was in his element. He asked the members to stand. Only Alfonso remained in his seat. There would be no reason for him to take the oath. The Cult was his destiny.*

*'I swear before God the Holy Spirit,' Father Romero paused to allow the others to repeat his words, 'That I will do all in my power to fulfil the code of the Cult of the Holy Spirit. I will obey*

the Master of the Cult in all things. I will support every other member to fulfil his or her duty to the Cult. I vow to remain silent about the Cult and its members.'

Alfonso closed the meeting and invited all to a feast at the encampment. There were fires and tables of food, lanterns, music and dancing. The members were ecstatic. The people thought that the feast was in honour of the work done so far but the members knew better. They were the chosen men. They would make this place fit for a proud people who had been brought to their knees by poverty and disease.

A month later there was another celebration, the wedding feast for Alfonso and Margaret. Their house was ready and they moved from the encampment into their new quarters. Everyone living in the villages or on the Codés lands was invited and everyone who could travel came willingly.

Manuel had acquired the most beautiful materials for the wedding clothes from Pamplona and Burgos. Alfonso's shirt was of bleached linen, almost white, his tunic and breeches were of black velvet and his boots of the finest black leather.

Lady Margaret's shape had changed but Morag, directed by Manuel, made her clothes to show that she was with child rather than trying to hide her swelling abdomen. Her dress was of white silk from the East, her cloak and shoes dark blue satin, her garments worked with silver and gold thread.

For the first time since she had left home Margaret wore the jewels she had brought with her. Her necklace of rare Scottish fresh-water pearls lay coiled on her neck and shoulders and was her link with her brother in Killhaven. Her ruby and emerald rings and her pendant of Irish gold on its long golden chain astonished the villagers. Her headdress, worked with amethysts and golden topaz, flashed in the sunlight of the afternoon and, as day turned to night, sparkled in the light of the fires and flares.

Father Romero could not conceal his joy at being invited to conduct the wedding in the church. Word had come from his Bishop that his Holiness the Pope wanted the marriage ceremony *to be less secular now, much more of a religious rite. The priest joined Alfonso's hand with Margaret's and pronounced them man and wife. They left the church still hand-in hand with Father Romero walking behind as they made their way through a great crowd of happy people to the ruins of the castle.*

*There were thirty tables laden with food, thirty fires for cooking meat and barrels of wine set up on stands, spigots in place. Minstrels in little bands roamed amongst the guests. There were acrobats and jugglers, jesters, stilt-walkers. On the edge of the feasting grounds there was archery, wrestling, fighting with wooden staves. In the centre a space was kept clear for singing and dancing to the minstrels' music.*

*At night fall the whole grounds were lit by lanterns on poles and hanging from hooks on the castle's ruined walls. The fires were stoked and the tables replenished. Flares and torches spluttered and hissed. Alfonso and Margaret wandered amongst the revellers and watched from the steps of the Castle's keep. It was a magical scene, a fiesta they would never forget.*

*Alfonso reaffirmed to himself that he would rebuild the castle. When these lands had been transformed it would stand as a symbol of his family duty to his people.*

*When the night was more than half gone he and Margaret retired to their bed-chamber and he sat on the edge of the bed knowing what was coming. Margaret began to laugh.*

*'You promised to open the satchel on our wedding night,' she said playfully, 'Now you have no choice but to discover the nature of the treasure and share it with your wife.'*

*Alfonso laid the satchel on the bed between them. The sealing wax was cracked and crumbling but still intact across the buckle. He crushed it between his finger and thumb nails and opened the bag. Inside a small board was wrapped in layers of the finest, softest leather Alfonso had ever seen. He turned the board over and the light in the room was suddenly intensified. It was as if the brilliance of the picture he revealed was the source of the illumination rather than the lamps.*

*Margaret gasped and knelt down beside the bed. With the back of her fingers she gently touched the surface of the picture and prayed to the Madonna.*

*'So this is from the ancient treasure of the Order of the Templar,' she said through tears of joy, 'It is a Holy Icon sent to guide us.'*

*The Icon depicted a golden bird soaring above a golden chalice. The background was of deepest sky blue, gloriously inlaid with images in silver filigree and decorated with precious stones inserted for dramatic effect. The bird and the chalice were not painted, their gold was the real metal.*

*The symbols depicted a splayed cross with three tiny rings on each of its four arms. Another representation, again in silver filigree, showed two Knights sharing the same horse and Alfonso explained that this was the traditional Templar symbol of poverty.*

*In a top corner was a picture of a Saint, or was it the Madonna?*

*The colours, gems and metals of the Icon glowed and shimmered now as if they were the only source of light in the room.*

*Lady Margaret lifted the Icon in both hands and prayed almost silent prayers. She asked for blessings for her marriage, her husband, her unborn child, and for the repose of her own soul. It had been a wrench to leave home in Scotland but she was certain now that this was where she should be.*

*Alfonso bowed his head and thanked God for his homecoming and the prospect of a glorious future in the* ............

--------------------------------------------------

Raoul had reached the bottom of the last page.

'There must be more.' he said anxiously, 'But I have searched through the contents of the chest and have not been able to find anything. The cover has been removed. Sometimes this happened because a binding had been so beautifully worked it became an artifact of great value on its own. The book was torn in two. I can find only the first section. There must be another part. '

As he put his type-written translation aside his hand trembled. He was tired, his face drained of emotion. No one spoke. The minutes passed in silence and at last Ramón rose, shook Raoul's hand and thanked him for his work. Doña Marie dried her tears and embraced her son with pride. Anamar took Ramón's hand and led him out of the house.

They walked in the moonlight to the bridge and sat on the parapet. The snow flecked peaks were still, the reflections in the river moving at a gentle pace. No words were needed but Ramón knew that, had Anamar not been with him, this would have been the loneliest moment of his life. Since he had been a boy roaming the lands of the hacienda in Navarre he had been preparing unwittingly for this instant.

It had been necessary to await the demise of his father. But that sad event had left him both the Manuscript and the responsibility for the Cult of the Holy Spirit. It had taken a death to reveal his destiny. Now he was ready for the next step, the search for the Cathedral of the Cult.

But the Manuscript had left so many questions unanswered. Should they find the Cathedral of the Cult, would it contain the Templar Treasure? And what was the Cathar connection? Could Alfonso have appointed the young Cathar, Pierre Ranisolles, to be a member of the Cult?

There was little sleep in the house that night. Raoul tossed and turned in bed and paced the room. Doña Marie lay on her back and traced her life since she had married Don Henriques. Anamar rose in the early hours and sat on the balcony, looking up at the mountains.

When eventually she went back to bed, Ramón smiled to himself. He was not alone. Anamar was more than wife, companion, confidante. Her Celtic spirit gave her a connection to the past. She had the ability to see beyond the limits of the practical world. She could understand without the words to explain. She had the strength to protect them both.

When first they had uncovered the existence of the Cult, he had been sure that it should be rejuvenated, now he was certain. He could feel the need of it now, as Alfonso had needed it then.

Next morning there was excitement in the air. The expedition party was due to assemble before noon. They would meet in the afternoon to prepare and pack. In the evening they would eat together and leave early next morning.

Ramón allowed his mind to check over the arrangements. The food and equipment for the expedition had been prepared to load into the lorry. He had telephoned ahead to Benasque to hire two pack horses for the duration of the venture.

Doña Marie and Madam Mons would look after the children. Guy le Blanc would make sure the farms, vineyard and forests were functioning properly. Maurice Cabanes would be responsible for the Bear Sanctuary.

Everything was ready. When he and Anamar went early to bed, they slept like tired children.

## RAMÓN'S EXPEDITION

It was a very early start but Doña Marie, the children and Madam Mons were all there to see them off. Raoul was to drive the lorry with Carlos and Raymond. Jules would travel in the car with Ramón and Anamar. By six o'clock they were on their way.

They used the new tunnel beyond Viella to cross the Pyrenees and arrived in Benasque at noon. Ten kilometres further they passed the Baños de Benasque, the impressive spa building high on the other side of the river. They reached the bridge across the Esera river where the dirt road became a track and the man who was supplying the horses was already there. It took half an hour to unload the truck, fill the panniers on the horses and pack the individual rucksacks.

Hardly a word was spoken. The expedition was underway. The horses were strong and easy to work with. Raoul took the halter of the lead horse and set off. Twenty minutes later he was struggling and called a halt. He had been setting too fast a pace.

Expectation carried their caravan of men, woman and horses up the great valley of the Esera River. They stopped to marvel at the Trou de Toro, the cavern of the Bull. They looked up at the great massif of Maladetta, the Evil One. By the end of the afternoon they had reached the Valle de Barrancs. They climbed up through the narrow canyon to the small grassy plan above. The best site for their camp was on the true right bank of the river, where Anamar had pitched her tent. She pointed out the big rock which marked the entrance to the cave system.

Ramón and Anamar pitched their small tent on a raised bank at the upper end of the plan. The others would sleep in the big tent which would also be used by all during the day, if the weather was bad. It was erected close to the river and beside the outdoor kitchen. A simple fireplace was constructed on the site Anamar had used. Stones were arranged as seats and a large flat-topped rock dragged into place as a table.

Raymond, Raoul and Jules took the horses back down stream to the forest and brought back two huge loads of wood, following Ramón's instruction, 'lying wood only to be taken'. Much nearer there were sticks and dead branches on the banks of the river, obviously washed down the valley at a time when the tree-line was much higher.

On their return the horses were tethered on long ropes some way upstream on another small plan. Anamar was amused to see a latrine hole being dug and a screen erected at a suitable distance downstream. It was obviously for her benefit. When she had been here on her own there had been no need for such elaborate measures to protect her modesty.

Before they cooked the evening meal and to the relief of everyone, Anamar suggested that they take a first look at the cave system. They had been waiting for the invitation. This was why they were here! In five minutes the party had assembled at the big rock, torches in hand, ready to explore.

But where was the entrance? They stood in a semi-circle on the steep slope below the boulder.

'Do we have to move the boulder?' Raoul was examining the massive stone.

Ramón reminded the party about the clues which Anamar had found in 'the missing document'.

**'Where the evil one stands above the cavern of the bull**
**Flows the secret river, born in the hidden depths of the sacred nave'**

He stood back and encouraged her to show them the way. Anamar faced the boulder and recited the third clue.

**'And at our hallowed sanctuary's door,**
**It is not enough to kneel and pray.**
**To lie and writhe is the only way.'**

Kneeling, almost touching its rough surface with her forehead, she said a silent prayer. She lay down full length along the base of the boulder, wriggled side ways and disappeared under it. The slope of the ground and the vegetation had been concealing the low opening below the rock.

Her torchlight revealed the chamber she had discovered when she had been here on her own. Encouraged by her shouts the others followed. Ramón was first, then Raoul, Don Carlos and Monsieur Raymond followed. Jules came last. The first chamber was as big as a room in a house. The ceiling was high. There was space for all of them.

Anamar led the way through a passage over a metre high and half a metre wide. The walls were smooth as if an underground river had flowed through it for millennia.

After twenty-five or thirty paces they reached the second chamber. It was much bigger than the first. To one side was a small pond, like a natural well, almost full to the brim with water. The cave's walls were dry and a shelf of smooth rock at knee height formed a bench long enough to seat them all. The torch beams flickered around the chamber, examining the floor, roof and walls.

It was Don Carlos who saw it first, The beam of his torch flashed on something metal in a niche above the well. On closer inspection it was a pewter drinking cup. Anamar was glad she had decided not to mention that she had discovered it on her first visit.

Ramón was excited beyond words. The pewter cup was proof that they were not the first humans to explore this cave system. The others gathered around, talking quietly, aware that they were uncovering history.

'This is almost as far as we go for now,' The echo of Anamar's voice mimicked her speech a fraction of a second behind, in perfect synchronisation.

'The roof has collapsed a few metres further along the passage. I've been able to see through a hole in the blockage. If we can clear the debris I'm sure this will lead on through the caves. If you want to see the spot, we can go forward two at a time.'

They took it in turns to examine the obstruction and filed back out of the system, squeezing through the gap below the big rock into the open air. No one, not even Raoul, dared doubt that this was the cave system which would lead them to the Cathedral of the Cult.

Next morning Jules rose at dawn before the others were awake and carried a spade and a crowbar up to the cave. Having carefully removed the vegetation below the boulder he excavated stones and soil to tunnel his way under the big rock and make access into the first chamber much easier. He worked carefully, leaving all the displaced material ready to be replaced when their exploration was finished.

Back at the camp two hours later he washed in the river, lit the fire and began to make bread for breakfast. Later they all climbed up to the cave entrance bringing the rest of the tools and equipment. There were two short-handled shovels, a sledge hammer, two plasterers' trowels in the shape of isosceles triangles, a length of rope, wicker baskets for carrying rubble and a big roll of cord to use as a guide to the way out, if the route became complicated. Most important of all were the paraffin lamps, two storm lanterns and two Tilly pressure lamps which gave a light as bright as electricity.

Ramón suggested that they should work in three groups. He and Jules would make a start on the collapsed roof, Anamar and Don Carlos would wait in the second chamber to pass out rocks and debris to Raoul and Monsieur Paul for ferrying outside.

Jules seemed to know what he was doing and the others followed his directions. He spent time studying the collapsed roof, tapping rocks, peering through the small hole. Then Jules, the practical man, started at the top of the rock fall and tried to remove one block the size of a man's head. He took the greatest care, but as he slid the rock out there was a little fall of rubble which neatly filled the space he had created.

He examined the wall on the left side and began again. It was slow and painstaking work but he was able to remove a number of stones and scrape away the gravel without causing a further fall. He had found the right place to begin.

To make the work easier they cleared the debris back to the second cave. It was tiring and dusty work and could not be rushed. They improvised masks to cover the mouth and nose and every hour or so they all came outside for a breath of fresh air and to let the dust settle.

Jules concentrated on clearing a narrow shaft. He worked without conversation, passing the debris back, his head and shoulders disappearing from view as he tunnelled deeper. Ramón made a ramp of rocks to help him reach the hole, extending it upwards as more of Jules' body entered the shaft. Another hour passed quickly and Jules appeared out of the hole, grinning. He pointed to the shaft and gave Ramón his torch.

Ramón climbed the ramp and poked his head inside the hole. He leant his weight on his elbows and shone the light into the shaft. Jules had broken through. Beyond the blockage, the powerful torch lit up a passageway similar to the one behind him. It opened out after a few metres to reveal another chamber, the floor of which was flooded with water. To the left hand side a shelf of rock, above the surface of the pool, led onwards.

It was now well into the afternoon and work was suspended to allow Ramón to tell the others the good news. While the food for the mid-day meal was being prepared they went through, one at a time, to see the progress.

Work started again about five o'clock and they brought any of the firewood logs which might be useful as pit props. Raymond and Carlos offered to cook the evening meal. Jules took his time at the blockage but when they stopped at eight for dinner, he had shored up the beginnings of a shaft over a metre high.

They washed in the river and celebrated the day's work with a ration of wine. The cooks grilled three small chickens and served them with green beans and a tomato salad. The fire and the lamps lit the encampment in an eerie light. Everyone was in a quiet mood, keeping excitement under control. They sat apart on the slope, looking up at the cave.

At the end of a day they would all remember as long as they lived, there was no great need for conversation in the camp. Anamar looked across at Ramón and he smiled. She thought he hadn't looked so happy for years.

Next morning Anamar was up first and made bread the way her Granny Mac would have made it - flat triangular farls cooked on a griddle, best when eaten fresh and warm. By noon Jules had cleared and shored a passage over half a metre wide and one and a quarter metres high.

Ramón decreed that, when they were exploring beyond this point, at least one member of the party must remain on the outside. It seemed a sensible precaution. For the first exploration Ramón led the way with a powerful torch and Raoul followed with one of the Tilly lamps. Anamar came next and Jules brought up the rear. Carlos and Raymond volunteered to stay.

The passage was wider than the one before and they filed into the next chamber, keeping to the rock shelf around the pool of water. Towards the back of the cave a cascade filled the pond with the captivating sound of falling water. To one side the over flow escaped through a channel.

The walls of the chamber were wet. Great clusters of stalactites hung from the roof. Beyond the pool the passage was low and narrow. After thirty paces it widened out and they had to wade through water ankle deep. At a Y junction, a line of large white stones had been set across the mouth of one shaft. Raoul speculated that someone must have brought the stones into the cave and had placed them here to indicate that this passageway was not to be followed.

But Ramón was already climbing into the next chamber which was over three metres higher than the flooded channel. He called for the paraffin lamp and it flooded the grotto with light. This chamber was small and dry. On the walls were carved inscriptions and names which were hard to decipher, specific years from the 13th and 14th centuries, an array of symbols depicting the Templar cross, a soaring bird, the Tau cross in the shape of a 'T' and, strangely, the crow's foot device which denoted a Cagot.

They could have spent time here recording the inscriptions but Ramón led on. They passed through a narrow passage to a cavern festooned with stalactites and almost choked with boulders. There were holes at each side and crevices which could have been squeezed through but they took the route ahead. Ramón exchanged his torch for the Tilly lamp and followed the stream against the water's flow. He climbed a ramp of rocks over thirty metres high. At its head a short passage led to a narrow slit between two rocks. In seconds he had squeezed through and found himself in a vast cavern. It took a few moments for his eyes to become accustomed to the diffused light of one lamp in such a huge space and to allow his mind to see the magnitude of his discovery.

'This is it,' he called back through the entrance slit. 'We've found the nave. Come and join me in our Cathedral!'

The others took it in turn to enter through the crack. Anamar let the men go before her. Jules slipped through without difficulty. Raoul's tall, angular shape made it much more difficult for him. When she joined them on the other side the men were silent, letting their vision adjust, gaping at this massive nave, awesome beyond their wildest dreams. Until they reached the slit their torches and lamp had flooded the passageways with light. Here their combined power could only illuminate this vast interior with a few brilliant, isolated torch beams in a subdued, mystical, background light.

Ramón had never considered himself a particularly religious man but his mother's faith had influenced his growing years and it was a shock for Anamar to hear him ask her, in a whisper, to dedicate this wondrous discovery to the Holy Spirit.

Without the slightest hesitation, and in a voice she remembered from youthful time spent on her knees, Anamar asked God to bless this revelation of the Cathedral, the spiritual home of the Cult of the Holy Spirit.

When they rose to their feet their eyes were more accustomed to the diffused light and they could appreciate the magnificence of this place. The cavern was as big as a cathedral with a broad ledge on the left hand side, ten metres above the floor. Raoul called this the Balcony. On the right-hand side a small fountain bubbled up from below and flowed away down a crack choked with pebbles.

There were strange rock shapes eroded by flowing water. The roof above the balcony was draped with stalactites. There were three large stalagmites, one over a metre high. Towards the back, a large, flat-topped rock looked as if it had been man-handled into place as an altar.

On the wall behind the altar stone a ledge about half a metre long had been carved in the rock at head height. Two large golden candlesticks were perched, one at each end. It was obvious that they were so placed to illuminate whatever had been displayed on the shelf between them. Raoul inserted two of their spare candles into the candlesticks and lit them.

They drifted away from each other, each on his or her own, exploring the great cave. Their separate lights flashed in eerie patterns, picking up the huge span of the nave, focussing on every detail of the cavern.

Listening to their muted conversation, Anamar suddenly realised that her companions were seeing this underworld with different eyes to her own. To them, this was an adventure, exciting, even dangerous. It was a journey of exploration through a fascinating cave system made all the more interesting because of its historical link to their Cult.

Had she been able to tell them her own thoughts, would Raoul or Jules, or even Ramón, understand? Would they even hear what she was saying? She had started from a different place. Of course the link with the Cult was intriguing and she was enjoying the adventure, but this was a magical world she had known all her life.

On her own expedition to find the cave, her Granny Mac had been her guide in the mountains. She had felt herself go back to the time when she was a child. Then she and her friends, Maureen and Eamon, had roamed the lower slopes of the Blue Stack mountains of Donegal. Her Granny Mac had told them tales of the 'conjurer', the wise woman who could make dreams come true. Who could cure ills with charms when the doctor failed. Who could reveal the future.

Her Granny Mac would have been at ease here in this extraordinary cavern. Her belief in God had never been compromised by her certainty that she lived in a world where fairies, wizards and conjurers kept the carlines and witches at bay. She had laughed when she heard the priest say that the wise woman only had her power because she had made a pact with the devil.

Granny Mac had told them about a cave in the West of Ireland which enabled the Fairy King of Munster to cross secretly into Ulster by travelling underground. He had managed to evade the leprechaun guards, had bought a pair of magic shoes made by the fairy cobbler of Ulster, and retraced his steps without a bother on him.

Anamar stared with the eyes of a ten year old at the roof of the cavern they called the Nave. The stalactites above the Balcony could have been built by leprechauns to keep demons imprisoned for hundreds of years. There was a splendid frill of white rock suspended below the Balcony which might have been carved by fairy masons. On the opposite wall there was a buttress in the shape of a grotesque giant's head.

Eerie passageways leading from the Balcony could be home to mischievous creatures waiting their chance to play tricks on the unwary. Nooks in the sheer walls might be hiding places for their treasures. A torch beam flicking across the upper walls made a horde of shadowy leprechauns scamper away from the light. It was a magical, underground world of weird shapes and sounds, fantastical, scary.

Anamar, the child, bent down and picked up a white pebble from the floor to have as a present for one of the little people, should she be discovered. As she straightened up, Ramón's voice brought her back from the world of enchantment. It was time to go.

They were all reluctant to leave but Ramón was aware that there were two others waiting patiently outside for their chance to come in. Raoul snuffed out the candles behind the altar stone and left them in place.

It seemed to take a long time to retrace their steps. When they reached the entrance, and without a rest, Ramón took Don Carlos and Monsieur Raymond back into the system. It was a remarkably different experience for him on this second visit. He resisted the temptation to tell the men what was coming next. It was so much better to let each of them make his own journey of discovery.

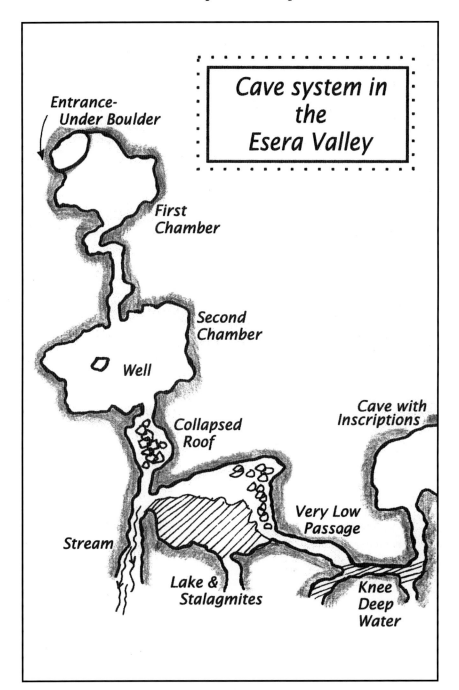

Entrance-
Under Boulder

Cave system in
the
Esera Valley

First
Chamber

Second
Chamber

Well

Cave with
Inscriptions

Collapsed
Roof

Very Low
Passage

Stream

Lake &
Stalagmites

Knee
Deep
Water

Carlos and Raymond marvelled at the eerie beauty of the chamber of the lake, with the unending splash of its waterfall and its roof adorned with stalactites. When they climbed the long ramp up to the slit which led to the cathedral, he stayed back and let them go on alone. Carlos was of stout build and had a nervous moment as he tried to squeeze through the narrow opening. He breathed out, forced himself sideways and plopped through into the Cathedral.

They were both overcome with emotion. Carlos fell to his knees in prayer. Raymond, head back, stretched out his arms to the vast space of the nave. Ramón sat down with his back against the wall and left them for half-an-hour, each on his own. Carlos climbed up to the Balcony and waved. Raymond let the water from the fountain well up and fall through his fingers.

Eventually they came back to embrace Ramón, to shake his hand, to thank him for a sublime experience they would remember all their days.

They retraced their steps towards the entrance, pausing to study the etched names and dates, inspecting the stalactites and stalagmites. Carlos picked up three pebbles and put them in his pocket. Raymond looked closely at the most beautiful of the stalactites hanging at head height in the second chamber. He was sorely tempted to break it off and take it for a souvenir of this wonderful day. But he glanced across and saw Ramón shake his head as if he could read his mind.

Carlos filled the pewter cup at the well and took a sip. The water was cool, not cold. There was a faint but distinct taste, fresh and clean, a tang not strong enough to be a flavour. If there had to be a water of life, Ramón decided, this was it.

Carlos drank deeply, threw the dregs against the wall and passed the cup to Raymond, as if this was a long-established tradition of the Cult. Raymond bent down to fill the cup and follow Carlos's actions. He passed the cup on to Ramón who, in turn, complied precisely.

The three men smiled at each other. In this simple way are serious rituals born.

When they emerged from Jules's tunnel into the totally different world of the mountainside, Ramón was dazed. It took him a few moments of struggle with reality to orient himself. Their underground adventure might have been a day dream. Anamar took his arm and they walked together down to the camp.

On the first evening the group had been highly excited, on edge, anticipating the adventure. By the second night they were tired but certain that they were in the right place. Now on the third night they were ecstatic but unsure how to celebrate.

Raoul cooked the food while Jules and Anamar waited for the others to return. He made soup from bouillon cubes, carrots and leeks. Two large, triangular tins of Jambon de York served with boiled onions in a white sauce would provide the main course. Dessert would be a huge Tarte aux Basque brought in a tin box. And again Ramón approved a special ration of wine - four bottles between the six of them.

The store of food carried up to the camp by the pack horses was proving its worth.

At breakfast next morning Anamar made double the quantity of the farls of Irish bread. Appetites were improving. Before they left for the cave, Ramón explained that the day would be devoted to improving the access through the debris of the roof collapse, mapping the cave system and recording descriptions of the sections they had explored.

Ramón was far from certain that the partnership would work but he decided that Raoul would help Jules with the tunnelling. He and Raymond would make the survey of the cave system, a section at a time, using the big ball of twine marked out with a knot every metre. Anamar and Carlos were given the job of recording descriptions of the chambers and each section of the connecting passageway. The work required all of them and the precaution of always having two on the outside was waived.

To his surprise Raoul found that he liked working with Jules. Although their job was physically tiring, it was far more interesting than he would have expected. They were finished by the noon break and joined the surveying party when they resumed. The work was finished by late afternoon but, before they left, Anamar and Carlos took them to a narrow passage off the cathedral cavern. It led to a small cave which they had discovered that afternoon and the others had not yet seen.

The cave was as big as a room in a house. As they entered their lights were caught in hundreds of little reflections from the walls and roof of the cave. The interior surface was completely covered with fragments of mirror and small pieces of coloured glass, dark green, yellow, ruby red, brilliant blue. And inserted in between, there were patterns of semi-precious stones and coloured pebbles.

Anamar remembered Deirdre Ryan, her friend and godmother of her oldest child, telling her about a visit she had made to the magnificent Amber Palace of Jaipur, in India. She and her father had been shown around the palace by a guide and he had brought them to a room perched on the roof. Once inside, the guide had closed the door, shuttered the windows and lit a candle.

Anamar rummaged in her rucksack for her emergency candle and matches and asked the others to switch off their torches. She paused before she lit the candle and let them feel the total darkness. She struck the match. It flamed and flared and lit the wick. She held the candle high above her head. The room was ablaze with gleaming, shimmering light. She began to wave the candle in slow circles above her head. A thousand flashes of light winked back. The gems sparkled. The coloured fragments of glass glowed.

As she circled the candle the cave began to move around their heads. Anamar moved the flame a little faster, and the cave began to spin.

The men gasped. Anamar circled the candle as fast as she dared. The walls and roof began to whirl. Or was it the watchers who were flying, gyrating around the flame like crazed moths? The flame fluttered. The melted wax flew. She moved the candle faster. The cave was spinning out of control. There were cries of astonishment and a yelp of joy or fear from Raoul.

Anamar gradually slowed the flame to a stop and held it steady to allow the spinning cave to settle.

When Deirdre had told her the tale of the room of a thousand twinkling lights Anamar had tried so hard to picture the scene. But, what had been fantasy then, was reality now and within her gift. She had the power to make the spell work.

Anamar snuffed the candle and the men switched on their lights. There was a flurry of conversation and they filed back to the Cathedral in silence. Carlos asked them to wait while he climbed up to the big ledge they called the Balcony. He began to sing in Latin, quietly at first, then gaining volume. It was the medieval Gregorian chant of the Benedictine Monks of the monastery of Santo Domingo de los Silos. Anamar had heard it on her pilgrimage to Santiago ten years ago.

She had gone to the village and attended Evensong at the monastery. The flowing cadences had left an unforgettable sound in her head.

The acoustics were perfect. Don Carlos had a tenor voice which filled a Cathedral older than any constructed cathedral in Christendom, older by far than the Church itself.

They were all deeply affected by the finding of their Cathedral. Raoul was like a noisy school-boy who had won a prize on Speech Day. Jules said nothing but this adventure had done more to restore his faith than all the priests he had met in his life-time.

Raymond's admiration was for the wonder of this natural phenomenon. Anamar sensed that this secret had been revealed at the right moment. Carlos was in ecstasy. He had always followed his faith religiously, taking it for granted. Now it was a reality from which he could never escape.

Ramón spoke to no one but held his wife's hand on the way back. Each had earned his or her own experience. Nothing would be able to take it from them. It would remain in their memories as long as they lived.

When they neared the hole excavated through the blockage, Raoul made sure he was leading the way. He was proud of the work he and Jules had done. The opening was as big as a doorway and as he reached it he lifted his elbows sideways to shoulder height, to show that even a big man like himself could pass through easily.

As he emerged on the other side there was a sharp crack. His left elbow had hit a vertical prop and he screamed in pain. But the blow had dislodged the support and it fell forward. Slowly at first, then with a rush and a dull roar, the rocks and debris from above poured down to block the passageway again.

Raoul was on the outside of the fall, the others trapped on the inside. They could hear his cries of pain. His elbow was broken, he yelled. The tools were on his side but he would not be able to use them.

Ramón asked the others to switch off all but one of the lights to save battery power and paraffin. As soon as the dust settled he and Jules examined the new collapse. Without tools it looked hopeless.

'Although we have no food,' Ramón said quietly, 'We have light, plenty of good water and the air is fresh.'

Anamar caught him by the arm.

'Now that you mention the fresh air,' she said quickly, 'When we were in the Cathedral, I felt the faintest breeze on the top of my head. There could be another way out.'

Ramón shouted to Raoul to tell him what they were doing and the five of them walked back quickly through the system to the Cathedral. Anamar stood still at the place where she had noticed the little breeze. Sure enough she could feel it. They could all feel it.

The air seemed to be coming down from above so they climbed up to the Balcony and searched the upper reaches at the back of the nave. There were crevices in the wall, but all were blank. There were little buttresses of rock at various angles. Ramón disappeared behind one. They heard him shout.

'I can feel the air. It's stronger here.' he called, 'I'm going to crawl into a crack. Don't try to follow me in case I have to come out backwards.'

The others gathered behind the buttress, listening to the sound of Ramón scrambling up the crack until he was out of ear shot. It seemed a long time before they heard the scuffling sound of him coming back.

'I don't know where it leaves us on the mountainside but I've found a way out,' he called. 'Follow me, one at a time.'

Anamar waited to be last in the line. It took ten minutes of steady crawling uphill and she emerged into the fresh air at the bottom of a deep cavity in a jumble of boulders. The light was fading quickly but once they had climbed out of the pile of rocks they could see they were within a hundred metres of their camp.

When they climbed back down to the big stone at their original entrance, Ramón and Anamar left the others outside and went in to find Raoul. He was sitting in the second chamber amid the debris of the fall, covered in dust, surrounded by the excavating tools. His back was to them. He was crouching over a lamp, cradling his injured left arm, staring at the blockage.

'It's all right. We've found another way out.' Ramón spoke quietly not wanting to startle Raoul but when he turned around he stared at them as if they were ghosts. He began to cry.

'I wanted to help but when I tried to dig the pain was unbearable.' It was as if he had not yet understood that the others had escaped. 'I'm doing my best but I can't hold the spade properly.'

Ramón managed to calm him and led the way out of the tunnel. Anamar had attended First Aid classes and she examined the damaged arm. She gently massaged the elbow with a herbal cream which she and Madam Mons had made for her First Aid kit.

She had found the recipe in a book of herbal remedies and had bought tincture of Arnica in a herbalist shop in St-Girons. Mixed with paraffin wax and honey it formed a soft white cream. The book claimed that the cream was effective for the relief of pain and inflammation and Anamar had used it successfully with the children. She folded a triangular bandage as a sling to hold the arm in place. Now Raoul had received personal treatment from Anamar and had the sling to show off his injury, he began to recover.

Anamar had acted like a professional nurse when she had been treating Raoul but he saw it quite differently. She had praised him for his translation of the Manuscript. She seemed to have enjoyed working with him on the tasks around the camp and in the caves. He felt he was receiving special treatment because of their relationship. It was annoying for Anamar but there was little she could do without causing an unpleasant scene in front of the others.

She decided to give the Arnica cream to Raymond and ask him to treat the elbow with it twice a day.

Carlos and Raymond, pestered with unwanted directions from Raoul, made the evening meal. They hard boiled eggs and served them with tinned anchovies, tomatoes and garlic mayonnaise. They grilled slices of pork as thick as a man's finger, boiled carrots and served them with tinned haricots verts. Dessert was tinned apricots and Pyrenean goats' cheese.

At the end of the meal they all found themselves sitting closer together than on previous evenings. They were enjoying the evening's ration of wine, discussing the day's excitements. Ramón began to laugh.

'I'd better tell you what I was going to do when the roof fell in.' he said smiling, 'Just in case any of you had been finding it difficult to remain calm, I had decided to tell you a story.'

'Do you know the origin of the English phrase, "Don't panic!"?'

'It's commonly believed that the 26-mile Olympic Marathon Race commemorates the run from Marathon to Athens by the Greek, Pheidippides. He was supposed to be the messenger who brought the news of the defeat of the Persians by the Greeks, and who then dropped dead as a result of his efforts. That's the fable. The true story is that Pheidippides actually ran 150 miles from Athens to Sparta in 48 hours to summon help against the Persian invaders. And far from dropping dead at the end, he lived to enjoy his achievement!

'Apparently the god Pan appeared to him during the run and, as a result of his helping Pheidippides, the god's standing was greatly enhanced in Athens. Pan had always been regarded as the unpredictable god of misrule, so in difficult times the cry became, "Don't Panic!".'

They all laughed and Anamar gave her husband a nudge in the ribs with her elbow.

'Just as well I remembered that cool breeze on my head, otherwise we might have been trapped in that cave for days, having to listen to you and your stories.'

Next morning Ramón took stock of the food and wine. Stores were low but sufficient. He announced his plans at breakfast. They would dig a new way through the roof collapse, make one last visit to the Cathedral, dine well that evening and strike camp the following morning.

Jules had already been back into the cave to check on the latest collapse. Although it was not obvious from the inner side of the blockage, he was able to see from the outer that the debris had fallen through a hole in the roof of the passageway. That gap was now blocked by two huge stones which had jammed together above it. It was his guess that there would be no further danger of rock falls here.

Jules was right. As the others worked at clearing the debris, Raoul rummaged in the store of food and discovered a tin of biscuits Madame Mons had made for them. He arrived at the cave entrance with the coffee pot in his uninjured hand and the mugs and the biscuits in his rucksack.

Rather than dumping the rubble outside the cave where it might have taken the attention of shepherds, they piled it up in a wider section of the passage between chambers and in the large second cave. By noon they were almost finished. One large flat rock remained to be moved. Everyone tried to help and they struggled to lift one edge and balance the rock on the opposite side.

As the stone was raised Raymond was the first to see underneath. His voice shook.

'Give me a torch!' he said hoarsely, 'There's a body under the rock!'

## THE CAGOT'S TOMB

The stone was much easier to manoeuvre on its edge. They pivoted it one way, then another and propped it against the wall of the passage. The lamps were brought forward. Now they could all see. In a depression under the rock lay a human skeleton. It was small, the size of a fourteen-year-old boy, lying uncrushed, in the foetal position in a cavity below the rock. There were remnants of leather clothing on the bones and a still-discernable symbol etched on the upper arm of the jerkin.

Held by a strap over one shoulder was a leather bag. From a waist belt hung the remains of what might have been a leather wine bottle.

'He's a Cagot,' said Ramón, 'There was once a colony of them living on the mountain near Mont L'ours-les-Cascades.' He pointed to the crow's foot symbol on the jerkin. 'That's the mark they were always obliged to wear.'

The party stood in silence before the skeleton.

Although the Cagot people were rarely discussed on either side of the Pyrenees, everyone in the party was aware of this mysterious, elusive and despised race. It was as if it was easier not to acknowledge their existence.

The Cagots were reputed to be small in stature, strange looking to others. Some said they were the descendants of the Visigoths. Their history was known through the oral tradition rather than the printed word. Ramón had found a reference to them in a 13th century manuscript, but had never seen a mention of them in any subsequent document. It was as if, in both Spain and France, there was a collective sense of shame for the way they had been treated over the centuries.

The Cagots were kept apart by unwritten rules. They were not allowed to marry outside their own people. In some areas they were not permitted to enter churches and had to watch the Mass through what was called a Cagot Window. In other areas they could enter the church but had to worship from the back, with the Host served to them by the priest on a long wooden board. They could not touch food in a market, go barefoot or enter a mill.

The Cagots could not own land. Their dwellings had to be outside the village, separated from it by a river or a forest, preferably both. They worked in wood as carpenters, wood cutters, coffin makers, barrel makers, cart makers, basket weavers. Some became masons and expert builders, others were accomplished sculptors in wood and stone.

They were exempt from taxes and military duty and could not take a position in either the Church or local administration. They could not be buried in consecrated ground so they were interred in shallow graves outside the village walls, on the verges of roads or on river banks.

A few Cagots became rich and influential and there were stories of the daughters of wealthy Cagots, with great dowries, being able to marry impoverished noblemen. In spite of 'Égalité' being one of the three noble aims of the French Revolution there were still Cagots at the beginning of the 20th century.

Ramón was the first to speak. He knew immediately what should be done.

'There is no need to move the body. We will pray for the Cagot's soul and replace the stone. His tomb will be where he died. But first we should look in his bag.'

He knelt down and opened the satchel without disturbing the bones. From inside he drew out a manuscript and placed it to one side. They would examine it later. There was no sign of weapons but Ramón's search disturbed the collar of the jerkin behind the neck bones. There was a glint of light on steel and the blade of a knife became visible below the remnant of clothing. It was a small dagger, still in a perished sheath, the blade as long as the span of a man's hand, the hilt worked in silver and finely etched. It had been hidden, hilt up, behind his left shoulder blade.

Ramón let the dagger lie across his palms while he examined it. Although he had never been a soldier, he had the warrior's fascination for a blade. Cagots were not permitted to bear weapons. This man must have had an important reason for carrying a concealed dagger.

'I don't think he'll have need of it now,' he said and slipped it into his rucksack.

The others joined him on their knees and they prayed for the repose of the Cagot's immortal soul. Taking care not to disturb the skeleton, they lowered the rock back into position. Ramón said the words that consigned the mortal remains to the tomb and Jules set to work to carve a cross on the top surface of the stone.

When Ramón gave him the document from the Cagot's bag, Raoul found it hard to hold with his one uninjured hand. Anamar saw his difficulty and opened it for him while he held a torch. The pages were of finest vellum inscribed in Latin. There was something familiar about this document. It was as if Raoul had seen it before. He translated aloud the first few words on the first page. They started abruptly, in mid-sentence ............ 'lands of his fathers'.

He shouted over his shoulder to Ramón,

'We've found it! This is the missing part of the Manuscript. Do you remember the words on the last page we already have? They thanked God for the homecoming and "**the prospect of a glorious future in the ............**" The first page of this document begins "............ **lands of his fathers**". The sentence is complete. The Cagot was carrying the second part of the Manuscript.'

They went through the passageways together and Raoul needed help to squeeze through the slit into the Cathedral. Ramón sat on his own at the back of the Balcony. Jules and Raymond wandered quietly around the great cavern of the Cathedral's nave. Carlos knelt near the altar stone and Anamar crouched down beside him - the one knowing why he was on his knees and the other wondering why she was not on hers. Raoul sat on a flat stone with his torch in his mouth, holding the Manuscript open as best he could with his knees and his uninjured arm.

They spent over an hour in the Cathedral and made their way out of the cave system, each in his or her own time.

Jules and Raymond refilled the space which had been excavated under the big stone to give easy access to the cave system. When the sods of the undergrowth were replaced only the closest examination would have shown that they had been removed. Access was restored to the original wriggle under the stone ........ 'to lie and writhe is the only way'.

With the exception of Raoul, everyone helped with the evening meal. He was allowed to sit on his own with a good lamp to continue his reading of the Manuscript. Ramón had already announced that after dinner Raoul would make an extemporary translation of the first few pages of the Manuscript carried by the Cagot.

On previous evenings the cooks had been able to select what they wished from the store but one special box had been kept to the side. It had been packed by Anamar and Ramón for the last evening. There were black olives in a jar, chorizo sausage, jamón de serrano and smoked mackerel wrapped in grease-proof paper. Two large sealed jars of cassoulet prepared by Madam Mons would provide the centre piece of the meal and to finish there would be Pyrenean goats' cheese and tinned peaches.

Ramón had given a deal of thought to the wine and had chosen three bottles of white from his Mont L'ours vineyard to be chilled in the ice-cold waters of the stream. To keep the balance between France and Spain there were three bottles of a strong Rioja style red from his father's vineyard in Navarre. And, only for this final evening, he had packed in straw in a wooden box six wine glasses.

To make this evening's festivities inclusive he had brought a fine old Cognac and a Patcheran liqueur. Honour would be shared and France, Spain and the Basque country were all acknowledged.

On this last evening they sat in a ring around the fire so that they could all join in the conversation. For the first time the tension had eased in the camp. They were much closer to one another than on any of the previous evenings. Everyone was smiling. They had fulfilled their greatest hopes. But now they had discovered their Cathedral they wanted to find the Holy Icon, the treasure of the Cult. Even before Ramón announced it, they all knew that there had to be another expedition to the Cathedral.

The first of the wine was poured before the meal was served. Anamar sat with her back against a bank and sipped the chilled white wine of Mont L'ours. It was a pale golden colour, fresh and clear, with a tang of peach and the clean taste of icy water from the peaks.

She let the men do the work. They were enjoying themselves. Ramón supervised the preparations for the meal. On previous evenings he had left it to others to do the cooking. To-night he intended it to be a feast here in the high valley, surrounded by the peaks. It was a perfect setting for a banquet beneath the stars.

Raoul tried to catch Anamar's eye but she smiled at each and every one of them. She shivered with pleasure as she sipped the wine. Ramón raised his glass to her and she returned the toast with a laugh she could never have allowed anyone else to hear at home in Ireland.

It was one of the most exhilarating evenings of her life. And Ramón caught her mood. He looked like a happy boy rather than the serious man who had led this expedition.

She arranged two places to sit and two small circular depressions in which to set their wine glasses while they ate. When the food was served Ramón brought Anamar's enamel plate with the first course and sat down beside her. At the end of the meal he rose to make the toasts.

'You have been drinking wine for pleasure,' he said gravely, 'But now you must take it for duty. It is time to celebrate what we have been able to do and salute the future. But one indulgence I can offer you. There is no need to rise for each toast. You have earned your seats.'

He asked them to drink to the Cult of the Holy Spirit, to the discovery of the Cathedral and to the Cagot in his tomb beneath the slab. He thanked them for their support and complimented Raoul on his translation of the Manuscript. He said that, without Jules, they would not have been able to penetrate the blockages. He looked at Anamar and thanked her shyly for solving the clues. Carlos recharged the glasses and raised his on behalf of them all. Since Ramón had become Master of the Cult their lives had all been changed, he said simply, and his voice quivered with an emotion they could all feel.

They took it in turn to rise and speak. Raoul said that it was a privilege to be with such wonderful people, that anything he had been able to do had been a reward in itself. And all the time he glanced towards Anamar, hoping for a sign.

Raymond said that he was a man of few words but this had been the most exciting time of his life. He hoped to come back here, the Cathedral was now his spiritual home.

Sensing that Jules might be uncomfortable at the prospect of having to take his turn, Raoul whispered to him that there was no need to speak unless he wanted to. Jules looked at him in amazement.

'Don't worry, Monsieur le Professeur, I am a showman, I have been a performer all my life.'

He turned and called into the darkness beside the big tent, as if he was calling his bear.

'Martin! Martin! Come into the light! The lady and the gentlemen want you to dance for them!'

He disappeared behind the tent and emerged into the lamplight from the other side. But he was now a huge creature, not a man. He lumbered towards them like a bear walking on his hind legs. He was Martin the bear as he entered their ring of seats and began a slow dance, lifting one leg and hopping on the other.

Anamar began to clap to the rhythm of the dance. The others joined in and the sound echoed around their narrow valley. Jules moved amongst them drawing them all into his entertainment. It was a mesmeric moment, reality suspended and fantasy in command.

Ramón was deeply moved by the spectacle of the showman becoming his bear. He had challenged the tradition of the dancing bear because of the barbarity of the training but this performance was pure theatre. Could they use it at the sanctuary to commemorate the tradition of the dancing bears of Ariège?

Jules lumbered behind the tent again and when he returned the performance was almost over.

'I miss my bear,' he said and wiped his face with his sleeve, 'Martin and I would dance together when we were on our own but never as part of a show. No one has ever seen me do the dance of the bears until we danced for you to-night.'

After the applause, the silence lasted until Anamar rose to her feet.

'Now it's my turn and you've been keeping me, like the good wine, to the last,' she said grandly. 'Jules has shown us how to dance like a bear. Now you must learn to dance in the Irish way.' She stood up and showed them a step, hop and step, on alternate legs to a tune without words,

'de-de, de-de, de-de-diddle-diddle,  de-de, de-de, diddle-diddle de..........'

She formed them into a ring, arms' length apart, hands on each others shoulders. They began to circle, slowly at first, then faster. She kept the circle spinning but this time, to suit Raoul, with right arms towards the middle, like spokes of a wheel. The finale was to take a partner around the waist and swing each other faster and faster until they lost hold of each other's waists and fell in a heap.

Had there been a shepherd staying out all night with his sheep, what would he have made of it? This group of men leaping about like dervishes, whooping and yelling, led by this wild woman who had them all in her power.

Anamar called a halt to the dance and she and Ramón refilled the glasses and rearranged the lamps. It was time for Raoul to begin his translation of the Manuscript found in the Cagot's satchel. They built a lectern of food boxes and hung a Tilly lamp from a tripod made of walking poles. Raoul cleared his throat and began, translating as he read.

'This is a reading from a text which is surely the missing part of the Manuscript and it follows on from the text found in the archive chest.' Having to do an extemporary translation was exciting for Raoul the performer. It gave him renewed confidence.

..........THE SECOND PART OF THE TEMPLAR MANUSCRIPT BEGINS

*By the end of a year Alfonso's lands had been transformed. The Cult met every month and the members had been chosen well. Margaret gave birth to twins, a boy and a girl, christened Robert after Margaret's brother the Earl of Killhaven and Maria for Alfonso's mother.*

*Trade was established with cities as far away as Pamplona to the North-East and Logroño to the West. The Cult's ship, trading out of Bilbao, had taken cargoes to France, England, the Baltic and the Mediterranean.*

*The villages were now restored. The irrigation trenches had been repaired and extended. The vines had been pruned and the vineyards weeded. The horses and goat herds were healthy. The poverty and starvation which had greeted Alfonso and his band when they had arrived had vanished.*

*Alfonso and Father Romero could see that the energy and enthusiasm of the members of the Cult had made the transformation. But Margaret knew better. The men might think that it was their skill and energy which was responsible but she knew better. It was the presence of the Holy Icon which had made the difference.*

*She believed that the Holy Icon had brought Alfonso to Scotland and to her brother's domain. It had drawn Alfonso and her together when she thought that her chance of marriage had gone. It had carried them safely by ship to this awesome land. It had given her the chance to have healthy children beyond the normal age of childbearing. And now it had transformed this huge and derelict estate into a land fit for kings.*

*At the end of Winter Alfonso was inspecting a vineyard when he was approached by the young Cathar, Pierre Ranisolles. One of*

*Pierre's jobs was to see that the pilgrims on their way to Santiago de Compostela were properly looked after in Codés del Camino. The road to Santiago, the Camino, passed directly through the village and nearly all the news of what was happening in the world outside their estate was brought by pilgrims.*

*That morning Pierre had met a group of pilgrims from Ariège and learned that the Inquisition was active again in that part of France, trying to uncover Cathar heretics. In past years they had carried out their inquiries North of the Pyrenees. Now they were investigating villages in the mountains near the frontier with Catalonia. This was where Pierre and his father had left his mother and his young brothers and sisters when they had fled the Inquisition a year ago.*

*He wanted to go back and bring them to safety here in Navarre, he said. He would go alone but if Alfonso would help him with a few men, pack horses and stores he would stand a much better chance of success. Alfonso spent the evening discussing the request with Margaret. Pierre was a good man. Alfonso had found him honest, loyal and hard working. Margaret admired his learning and his skill as a scribe. She enjoyed his company, she respected the way the people turned to him for advice rather than Father Romero.*

*Alfonso's instinct was to help the Cathar. He would lead the party himself. He would take thirty of his best soldiers. Then it was Margaret's turn and to his amazement, she agreed. A man like him needed to meet challenge half-way, she had reasoned. But there were two conditions. James Lamont must go with him and they must take the Holy Icon.*

*Alfonso and James might be a formidable partnership but, for such a journey, Lady Margaret was certain, they needed the Holy Icon. It would ensure the success of their mission and would bring them safely back to Navarre. Alfonso decided to take his friend Hassan and not only because he was a powerful warrior. Hassan had travelled the roads of Spain and France with the merchant Bin-Rahman. He would be their guide.*

*While Alfonso was away Lady Margaret would be in charge. Le Poing, the Fist, the wily innkeeper from Brittany, would be her* right-hand man and Manuel Diego Bin-Rahman. the merchant, would be her left. The preparations took almost two weeks. The members of the party were mounted and there were twenty pack mules to carry their baggage. Alfonso himself carried the Holy Icon. As on all his travels since leaving the Holy Land, it would stay in his keeping, day and night.

The improving weather of early Spring allowed them to make good time. They followed the Camino de Santiago as pilgrims would have done on their way home through Estella, Tafalla, Sanquesa and Tiermas to the important town of Jaca. There the Camino turned North to cross the Pyrenees but Hassan advised that they stay on the South side of the mountains for a few days longer. The roads were in reasonable repair, the villages were friendly. Alfonso had decreed that they pay their way, buying provisions as they went. They paid their respects to the warlords through whose lands they travelled. In fifteen days they reached the foothills of the Pyrenees.

Beyond Ainsa they entered a narrow gorge, a deep crack in the mountain, with a torrent of a river below towering cliffs on either side. It was a dangerous, eerie place, ideal for an ambush. They stayed in close formation, travelling quickly, with two outriders ahead. The gorge twisted to the North and led out into a wider valley and the town of Benasque.

Hassan advised that they use the Port de Benasque to cross the Pyrenees into France. If they continued on the southern side of the mountains to the Catalan town of Puigcerda they would draw too much attention to their party. The Port de Benasque was used much less frequently. It would mean that they could enter Ariège from the French side of the mountains rather than directly from the Kingdom of Catalonia.

Beyond the town of Benasque, at the foot of the highest part of the range, they saw a small village in the forest on the other side of the river. The ground was rocky, clusters of thorny shrubs and trees surviving in an iron-hard land. A wooden bridge gave access to the village. The houses were small and neat, built of wood, linked together around a square. Cattle and goats grazed in forest clearings.

*The people were small. They seem frightened, running back into their homes when Alfonso's party approached.*

*As the troop drew level with the village an older man emerged from behind a wall, crossed the bridge and bowed to Alfonso. He was tiny, a little stooped figure in a cloak with the mark of a crow's foot.*

*'We beg your help, lord', he said fearfully, 'My son has been killed and my grandson taken hostage by three brigands from across the mountains. We have paid the ransom but now they want more and we have nothing more to give.'*

*He pointed towards the hills. 'They are hiding on that mountain an hour's walk away. They say they will kill my grandson if we do not pay by sunset to-day.*

*Alfonso and his men were familiar with these people of the mountains. They were Cagots, descendants of the Goths, living apart from others in forest villages, not allowed to marry outside their own people, not allowed to bear arms or touch food in a market. They were skilled craftsmen in wood and builders of renown. They were all required to wear the mark of the crow's foot on their clothing.*

*Alfonso called a halt and spoke to James. Orders were issued and four of the soldiers rode off towards the brigand's lair. The rest of the party dismounted and the villagers brought water, bread and cheese. They had little, but what they had they were prepared to share. Alfonso smiled to himself. It mattered nothing to him that there were laws which kept these Cagot people apart. He would take them as he found them.*

*Within two hours a cloud of dust on the mountain trail showed that the soldiers were returning. One of them had a bag with the first ransom which had been paid and he had the Cagot boy behind him on his horse. Each of the other three soldiers had a brigand tied to his saddle on a long rope. As the horses trotted the bandits had to run or be pulled off their feet and dragged.*

*The boy ran to his grandfather and James presented the three brigands to Alfonso who was sitting in the shade of a tree.*

*'You should all die,' Alfonso said without rising, 'But to-day we will be merciful. The ransom you extorted will be refunded to this village with any money you have of your own. You will each lose the hand of your sword arm. If you approach this village again I will have you hunted down and killed wherever you hide.'*

*James took the men outside the village and supervised the punishment. To Alfonso's amazement the Cagot men and women tended the bleeding stumps of the brigands' arms. They had approved of the punishment but now it had been administered they were showing compassion.*

*Alfonso's party camped for the night at the village, paying for their food and wine. They left at dawn and followed a trail up a great valley, climbing towards the ridge to the North. They dismounted at the steepest part and led their horses over a narrow pass across the main range of the Pyrenees. That night they camped on a grassy alp between three beautiful lakes. According to Hassan, they were only a few hours above the town of Luchon.*

*In the morning James wakened Alfonso with a smile.*

*'We have been followed across the mountains, Don Alfonso. The Cagot boy we saved wants to come with us.'*

*The Cagot boy was called Redcared. He was dark haired, olive-skinned and a head shorter than a Spanish boy of his age. Although he was small he had the build of a tumbler. He could climb trees and cliffs like a spider. He was intelligent, willing, unfailingly cheerful. Over the next few days it became obvious that his shyness was simply the wariness of the serf in the presence of his masters. In a short time the soldiers began to treat him as one of their own, as their talisman.*

*Redcared told Alfonso that his grandfather had given him permission to leave. He made Alfonso laugh, asking if he could be his servant. What need was there for a servant on the march? But Redcared changed Alfonso's mind. Within days he became his master's indispensable retainer, his young squire.*

*The town of Bagnères de Luchon was a marvel to them all. It was the first habitation of any size they had passed through on their journey but their arrival caused little stir. The local people were used to travellers. Merchants, noblemen and their followers came here for the thermal baths built by the Roman Emperor Tiberius a thousand years before.*

*Hassan led the party North to the great cathedral of Saint-Bertrand-des-Comminges. Before they entered to make their devotions Alfonso took Redcared to one side and cut the crow's foot device from the boy's cloak with a sharp knife.*

*'When you travel with me,' he said 'You are one of us. No crow's foot will stop you going where we go.'*

*Inside the magnificent monastery Redcared was nervous. He had never entered a religious building. It was forbidden. The church in Benasque, near his home village, had a small, low window placed to let the Cagots see inside during Mass but they were not allowed to enter at any time.*

*Travelling East it took two days to reach Foix. They kept away from the great castle on the hill and camped at the southern edge of the town for two nights. It allowed Hassan to make contact with Arnaud de Foix, a merchant with whom he and Manuel Diego had done business many times. Arnaud specialised in the carriage of goods to or from Catalonia on the other side of the Pyrenees. The merchant was mercenary, according to Hassan but honest.*

*Arnaud de Foix confirmed Pierre's fears. The Inquisition was again active, spreading their intelligence net-work and interrogations further afield. The merchant knew the village in the mountains to which Pierre and his father had taken his mother and family. They were in danger. An Inquisitor had been appointed and had already started his work. But it was to their advantage that he was an exceedingly methodical man. It would take time to smoke out the heretics. Answers would be checked and rechecked with the results of other interrogations. Nothing would be done quickly.*

*Arnaud advised that Alfonso's party should have a plausible reason for being here in Ariège. There were professional spies in the pay of the Church. There were church employees and laymen ready to inform on others in the hope that they would be granted earthly recompense or heavenly reward.*

*Arnaud suggested that they should let it be known that Alfonso wished to buy expensive goods, noble metals, precious stones, amber, coral, pearls, silks, furs, incense, pepper and spices. This would explain why they were travelling with a strong company of men-at-arms. Arnaud, always on the alert for a business opportunity, suggested that, to add to the realism to the story, perhaps Alfonso would like to buy some of his wares. He just happened to have some items of the highest quality which might be of interest to him.*

*Alfonso had to turn away to hide his smile. On the day they had set out on the journey he had promised himself that he would bring back some wonderful gifts for Margaret. Now he had an opportunity. Hassan helped him choose silks and furs and he selected enough precious stones to make a necklace for Margaret and a smaller one for Maria when she was old enough to wear it.*

*He also bought two daggers, each with a sheath. One was for his son, Robert, when he was old enough to wear and wield it. The other was a gift for the boy, Redcared. Cagots might not be allowed to carry weapons but Alfonso had decreed that, within his band, every man should be armed. His instincts told him that, when the boy had learned to use the weapon, no one in the party would be faster with the blade or quicker to his lord's defence than Redcared the Cagot.*

*Before they left they restocked with provisions and Arnaud de Foix was, of course, happy to supply their needs.*

*Pierre led them up the valley towards the mountains and the village of Castells where his family were living. He knew the route well. Cathar shepherds traditionally used it when they were taking their flocks to Winter on the southern side of the Pyrenees.*

*Alfonso's party camped away from the road, behind a low ridge, an hour's walk from Castells. When it was almost dark Pierre and Hassan set off on foot towards the village and returned before dawn.*

---

Raoul paused in his translation. He had been speaking for half an hour with only the briefest of pauses for a sip of water or wine. For the present it was enough. The conversation buzzed like a swarm of demented bees. They all had opinions, questions to which they knew there were no ready answers.

Would this new Manuscript tell them what had happened to the Holy Icon? Did Alfonso manage to rescue the Cathar family? Was the Cagot, whose skeleton they had found in the cave beneath the slab, the boy, Redcared? Was the dagger which Alfonso had bought for Redcared, the same blade as had been hidden in the remnants of the clothing on the corpse?

They talked for another hour before anyone thought of going to bed and when they did so, Raoul fell asleep as soon as he lay down. The others stayed awake, their minds racing until the darkest hour before dawn.

The camp was struck and cleared and they had a breakfast stop on the way down the Esera Valley. As arranged, the horses were returned to their owner when they reached their vehicles parked near Baños de Benasque. It was a long drive back to Mont L'ours-les-Cascades but the spirits were high. When they crossed the frontier into France Ramón telephoned home to confirm that they were on their way.

Doña Marie and Madam Mons had been planning the welcome home meal since the day the expedition had left Mont L'ours. The party arrived in the late afternoon and it was decided that they would not have dinner until nine o'clock. Don Carlos and Monsieur Raymond were invited to stay the night. Jules left immediately for the Bear Sanctuary to check that all was well. In the early evening Ramón and Anamar sat with his mother and the children under the big tree behind the house and told them of their adventures.

When they assembled for dinner the first course was an array of tapas, which caused even Ramón to smile with pleasure. When his mother entertained, no trouble was too much. She took great pride in presenting a feast of titbits, Spanish, French, Italian and Oriental, from snails in garlic butter to stuffed quails' eggs, morsels of smoked fish, cured ham, sun-dried sweet red peppers, tiny wedges of pizza, mushroom vol-au-vents, Chinese spring rolls.

For the main course there were two large chickens roasted in the famed style of Poulet de Bresse with separate green and tomato salads in the Spanish style. For dessert Madam Mons had surpassed herself. She presented a huge, oval silver platter displaying her art as a pâtissière  There was a circular Tarte aux Basque and an array of beautifully glazed, individual French fruit tarts.

The food on the expedition had been excellent but hunger, sharpened by the days of work on the mountain, ensured that this feast to honour the intrepid adventurers was properly appreciated.

Before Carlos and Raymond left next morning, the next meeting of the Cult was arranged to take place in one month's time at the hotel in Aulus-les-Bains. There would be a session in the afternoon which would allow all the members to hear the story of the expedition's discoveries. In the evening, after dinner, there would be a formal meeting of the Cult to agree plans for the future.

## THE FLIGHT OF THE CATHARS

If Jules was pleased to find that all was well at the Sanctuary, he said nothing. Maurice Cabanes, who had been looking after the bears during his absence, expected no praise, but was accorded a nod from the montreur d'ours which would have to do in lieu. Maurice had recorded twenty-two visitors to the sanctuary during his tenure and that had brought the total since opening day to over two hundred and fifty.

He also reported that there had been an approach on behalf of the University of Toulouse. A professor from the Zoological Department had spent a day at the Sanctuary and was seeking permission for his first-year students to make a study of the bears.

Jules was suspicious. He had lived with bears all his life and doubted that this study by scientists would be of any benefit to the bears or the Sanctuary. Ramón explained that the students would be observing from outside the perimeter fence, making notes on the behaviour of the animals but not interfering with the pattern of their lives. Jules was not convinced.

Since their return Ramón had been thinking of the Dancing Bear Show which Jules had used to entertain them at their camp. Then, he had felt that this might have amused the visitors, particularly the children. It would also have shown them, in dramatic form, the traditional role of the montreur d'ours. Now, he had second thoughts. The main purpose of the Sanctuary was conservation of the species. Such a show might be a distraction.

When he mentioned his concern, Anamar agreed. She had already discussed her thoughts for a Christmas Show at the school with Jules. The showman and his Dancing Bear Act would be part of a performance which would include stilt walkers, jugglers, musicians, dancers, tumblers. They would make bear costumes and papier maché bears' heads for Jules, who would play the big bear, and the twins, who would play the young bears. Deirdre could be the showman, the 'montreur d'ours', with a tail-coat, a large drooping moustache and a big black beret. At first Anamar had produced a big-brimmed black hat but Madame Mons had been insistent - the hat denoted a gypsy 'montreur d'ours'. The men of Ariège wore the beret!

She would speak to the school-master. Doña Marie and Madame Mons had agreed to help with the costumes and the props. They would let it be known that there would be an entertainment at Christmas, but the Dancing Bear Act would be kept as a surprise for everyone not involved and that would include Ramón.

The meeting of the Cult was easy to organise. When Ramón telephoned to make the booking Monsieur Paul Huguet, the proprietor of the hotel in Aulus-les-Bains, had prepared a menu in anticipation of the booking. His suggestions were approved and the other arrangements fell into place around the banquet.

Raoul worked hard to complete the translation of the Manuscript. Ramón had made it clear that it must be ready for the meeting and that Raoul would be invited to read it aloud.

The investigation of the Cult's accounts by Don Carlos Conde and Monsieur Raymond Bodelot showed conclusively that the Treasurer, Monsieur Mark Decuré, had been embezzling the Cult's funds over the past five years. Ramón telephoned the bank and left a message, summoning him to a meeting.

But Monsieur Decuré did not turn up for the interview. When they tried to contact him at home, his telephone had been disconnected. Don Carlos discovered that he had resigned from his post at the bank and retired to French Algeria.

Ramón began the meeting by introducing a new member. He described Jules Laurent as 'the practical man' whose work on the expedition had been crucial to the discovery of the Cathedral. Jules was awed by the proceedings. He had never been present at an occasion like this.

On the expedition the others had treated him as an equal but the Great Revolution had changed little in Ariège. The old order still prevailed. Now, at this formal gathering, these men in their gentlemen's clothes were inviting him to become one of them. He leaned forward with a little bow, shook Ramón's hand and sat down without a word.

Ramón announced that, as the Cult's accounts were not in order, and Monsieur Mark Decuré had fled the country to live in Algeria, he was now appointing a new Treasurer, Monsieur Raymond Bodelot. Copies of the accounts were distributed. They were all agreed. The former Treasurer had been systematically embezzling their funds, making false entries, claiming for expenses not incurred, withdrawing cash without explanation. And now he had left the country, presumably with their money.

Ramón decreed that Monsieur Decuré should be confronted and the funds recovered. He asked for a volunteer to go to Algeria with the new Treasurer at the Cult's expense. Monsieur Paul Huguet was first to raise a hand. The hotelier had lacked enthusiasm for the Cult at the previous meeting, seeing it only as a source of business for his hotel. As a fellow member of the Cult he had known Monsieur Decuré for years and had never liked him, now he was incensed at this blatant breach of trust.

Refreshments were served and Ramón introduced the story of the expedition to the Cult's Cathedral. He explained how Anamar had found the cave and deduced how it could be entered. He invited those who had been with him to tell the tale. Monsieur Raymond described the caverns. Jules related how they had tunnelled through the blocked passageway. Don Carlos recounted their discovery of the Cathedral Cave at the very heart of the underground system. Anamar narrated the story of the Cave of Spinning Lights and its link with the Amber Palace of Jaipur.

Ramón reported the finding of the skeleton of the Cagot, entombed with what had proved to be the second part of the Manuscript. He summarised the beginning of that document which had been read by Raoul at their camp. He invited him to continue the translation from the place where Alfonso's party were camped near Pierre's family village in the Pyrenees.

In a theatrical whisper Raoul began to read.

### ............THE SECOND PART OF THE MANUSCRIPT CONTINUES

*Hassan and Pierre Ranisolles returned from the village to Alfonso's camp while it was still dark. They had made contact with Pierre's family. The Cathars had been accepted in the village by the priest but the Inquisitor had arrived three day before. He was installed in a house beside the priest's and had begun his interrogations already.*

*The villagers had another cross to bear. A poor harvest had created a serious shortage of food. Everyone was suffering. Some were starving. Families were supporting each other but help was needed if they were to survive.*

*The priest was an elderly man who had seen the Inquisitors at work in other places and had not been impressed by their methods. He was sympathetic to the Cathars as people, but not to their cause. He admired the selfless work of the 'Parfaits', the lay-leaders of the Cathar Church and was aware that Pierre's family were Cathar refugees, but he had no intention of informing the Inquisitor that there was an heretic family in their midst.*

*Alfonso knew that it would be difficult to keep secret the presence of his party in the area and he decided to act that night. They moved as soon as it was dark. James detailed two men to secure the Inquisitor's residence from the outside and to ensure that those inside were barricaded in for the night.*

*Alfonso met the priest and told him of his mission. He offered food for the villagers. This elderly man of the cloth smiled grimly to himself when he was told that the Cathars were fleeing the Inquisitor. Food for the starving was more important than assisting the interrogator in his work. He joined Alfonso and Hassan in distributing supplies to all the families. There was grain, salt, dried vegetables, salt-beef and cured pork, dried beans, enough, if carefully eked out, to last the village for months. Alfonso knew he could readily restock his supplies when they reached Puigcerda on the other side of the mountains.*

*Pierre assembled the family party, his mother, two older sisters and four younger brothers, the youngest eight and the eldest thirteen. But there was an immediate difficulty and Pierre had to seek Alfonso's help. His mother, Madame Ranisolles, was refusing to flee to Navarre. It was too far away, she said. It was a foreign country beyond the Kingdom of Aragon. She could hardly make out what the men from Navarre were saying. She knew about Catalonia. Her brother had fled there the previous year.*

*When she had heard that her husband had been killed by brigands on the pilgrimage to Santiago, Blanche Ranisolles had assumed the leadership of the family. Of necessity, she had become a farmer and the whole family helped to tend the small-holding she had been able to rent. She was a small, matriarchal figure with sturdy legs and arms as strong as a man. Her weakness was her feet. She hated walking and, although she disliked riding, it was a relief to learn that she would be making this journey on horse-back.*

*This village in the mountains suited her. The people were friendly. The Winters might be hard but the Summers were never as hot as the valley below. But Pierre was right. Now that the the Inquisitor had come, it was time to move again. Her brother had taken his family to a village called Balaceite to the South of Catalonia and near the town of Morella in El Maestrazgo. Her brother would welcome her and her family. He and she had always been close when they were children. He would help her find a place to live where she could farm in peace.*

*Alfonso laughed when she announced her plan to go to Balaceite.*

*'How many days to Morella?' he asked Hassan.*

*'Fifteen, if the mountain roads are in good repair,' was the cheerful answer but they both knew that, given this party, it was only a guess.*

*They left before dawn. Alfonso had brought enough mounts, Madame Ranisolles on a quiet mare and her daughters and sons on ponies. There were four pack mules to carry their possessions. They had no fear of pursuit. Before the news reached the nearest town, Font-Romeu, and a company of soldiers arranged to pursue them, they would be across the mountains and into Catalonia, outside the jurisdiction of the French Comte de Foix.*

*When they reached the crest of the Pyrenees, they turned off the main route at the village of Carol. They reached the town of Puigcerda, built on a hill for protection, and the gate keeper allowed them to enter as soon as he saw that Arnaud de Foix was in the party.*

*'One of my men,' Arnaud said quietly as they passed through the walls into the heart of the town. 'He is my eyes and ears in Puigcerda.'*

*They dismounted in a plaça below the town's massive bell tower, built to dominate the town and warn the people of impending danger. The market had just opened. The stores had to be replenished and Arnaud the merchant amazed even Hassan by the cheap prices he could negotiate for best quality produce. It would take time to buy and assemble the food and Alfonso wandered around the market. He was a man of the country but, on his travels, he loved the urgency and bustle of towns.*

*The quality of his breeches, jerkin and cloak marked him as a man of wealth. His fine sword left no doubt that he was a warrior. But it was his stature and bearing which ensured that Alfonso was treated as a nobleman. He was comfortable here, strolling around stalls laden with grain, vegetables, salt. He examined the sythes, mattocks, spades, tables and chairs all made by the men who were selling them.*

*He sat down on a log seat outside the inn to order wine and a roasted chicken. It was such a pleasure after travelling so far to watch the life of Puigcerda swirling around him. The stalls were busy. There was the smell of cooking food, the fresh aroma of fruit, the scent of cut wood, the acrid reek of animal dung.*

*Everyone seemed to be in a hurry. There were noisy arguments, sometimes spilling over into a brawl. Some farmers arrived late to find that there was nowhere to hawk their produce except on the thoroughfare. There, the people tramped over the wares and jostled sellers out of their way. There were beggars, jugglers, contortionists. But Alfonso was the only one who was watching. Everyone else was involved.*

*This was what he missed most when he was at home. He sat back and promised himself that he would spend more time in Codés del Camino when he returned. Codés was only a village but it was on the Road to Santiago. On some days over a hundred pilgrims would pass through on their way to the City of St James. He would build a new inn there for pilgrims. Le Poing would be set the task of designing and building it.*

*The present inn could be used for ill or injured pilgrims who needed to stay longer. Margaret would welcome the chance to talk to them. He and she would have their own quarters at the new inn. It would allow them to entertain persons of rank who were passing through. Le Poing would be able to inform them of the imminent arrival of such personages.*

*In his days as a warrior monk Alfonso had been based at the great Templar castle at Ponferrada. Times had been quiet and there had been little contact with pilgrims. From his own experience, Pierre had explained to Alfonso that the Camino de Santiago was famous for two reasons. The first was obvious. It was the recommended road to the tomb of Saint James.*

*But the second reason was of equal importance. The Camino allowed news to travel quickly in both directions. Details of wars and alliances, tittle-tattle about royalty and eminent churchmen, were passed from mouth to ear. Pierre had explained how stories of miracles, architecture, building skills, songs, philosophical ideas, religious beliefs, even heresies sped along the Camino from village to village, from pilgrim to pilgrim. Tradition had it that this was the old Roman Road to Northern Iberia. Now it was one of the most important roads in Spain. Margaret would be delighted. The Camino would be their window on the world.*

*Walking back to join his party Alfonso felt elated. He was looking forward to the journey south through Catalonia. The merchant's work was done, the stores delivered and paid for. Arnaud intended to stay in Puigcerda for a few days. He would join a mule train carrying salt back over the mountains to Foix without drawing attention to himself.*

*In the afternoon Alfonso's party climbed the narrow streets of the village of Alp, past the open door of the church, Sant Pere d'Alp and followed the ancient track which would take them across the mountains of the Sierra de Cadi.*

*The path was narrow and James kept the horses and mules in single file. A narrow gorge led upstream through the bushes and across the water by a ford. The steep ascent on the other side brought them out on a spur and the high pastures. A shepherd hurried his herd of goats across a rocky flank of the hills and well away from their track.*

*It was fortunate that Hassan knew the way. He had been here twice before and was aware that the path turned and twisted, doubling back, still climbing but giving the impression that they were heading any way but directly across the mountain range above them. Of the three trade routes between Puigcerda and Barcelona, this was the hardest and thus the least travelled, and that made it the safest road for the fleeing Cathars.*

*Pierre knew that his mother and the family were finding the mounted travelling very difficult. The party dismounted on the steeper stretches, staying together but no longer a disciplined corps of men-at-arms making good time. Alfonso saw Pierre's concern and told him that there was no need to worry. After a few days their little caravan would move as if they had all been born to the life of the traveller.*

*Aware that Blanche Ranisolles was glancing at him anxiously, Alfonso called a halt in the early evening below the Coll de Pal. As they camped, the family made the soldiers laugh by opening all their baggage to find the few items they needed for that night.*

*Hassan and Redcared helped Pierre make a shelter while his brothers gathered wood for a cooking fire. Pierre was exhausted. He felt himself responsible for the family but it had been a long day for all of them. They were not trained to fend for themselves on a journey. He asked Alfonso if Hassan and Redcared could help him with his mother and the others, assisting them on the difficult parts, helping them on and off the horses, showing them how to manage their baggage.*

*They rose at dawn but even with help the family found it hard to cook, pack and load the mules. The morning was half gone before they could make a start. But the young boys were learning quickly from Redcared. Before the day was over, he had become their leader within the group.*

*It was a dark, damp day, slippery underfoot and cold even when they were on the move. The mountain range they must cross presented a wall of black cliffs reaching up to grey streamers of mist between the peaks. It looked impassable. But Hassan knew that there was a pass and that the rough track climbed relentlessly towards it.*

*There was no sign of other travellers, nor was there any habitation, not even a shepherd's shelter. Perhaps the man who had seen them on the previous day had warned others to let them pass. Bursts of rain swept in from the North-West in great gusts. They rose above the trees and tackled the last steep stretch to the pass.*

*The mist cleared and they saw the gap. This was as high as they had to climb. At the crest they were amongst the formidable mountains of Cadi, not as high as the snow-capped Pyrenees but rugged and rocky. From below, the range had looked impenetrable but the Coll de Pal was the way through. As they crossed , the clouds dispersed. They left late Winter on the North side for early Summer on the South. Now, there was shelter from squalls of rain riding on the wind. It was a different day, a different country.*

*The sunshine dried their clothes and raised their spirits. Now she had crossed the mountains, Blanche Ranisolles was no longer anxious that they might be caught and returned to France to face the Inquisition. She smiled and jested with the soldiers, claiming that the party was travelling far too slowly for an accomplished horsewoman like herself. Her happy mood spread throughout the caravan.*

*Rather than arrive in the town of Baga in the evening Alfonso called a halt during the afternoon.*

*In the morning he sent Hassan ahead to say that they were a trading party travelling South towards Barcelona. When he returned, Alfonso and James rode at the head of the party, followed by the men-at-arms and the pack mules, with Pierre's family at the back like camp followers.*

*Baga was a small, walled town at the head of a fertile valley and below the main ridge of the Sierra de Cadi. The walls were massive. At the upper end a circular watch tower with a strange single-pitched roof looked up to the mountain and across the valley.*

*The party passed through the huge doors in the town walls and Alfonso was welcomed by the agent of the Duc de Baga. Hassan met a local merchant who had sold him goods last time he had been here. The Duc himself was away in Barcelona but it was his policy to encourage trade and his agent, who proved to be the brother of the merchant known to Hassan, was determined to make the most of this opportunity.*

*The town was built on a rocky ridge, tightly packed into the space within the walls. Steep steps in narrow alleyways led from one plaça to another. The houses were fortified, built of stone with wooden frames. Some were four or five storeys high with protruding wooden balconies. Above the doors of the most impressive houses were stone plaques with coats of arms. The main plaça was so deeply arcaded that Alfonso's men from Navarre wondered at the strength of the pillars which held up the protruding storey. The people came out to see the new arrivals but stood back to give them room to dismount.*

*The local merchant assured Hassan that this was a time of peace and arranged that they could camp outside the walls, beside the river and the mill.*

*Hassan bought provisions from the merchant and Alfonso was invited to eat with him and his brother, the Duc's agent. James and Hassan accompanied Alfonso and they were treated to a fine meal of boiled fowl and roasted cabrito, the meat of the young goat. The wine was poor but as he did his duty and sipped at his goblet, Alfonso smiled at Hassan, who drank no wine, and James, for whom wine was more essential than food.*

*Alfonso admired the way in which the Duc's agent and his brother combined business and pleasure. It was late when the merchant went upstairs and returned with a bag of precious stones. Some had been found in the mountains above but others had been acquired by trade. This was his most valuable merchandise, he said, and he was willing to buy, sell or trade.*

*It was Hassan's turn and Alfonso let his own merchant do the dealing, with no more than a nod or a shrug or a purse of the lips to indicate his wishes. Hassan gave three cured wolf skins and a sum in gold for a leather bag of the precious stones. The other stones would make beautiful gifts but Alfonso was enthralled by the amber and pearls. He could see these set in necklaces and worn by Margaret. She loved jewellery. The stones would be lustrous on her skin. But he said nothing. If he showed his desire to buy, the price would rise. Hassan was dealing for the stones as commercial commodities, not beautiful merchandise.*

*When it came time to part both sides seemed pleased by the bargaining and the local men walked with Alfonso and his friends down to their camp by the river.*

*In the morning Hassan guided the party out of the main valley and through the villages of Saldes and Gósol down to the town of Berga, at the foot of the mountains. It was much longer and involved more climbing than the direct route but the track was good and the villagers friendly. They avoided the castle of Berga on the previous advice of the merchants in Baga and for four days crossed wooded mountains, flat plains and rolling hills. The villages were on high ground and fortified, the castles clamped to the summits of rocky outcrops.*

*The climbs were steep but the view from the ridges allowed them to see where there might be danger ahead. However, Alfonso was aware that it also enabled the local people to see them from a long way off and he decided to stay away from settlements.*

*Near the fortified town of Montblanc they were short of water but the gates in the massive walls were closed by the guards as they approached. Half a day's ride later they reached the most famous monastery in Catalunya, Santa Maria de Poblet, set behind high, battlemented walls in a huge forest. The monastery was known to be wealthy from the rents of farms and having been richly endowed. The Abbot had control of one of the greatest fortunes in Spain. There were, however, tales of strange practices within the walls.*

*Alfonso's party had finished their last drops of the water and it was imperative to replenish their supplies. When they approached the monastery's towered gates they were surprised to be welcomed and offered a camping ground within the walls.*

*They were able to buy supplies of food and water for the party and Alfonso and James were invited to eat with the Abbot. Within the inner walls they admired the cool courtyards and cloisters, the scriptorium, the library, the refectory and the extensive wine cellars. But it was the wonders of the Cistercian architecture of the Abbot's church which held them enthralled. There were soaring arches and columns, intricate carving in stone. There were tombs of kings, queens and nobles on the sides of arches as if to save space on the floor. Five chapels radiated from the central nave and aisles with each one as perfect as the others. Religion must be strong in such a place as this, Alfonso mused to himself. But what of the scandalous tales of debauchery?*

*At the Abbot's table the food was good and there was wine in abundance but the prelate's talk was of royal schemes and plots and, much as Alfonso encouraged the Abbot when the wine was flowing, there was no mention of the bacchanalian carousing or the lewd stories which were the talk of Christendom.*

*On the next day, on a ridge amongst the mountains of the Sierra de Montsant, Alfonso rode around the curve of the red-stone wall of a church, passed through the open gates of a fortified village and found himself in the main square of Parades. News of the approach of a strong party had preceded their arrival and the villagers came out to greet them and offer the good water from their well in the middle of the square.*

Ramón felt that Raoul had been reading for long enough. He called a halt, thanked Raoul and suggested that he continue next morning after breakfast for any of the members who wished to stay to hear it. Liqueurs were served and  Ramón sat back listening to the buzz of conversation, knowing they would all stay for the reading next morning.

He was right. At nine o'clock they were all in their seats. Raoul had his audience. He was the actor again, refreshed, beaming at his patrons. He reminded them that he had stopped the reading at the arrival of Alfonso's party in the village of Parades. He began again.

...........THE SECOND PART OF THE MANUSCRIPT CONTINUES

*Alfonso announced that they would spend two nights in Parades and that there would be a feast on the second evening to celebrate their safe passage thus far. A pig was bought and the roasting began in the afternoon. Hassan smiled to himself, wondering if it had been forgotten that he could eat no pork. He looked beyond the roasting pig and caught the eye of Blanche. She pointed to the fowl she was cooking at a smaller fire and smiled.*

*The villagers were invited to join them. There was a barrel of wine, music and dancing. A board table was erected and Alfonso sat at its head with Pierre on his right hand and Blanche on his left.*

*Alfonso was pleased to see that James was attracted to one of the local women. Since he had arrived in Scotland, he and James had been soldiers together and they were still close friends. Now, he had a wife and children but James had neither. His comrade was a serious man, sometimes too serious, too diligent. He liked the company of women in the evening but when morning came they found him gone. But he had been a man on his own for long enough.*

*Next morning they broke camp late and when they left the village the woman came too, sitting behind James on his horse. Beatrice was no longer in the first flush of youth. She was the same solid build as Blanche Ranisolles but taller. Her black eyes shone with pleasure. Her black hair gleamed. Her features had shown her strength of will. Now they showed her joy in a radiant smile. Her every gesture proclaimed that this was the happiest day of her life.*

*By Hassan's reckoning it would take five or more days to Balaceite, the village near Morella which was their destination. Alfonso decided that it was time to divide his party in order to allow Pierre to make contact with his relatives without undue ado. Alfonso would go with the family accompanied only by Hassan and Redcared. A messenger was sent ahead to tell Pierre's uncle that Blanche and her family were on their way. James would ride with the rest of the soldiers at least one day's travel behind.*

*Before they parted, Alfonso changed his nobleman's clothes and dressed as a merchant. He exchanged his half-Arab steed for the mount of one of the soldiers. Each day the going became more difficult. Blanche Ranisolles and her children were weary of travelling.*

*They climbed for half a day, crossing ridge behind ridge, reaching into the heart of the mountains of Montsant. Days later they passed through a series of three deep gorges before they came to the town of Valderrobres. The road was rough, at times following the river at its very edge. As they emerged from the third chasm there were mountain peaks of sheer rock on the sky-line like church towers or impregnable castle keeps, but on a huge scale. Alfonso had never seen such mountains, like the teeth of a giant animal. Beyond the gorges the land was dry but they had replenished their stock of water and passed by Valderrobres.*

*Hassan asked the way to Balaceite, the village to which they were headed and they left the road for a track. It led into a narrow gorge in deep shade. At the upper end they emerged into the bright glare of the mid-day sun and into an oven-like heat. The rock was red or white. On the track the red was crushed to red dirt - the white ground to a powder so fine it startled upwards every time a foot or a hoof moved. It formed a moving white cloud around the party. On what should have been the last day, the going had never been harder.*

*The road had been washed away in places by the Winter rain and not yet repaired. The river beds were dry. There was neither shade nor water. The cloud of white dust stung the eyes. For those at the front the way ahead shimmered in the heat. The mules were fractious, the horses in a lather of sweat. By late afternoon the family members were exhausted. It was clear that they would not reach the village before dark.*

*A small ravine gave partial shade from the baking heat of the late afternoon and Alfonso decided to camp for the night. A foraging party found a trickle of water further up the ravine and a few sticks of dead wood to light a fire. That night the sky was clear and deepest blue, the air cold. They lay out under the stars and talked quietly. A tiny comet laid a long, silver trail across the heavens and vanished below the horizon. A breeze gusted across the silent land. Pierre and his family were on one side of the depression and Alfonso, Hassan and Redcared were amongst rocks some distance away. The encampment fell asleep.*

*At first light Alfonso was startled awake with a hand gripping his shoulder. He reached for his sword. It was gone. Hassan was kneeling beside him, asking him if all was well. He sat up and found his jerkin slit. A dead man lay beside him with a dagger through his throat and in his hand Alfonso's own sword.*

*He shivered.*

*Hassan hurried across to the Ranisolles family to see if all was well and found them undisturbed. They had heard nothing. The sound of almost silent sobbing caused Alfonso to look around. Redcared was sitting behind him, his hands hiding his tears. It was his dagger which transfixed the dead man's neck.*

*Redcared knelt beside Alfonso like a penitent and related what had happened. He had been wakened by the low sounds of two men searching through Alfonso's belongings. They had opened the satchel but left it to one side when they saw that it contained only a picture painted on wood.*

*Redcared had heard one whisper,*

*'This is the leader. He will carry the gold. His purse is underneath his head. If we try to move him he will waken. We must kill him first.' And silently he had drawn Alfonso's sword from its scabbard.*

*Redcared had crawled towards the robber from behind and, as he lifted the sword to make his lunge at Alfonso, Redcared had stabbed him through the throat with his dagger. The sword had slit Alfonso's jerkin. Hassan had wakened and jumped to his feet but the dead man's companion had ridden off.*

*Alfonso moved over to Redcared's side and put an arm around his shoulders. The Cagot boy struggled for breath, his sobs came in louder bursts and then stopped. He dried his tears and stood up.*

*Later, as the others prepared to leave, Alfonso retrieved the dagger from the dead man's neck. He took Redcared to the trickle of water higher up the ravine. They washed the dagger clean of every trace of blood. The boy dried it with the tail of his shirt and slipped it back into its sheath.*

*They were both thinking of the hours they had spent training with their daggers. To Redcared it had been a game, throwing at a target on a tree, practising to cut and thrust, to feint, laughing when the blade came close enough to cut the clothing.*

*As a young soldier Alfonso had recognised the dagger as the ultimate close-encounter weapon. It was different from an arrow or a spear, even a sword. With other weapons there was space between the killer and the would-be killed. The dagger was different. It provided death at its most intimate, as close as an embrace. No man could ever be the same again after such an act. Redcared was no longer a boy. His dagger was no longer a toy.*

*Alfonso took him by the shoulders and looked him in the eye.*

*'I owe my life to you,' he said quietly, 'From this day onwards you will be my guardian angel, Redcared, El Angel.'*

## THE CATHAR PILGRIMAGE

*The body of the thief might have been left for the wolves but Redcared begged for a burial. Pierre and his brothers helped him dig a shallow grave some distance away from the camp and they piled the biggest rocks they could find on top of the earth. Blanche Ranisolles stood beside the grave and said a prayer for the soul of the robber. Now they were ready to go.*

*As they moved off towards the village, Alfonso sent Hassan back to find James. The second thief must be caught and punished.*

*Balaceite was further than they had reckoned. Perched at the head of a remote valley, it could be reached only by a long stretch of poor road which terminated at the village. All around there were white cliffs and red rocky knolls. Red and white boulders fought for supremacy on the hillsides. It was a wild landscape with pinnacles of rock like ancient citadels. They had come to work a stone-hard land.*

*But Alfonso and Pierre agreed that the location was suitable. It was in the very heart of inhospitable terrain, well away from towns and trade routes and at the end of a track which served it only. The town of Morella was a further day's journey to the South. To farm here would be a struggle for survival but its location made Balaceite a perfect place for the Cathars.*

*It was mid-morning when the party reached the village. A tall, thin, slightly-stooped man dressed in black and wearing a black beret was there to meet them. Jean de Pires was pleased beyond words to be welcoming his sister and her family to his adopted village. He wept with tears of joy. The elders were there too, to greet the new family. Jean de Pires was highly regarded, not least by the priest. Numbers were important to survival in this land. Work in common, such as building, maintaining irrigation ditches, shepherding, harvesting, olive and fruit picking, needed the combined effort of all the community.*

*Blanche would have no difficulty in renting a small-holding. There was a vacant house needing repairs. Work to make it habitable had already been started by Jean as soon as he had heard of his sister's impending arrival. But the villagers were shocked to hear of the attack on Alfonso, so close to their own homes. The brigands had been terrorising the district and, when James arrived to mount the search for them, two of the local men volunteered to act as guides.*

*Before they left the soldiers were ordered to dismount and given time to rest and eat. One of the horses detached itself from the herd and wandered across to Alfonso. It stood beside him and nuzzled his hand. Alfonso's half-Arab mare, Estrella, the star, had decided that she had been parted from her master for long enough and was now asking him to have her back. The soldier who had been looking after her smiled, fetched his own horse from the tethering post and transferred the saddles and bridles.*

*James and his party arrived back in the village before dark. The brigand had been caught and executed. In their mountain lair the two thieves had accumulated a horde of stolen money and goods, silver coins, church goblets, harness, saddles and large amounts of food. There were leather bottles of wine and clothing. Nearby two horses were tethered. After a word with Alfonso, James presented the horses, harness and saddles to Blanche Ranisolles and delivered the rest of the brigand's booty to the priest for disembursement within the village.*

*Alfonso decided to stay for a week to rest the horses and mules and stood the men down. He and his party made camp outside the village.*

*After a few days he was satisfied that this was a reasonable place for Pierre's family to settle. Jean de Pires had come here three years before and was now one of the leaders of the community. He had been hounded from his home in Ariège by the Inquisition for his Cathar beliefs but he had never lost his faith in God. He believed that all men had the right to follow their own religions be they Christian, Jew or Moslem. The arrival of his sister and her family was a gift from God. He had no sons of his own and hers would be the future of the village. He felt deeply indebted to Alfonso and his men for ensuring their safe passage to Balaceite.*

*On the third day Jean talked to Blanche and together they went to see the priest. Father Hernandez was amazed and delighted to hear what they had to say. They were proposing a pilgrimage, with his help and guidance, to give thanks to God for the safe journey of the Ranisolles family to Balaceite. It would begin at dawn in one week's time. They would assemble at the ravine where they had spent the last night of their journey and where Alfonso's life had been spared. There would be prayers of dedication and pilgrim vows. Father Hernandez would lead the pilgrimage. All the villagers would be invited to join the walk. Their route would take them back to Balaceite for Mass in the church.*

*Father Hernandez was proud to be involved in the organisation of the pilgrimage. This was the most important event to take place in Balaceite since he had been ordained here as a young priest. These people had consulted him before announcing news of the pilgrimage. They had travelled a long way. They had come to Balaceite as strangers. He was well pleased with these new arrivals.*

*The priest was not a worldly man. This was his place and he had rarely been away from it. His education had been to grow up here, away from cities and towns. The old priest who had ruled this village with a rod of iron had chosen him to be his successor shortly before his death. Father Hernandez's way was not the way of his predecessor but his life was dedicated to the Lord's work.*

*He had been sheltered from new ideas. He regarded innovation with suspicion. Such notions always seemed to confuse men, making them dissatisfied with their God-given lot. He treated directions from on high as suggestions, not orders. It was not that he disregarded his Bishop's instructions. He simply felt that they were not necessarily meant to be implemented in his village.*

*He took people as he found them and these Cathars were far more pious than his own flock. Jean de Pires had been here for years and he was a good man, the most devout man in the village. He knew that the Cathars were being persecuted as heretics in France, but then the priests there ministered under rules which could be very different from those which applied to his fellow clergy in El Maestrazgo. They were more strictly controlled by their bishops. They were expected to be celibate. South of the Pyrenees these conditions did not always apply.*

*In a rare moment of vanity Father Hernandez decided to invite the priests of two neighbouring villages and Father Sanchez, a senior cleric in Morella. He allowed himself a little smile. These fellow pastors regarded him as their poor relation within the Church. But this pilgrimage was not just another Feast Day. It was a new event which had come from a real journey. It could be celebrated annually, growing year by year, bringing pilgrims from afar like the great pilgrimages to Jerusalem, Rome and Santiago. It could become one of the most important religious festivals in El Maestrazgo.*

*Before the chosen day the pilgrims were instructed by Father Hernandez. They must go fasting from mid-night on the day before the pilgrimage. They must present themselves at the starting place, at dawn on that day, to be blessed as pilgrims. They must go on foot, barefoot if they wished, and attend Mass in the church on arrival at their village.*

*On the evening before, the pilgrims began to assemble on the rising ground above the ravine. They sat by families in a large ring, talking quietly, trying to rest. Blanche Ranisolles asked her children to gather rocks and build a cairn on a little mound to mark the site of their last camp on the way to Balaceite. Others began to help and soon the pile of stones was the height of a man. In the last hour before dawn Alfonso arrived with James, Hassan, Redcared and the soldiers. James's woman, Beatrice, followed her man, two paces behind him. This was not an affirmation of woman's place. It was much more important that she claim her position with her man, as of right. The four priests arrived last, just before the red rim of the sun appeared above the horizon.*

*Father Sanchez, the cleric from Morella, was also accompanied. Before he had been appointed to Morella, he had ministered in a village in the great Pallaresa fastness of the Pyrenees. In this remote mountain valley it was accepted that a priest might have a house-keeper who was also his concubine. There was a civil ceremony which allowed the priest and his woman to be married. The rite was not recognised by the Church but vows were exchanged, dowries presented, and if there were children, they could be named as heirs to their parents' estates.*

*In Morella no such libertarian system prevailed. Father Sanchez had to be discreet. The parishioners were tolerant of his situation but it created a circumstance, within which an authoritarian priest of his calibre had to tread softly in matters of contention. No doubt his bishop was aware of the issue, but as long as the priest's 'wife' was away when His Grace made a visit, no action was taken.*

*Father Sanchez was attended by his 'wife' who had insisted that she be allowed to be a pilgrim. When she arrived with her 'husband', the priest, her point was made and she slipped quietly amongst the crowd and left him to his duties.*

*The four priests stood in a line on the mound beside the cairn of stones and the pilgrims knelt for the blessing. Father Sanchez spoke first, demanding humility and obedience. Father Hernandez was content to be last, asking for contemplation and prayers. As the blessing ended Alfonso felt he could hear his wife's voice whispering in his ear.*

*'Show them the Holy Icon,' Margaret was saying, 'Raise it as a banner. These people need a sign that God is with them on their pilgrimage.'*

*She was right. It was time for the Icon to emerge from its satchel. Alfonso undid the clasp, unwrapped the picture and attached it to one end of a long walking pole like a pennant. He gave the pole to Redcared.*

*'I cannot do it, my Lord.' The Cagot boy's face had lost its colour. 'When my people carry an emblem like this on a procession it must be covered with a cloth.'*

*Alfonso smiled. His voice was low but insistent. Redcared trusted Alfonso above all his Cagot ways. He raised the pole and the sun's low rays flashed on the Holy Icon as if it was on fire. The crowd*

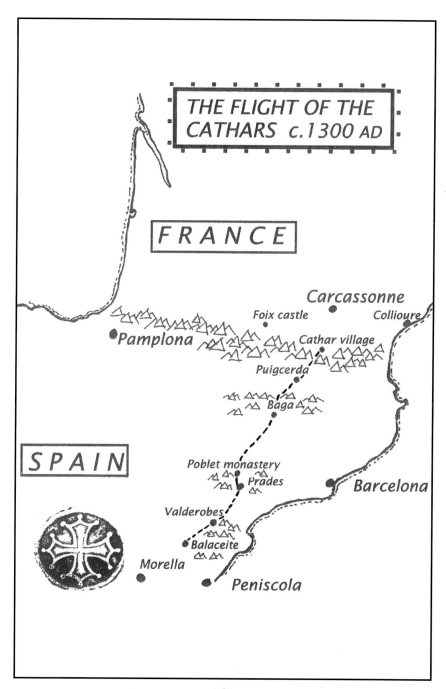

*gasped. There were shouts of amazement. It was the most beautiful picture any of them had ever seen. They sank to their knees, the people first, then the priests. They all prayed until Father Sanchez rose and waved them to their feet.*

*The four clerics formed a line abreast with their backs to the people, ready to lead the pilgrimage. They were followed by Blanche Ranisolles and Jean de Pires and they insisted that Redcared walk between them with his banner. Alfonso and Pierre led the main body of pilgrims with James, Beatrice and the soldiers at the back. Almost unnoticed, Hassan followed a little way behind. He had sat on his own behind a large rock during the blessing, now he wanted to accompany the pilgrimage.*

*Father Sanchez set a slow pace, his brother clerics allowed him to be a stride ahead as befitted his position. His feet were taking him on pilgrimage but his mind was fixed on the Holy Icon. Who was this noble-man from Navarre, Alfonso Barriano, Marqués de Barra? And why was the Icon in his possession?*

*It was the most magnificent religious artifact Father Sanchez had ever seen. Unlike his brother priests he was well travelled. He had ministered in the North of Aragon. He had served Mass in Foix in France and in Malaga, Cadiz and Valencia. He had been to Rome, attended Mass in St Peter's and seen the treasures of the Vatican. This Icon was a thing of beauty. It was a Holy Relic beyond price. It must be one of the great treasures of Christendom. Such religious paintings would only be held by rich and powerful rulers or high church dignitaries.*

*But Father Sanchez was also aware of the mystical power of such a divine relic. There was nothing like it in the length and breadth of El Maestrazgo. If only he could secure it for the glorious new church, Santa Maria La Mayor, being built at the foot of the castle. For centuries Morella had been one of the most important towns in Spain but since Don Blasco de Algón, leading the troops of James the Conqueror, had recaptured the town from the Moors, its power and influence had grown dramatically.*

*James the Conqueror had granted its inhabitants the honourable privilege of allegiance. Expanding trade and the patronage of the*

*Church had ensured prosperity. At the request of the local people, the Franciscans had built the Royal Monastery of San Francisco in the town. The new church, Santa Maria, was already being called the 'Archpriest's Church', even though it was still under construction, such were the formidable difficulties of preparing the chosen site. But it was due to open within the next few years. Father Sanchez could imagine himself presenting the Holy Icon at the dedication of Santa Maria La Mayor. He stiffened his shoulders to prevent a shiver of excitement shaking his whole body and concentrated on the pilgrimage to Balaceite.*

*The procession rumbled onwards towards the village. Young men, prompted by their mothers, offered to carry the Holy Icon to give Redcared a rest but the Cagot boy would give up the relic to no one. If his parents could have seen him now they would have been amazed; a Cagot accepted by these priests, the people and the soldiers; his lord, Don Alfonso requiring him to carry the Icon and insisting that he should not wear the crow's foot mark.*

*They reached the church in Balaceite and filed inside for Mass. The Holy Icon on its pole was placed against a wall at one side so that it was within the view of both clergy and supplicants. Father Hernandez invited Father Sanchez to lead the celebration but, even as he accepted the honour, his brother priest was thinking only of the Holy Icon.*

*There was no work done in the village that day. The children played. The adults stood in little groups talking quietly, discussing the pilgrimage, going into the the church again to see the Icon. Some were euphoric, caught in a mood of joyful devotion, others in a state of high excitement. A few of the men feigned indifference but took great care to be seen to be involved.*

*Father Sanchez wanted to speak to Alfonso about the Icon but found himself unable to do so when he had the opportunity. Instead he talked to him about his journey home. How long would it take to ride back to Navarre? By which road would he go? When did he plan to leave?*

*Alfonso was surprised to find the priest so pleasant to talk to. First impressions had not been good. The cleric had been aloof, on his dignity. Now they had made the pilgrimage together, he was good company. They talked like comrades-at-arms, telling each other of escapades in France and Spain when they were younger. Suddenly Alfonso stopped in mid-sentence. He had begun to talk about his flight from Brittany to Scotland when he became aware that this was not a conversation between two men of the world. The priest was leading him on, trying to discover who he was.*

*The three visiting priests left in the late afternoon but not before Father Sanchez had again paid his respects to the Holy Icon. It was still in the church, still propped against the wall where he had directed Redcared to leave it. He knelt before the holy image and prayed one silent prayer over and over, like saying the Rosary.*

*'Lord, Lord grant me the custody of this hallowed image in Thy Name,. Its place must be in Santa Maria La Mayor where every stone we lay is testament to Thy Glory.'*

*His voice was quieter than a whisper. He crossed himself twice. Although his lips moved there was no sound as he mouthed his innermost thought.*

*'Let it be in my charge, Lord, not tied in a sack, doomed to travel the roads in the custody of an itinerant man-at-arms.'*

*As he rose to his feet he felt himself surprised by a fleeting pang of guilt. He had sinned by coveting control of this sacred relic. But as quickly as this scruple slipped into his mind, he cast it out. He would have this Holy Icon for the glory of God.*

*There was a rustle behind him and he turned. Alfonso was standing in the doorway, the space filled by his frame, no longer a penitent pilgrim, now a soldier once again. Father Sanchez rose and smiled and Alfonso moved aside to allow him to leave the church. The other priests were waiting for him and they rode away from Balaceite, two of them in spiritual ecstasy, the third oblivious to the presence of his 'wife', obsessed by the holy artifact which had transfigured the pilgrimage for them all.*

Ramón rose to his feet and held up his hands to show that the reading had ended.

'Next time we meet you will hear more. But we have imposed on Raoul for long enough this morning. We are in his debt. His translation from such an ancient text has been admirable. This Cult of ours will enrich the lives of all of us.'

## THE CHRISTMAS SHOW

As the days shortened into Autumn, Ramón found himself busier than ever he had been at this time of the year. He was preoccupied with the affairs of the Cult and the expedition, but that was time willingly spent.

The population of the Sanctuary was increasing. A wild life charity in England had heard of the plight of three bears in an Hungarian circus touring France. The bears were old and suffering from poor treatment. The charity bought the animals and, by prior arrangement, had them delivered to Mont L'ours with a substantial donation towards their keep.

An agreement was signed with the University of Toulouse. It allowed the University Department to mount an observation project over a period of two years, in return for help with the Sanctuary's educational programme. Jules was still not convinced that the academic findings would be of any value, but if Ramón approved he was prepared to accept their presence.

'These experts have read it all in books,' he would say to Ramón, 'But they have never lived with bears.'

The new Treasurer of the Cult, Raymond Bodelot, and Paul Huguet, the hotelier, set off to travel to Algeria to find and confront the former Treasurer, Monsieur Decuré. Bodelot had recently been left a small private income, large enough to allow him to retire from his post in local government and this was the low season for business at Huguet's hotel. Both men could afford the time for such a venture.

It was a difficult journey, fraught with danger. Algeria was in the grip of insurrection. Local nationalists were in open revolt. A faction of the French Army, allied to the militant French settlers, 'les pieds-noirs', were fearful that President Charles de Gaulle would abandon Algeria to the Algerians. There were riots and demonstrations in Algeria. There was hysteria in France, followed by massive strikes. The dissident army faction and 'les pieds-noirs' threatened to bring civil war to France itself.

Bodelot and Huguet travelled by train through Spain to Algeciras, near Gibraltar. They crossed the straits to Tangier in Morocco and, using a French army colonel known to Bodelot as a contact, and travelling light, they traced Decuré to a settlement on the outskirts of Oran. His house had been a fine building, in a grove of trees near the sea, constructed around a courtyard for security. But it was now damaged and deserted. The gates were locked and the windows boarded over.

They were too late. The house had been attacked and Decuré killed by insurgents as a reprisal for an assault by 'les pieds-noirs'.

Locals told them that Decuré's son had come to clear up his father's affairs and had taken what was left of his possessions back to France. But no one knew his home address. It was Huguet's idea that they should contact the local leader of 'les pieds-noirs'. Huguet guessed, correctly it transpired, that Decuré had been an active supporter of the settlers. When they reached the faction's offices he hinted that they were the bearers of good news and that, now Decuré senior was deceased, they needed to contact his son and heir. The leader ordered a clerk to find Decuré junior's address and dismissed Huguet and Bodelot with the air of a man who had much weightier burdens to carry.

The clerk had known Decuré as an important official and they left the building with an address and telephone number for Decuré junior in Argelès sur Mer, a village in France between Perpignan and the Spanish frontier.

It took Huguet and Bodelot four days to travel back to France. They decided not to telephone beforehand and arrived at Decuré junior's home in Argelès in the evening after dark. When he opened the door, the young Decuré was hostile, suspicious of these two men who had followed his father all the way to Algeria and had now traced him to Argelès. Bodelot did the talking. He explained their mission and made it clear that they were not seeking to bring disgrace to the family. Their assignment was to recover the missing funds from their Cult's accounts.

Decuré junior brought them inside. The children were in bed. He introduced his wife. Over coffee he described his arrival at his father's house in Oran. The safe had been opened and all the money stolen, only a few meaningless papers remained. He seemed sincere. Huguet and Bodelot glanced at each other. They believed him. The father had been arrogant and impatient but the son was a different man and it was as if he had known his father well enough to have been expecting such a visit.

After an hour they took their leave. Their mission had failed. The Cult's funds could not be recovered. As they shook hands on the door step Decuré junior remembered something which he thought might be important. There had been a parcel in his father's safe. It contained pages from an old document, wrapped in brown paper. The pages were hand-written in Latin, undamaged by the forced opening of the safe.

'They make no sense to me,' the young Decuré said, 'Would you like to have them?'

Neither Huguet nor Bodelot could read the Latin script but it seemed likely that these papers were the property of the Cult. They travelled on to Mont L'ours next morning and presented the brown paper parcel to Ramón with an apology for the failure of their mission. Decuré had removed more than funds from the Cult. At some stage he must have taken these pages from the archive trunk. Ramón was pleased but half an hour later, when Raoul had checked the parcel, he was ecstatic. This was far more important than the stolen money. There was no doubt, these pages were the final part of the Manuscript, the Postscript.

---

The first big white flakes fell before the end of October. By mid-November the peaks were plastered and the snow line was five hundred metres above the village. Ramón was so engaged in his own affairs he failed to notice that his wife, his children, his mother and his house-keeper were all involved in rehearsals for a sketch about Dancing Bears. To explain the dramatic activity around the house Anamar told him half the story. She simply said that they were preparing items for the Christmas concert at the school. Her husband had nodded encouragingly and wished them well.

Anamar had discussed the entertainment with the school principal, Monsieur Jacques Decot and his assistant, Mademoiselle Marie Claire de Pau. The three of them would act as producers, with Doña Marie and Jules Laurent helping to train the children.

Madame Mons would organise the making of the costumes and props. Doña Marie and Anamar would develop the dance routines, Jules would teach the stilt walkers. Mademoiselle Marie Claire was musical, she would train the singers and musicians. Monsieur Decot had been a fine gymnast in his youth. He would coach the tumblers.

When Raoul heard about the show he offered to teach the jugglers. At university, student fashion had insisted that it was important to be an expert at something other than studies. A street performer had taught Raoul the art of keeping four balls in the air at the same time. Anamar and Doña Marie were sceptical but he proceeded to demonstrate his skill with three apples and an orange and was allowed to join the troupe.

Ramón made two five-day visits to his father's hacienda to arrange for the running of the estate. His father's most senior servant, Pedro Conde Parrado, now in his sixties, had been in Don Henriques service since he had been sixteen. They had fought together in the Civil War. Next to his parents, Parrado had been the greatest influence in Ramón's life. They had played together when Ramón had been a small boy. They had worked together at harvest time and picked grapes in the vineyard. Parrado had taught him to ride and to shoot. They had walked the furthest marches of the estate and ridden the mountains above.

Parrado was familiar with every aspect of the estate and he was now entrusted by Ramón as his agent in all matters pertaining to the hacienda. Together they appointed new staff and promoted the most loyal employees. Ramón visited the notary and the bank in Logroño and discovered, that in addition to the lands and vineyard, he had been left a very considerable sum of money. He arranged to visit Parrado at the hacienda for two or three days each month and gave his agent full authority to act on his behalf in his absence.

Doña Marie accepted an invitation from Anamar and Ramón to make her home with them in Mont L'ours. Living on her husband's lands in Navarre had been the happiest time of her life, but now her husband was dead and she was ready to return to her family home in Ariège. Her grandchildren were there and they were now her chief interest. There was fun and laughter in the house. There was always something exciting happening in Mont L'ours, like the Bear Sanctuary and the Christmas show. Ramón and she had always been close but she had been amazed to discover how quickly she and her daughter-in- law had become firm friends.

Ramón paid a substantial sum into a new account for the Cult. He met the Treasurer, Monsieur Bodelot, to set up new banking arrangements. At Bodelot's suggestion, they agreed that a weekly summary of the current state of the account would be sent to Ramón directly from the bank.

While Ramón was away, everyone in the troupe was enjoying the preparations for the Christmas performance. Raoul had two boys and a girl to train as jugglers and it was hard work. He wanted the children to perform individually and then as a group. But four balls proved too difficult for the individual part of the act and he had to settle for three. Getting them to function as a group was even harder. Then he had an idea. He would join the children. The four of them would stand as the corners of a square and juggle the balls from one to another in a clockwise direction. This was much better, he said to himself, he had been born to perform on a stage.

The school principal, Monsieur Decot and Jules Laurent built a stage, about fifty centimetres high, at one end of the hall beside the school. From scrap wood they fashioned a set of steps to give access to the stage from the front. They rigged up curtains improvised from two lorry tarpaulins at the front of the stage. These were suspended from an iron curtain rod and curtain rings which Jules produced one evening and, about the source of which, he encouraged no questions.

Marie Claire was making good progress with the musicians and singers. Monsieur Decot had formed two groups of gymnasts, one of boys and the other of girls. The Dancing Bear sketch was being developed behind closed doors. No one who was not involved in the act would be allowed to see it until the night of the show. But the papier-maché bear-masks were proving difficult to make.

After a few disappointing experiments Doña Marie and Madam Mons developed a technique. They started with two different sized footballs, a large one for Jules's mask and the smaller one for the masks to be worn by the twins. The balls were used as templates to make the interior shape concave. One half of its surface was greased with petroleum jelly and covered with a layer of tissue paper. Newspaper steeped for a week in a solution of wall-paper paste and water was applied, layer by layer, over a period of days to allow time for one layer to dry before another was added.

The ball was removed once the initial layers had hardened and the eye-holes were cut after careful measurement. The features of the bear were built up on the outside with wodges of the soaked newspaper added like a sculptor would add lumps of clay. The masks were left for a week to dry in a warm cupboard and were then ready to be sandpapered and painted.

The producers suggested that the stilt walkers should also be trained in secret to make their first appearance as dramatic as possible. Jules obtained permission to use a barn on the edge of the village and he and the four children began by making the stilts. All spectators, even the producers, were excluded from the training sessions.

By the end of November the snow-line was down to the outskirts of the village. At the beginning of December a heavier fall covered the river banks, lay on the parapet of the bridge and sat precariously on the steep slate roofs of the houses, school and church. The roads and the square were cleared but a frost ensured that the snow lay. The village was hard frozen into the Winter landscape.

Raoul followed Anamar one bright, icy afternoon as she walked along the path beside the river, heading upstream into the mountains. When he caught up with her they talked about how the Winter changed their lives here in Mont L'ours. They had been working together for weeks on the preparations for the Show, part of a happy team of adults and children. Anamar was impressed by Raoul's efforts to make the performance a success. He was popular with the children, willing to do more than his share of the hard work, helpful to Madam Mons with the costumes.

He and Monsieur Decot had become walking companions and each week-end they tramped the hills using Anamar's mountain walking guide to the area. At one stage Anamar had thought that Raoul and the assistant teacher, Marie Claire, were becoming close friends but then he was always so charming to women, young or old, it was hard to tell. On the way back down the path his tone changed and he began to speak in English.

'This is all a pretence,' he said resentfully, 'I am involved in this children's entertainment only because of you.'

Anamar increased her pace as if walking faster would make it more difficult for him to continue this dialogue. Her cheeks were burning. She felt her anger rise. Had he not listened to a word of her reply when he had spoken this way before? What more could she say?

The snow flew from their marching feet. Raoul ran ahead and stopped to turn and face her.

'You must listen,' he said firmly, 'I am not proposing some casual affair. Your husband is too old for you. I can give you freedom and excitement. We could live in Paris, or Dublin, wherever you wanted. Our life together would be a joy.'

'I can find the patience for this children's party but we are not children. I cannot believe that you have no yearning to share your life with me. We are young. We have the desires of youth. Your husband cannot treat you ........'

Anamar held a gloved hand up in front of his face to stop the outburst. But she was too enraged to speak. It was obvious that her anger, which had not stopped Raoul in the past, would not do so now nor in the future.

While her hand was raised in front of him Raoul was transfixed. He could neither move nor speak. Anamar took a deep breath and listened to the sound of it break the silence of the snow enveloped valley. There had to be another way. And then she understood. Men hated to fail on the chase. Trying to evade Raoul's advances had only inflamed his infatuation.

She placed her hands on his shoulders, keeping him at arm's length and allowing him physical contact in one firm gesture. She laughed aloud.

'I have a friend in St-Girons,' she said coyly, 'I can confide in her and she will be able to explain to me the power of your Latin amour. You must meet her.'

In spite of the cold Raoul felt his cheeks flush. This was the first time she had acknowledged his feelings. Anamar stepped back and smiled. Celestine would know what to do with this suitor.

'I'll invite her to come and stay for a few days,' she said brightly, 'She knows Ramón and we can go walking together. You'll enjoy her company.'

Back at the house, and as soon as Raoul had gone to his room, Anamar telephoned Celestine. She had to wait while the operator tried to connect the call.

Anamar had first met Celestine when she had stayed at her hotel on the fourth day of her pilgrimage to Santiago ten years before. They had enjoyed each other's company and when she had married Ramón and come to live in Ariège Celestine had become a friend.

Madam Celestine D'Abrat had been a beauty in her youth. Now in her forties, she was a handsome, well-groomed woman who looked after her appearance and figure. She had a deft feeling for style which Anamar admired but regarded as beyond her own aspirations. For her part, Celestine admired Anamar's sense of adventure and her ability to be a wife and mother and still retain an independence of spirit.

She was delighted to hear from Anamar and intrigued at the urgency of the invitation to have lunch with her in two days' time.

Anamar loved driving and enjoyed the journey through the Winter landscape on the morning of their lunch. The snow was deep but the roads were clear except for icy patches in the shade of cliffs or trees. The latest fall had frozen on the way-side bushes. It hung in icicles above humps of powdery granules hiding rocks and vegetation at either side.

Celestine had booked a secluded table at a restaurant.

'Why the great hurry, chérie?' she asked, eyebrows arched and before they had sat down.

Anamar admired her friend's well-cut, fine wool suit in a dramatic shade of red, with a cream, ruffled shirt and black cape, gloves and handbag. There was no concession to the cold outside. She waited until they had settled into their seats and ordered white wine as an aperitif.

'I need your advice,' she said, allowing her face to show her worry. 'I have an admirer, an unwanted suitor who will not take "No!" for an answer.'

Celestine began to laugh quietly, rocking gently back and forth in her chair, as if this was a truly unbelievable scenario. 'Tell me about this man,' she said as she lifted her head, 'Is he tall, dark and handsome?'

'Well he's fair, not dark,' Anamar said seriously as if unaware of Celestine's teasing, 'But he's certainty tall and handsome. He is also young, about my age I should think.'

'Excellent, chérie, older men are fine as friends but I prefer young men for affairs of the heart. I presume you want me to distract his attention.'

Although she had known Celestine for years her friend's direct approach could still amaze her.

'I hadn't thought of that,' she said untruthfully, 'I just wanted your advice but, if you find him agreeable, why not?'

By the end of lunch the arrangements had been made. Celestine would come to stay at Mont L'ours after the next week-end for the nights of Monday, Tuesday and Wednesday, the three slackest days of the week for business at her hotel.

Raoul had met Celestine briefly before as a friend of Anamar's but, when she asked him to go to St-Girons to collect her, he was unprepared for the alluring vision who emerged from the hotel.

Celestine spent time on her appearance every day but this morning was exceptional. She had made an early hair appointment, spent an hour on her make up and dressed in a style which managed to combine city chic with the practical clothes she needed for a stay in the country. She wore a woollen skirt and a bolero jacket in fawn, with a pink fleck, over a pale pink blouse. The practical items were her smart laced-up shoes and a well-cut English trench coat by Burberry, with epaulets, firmly belted to show her figure off to best advantage. There was one shop in Toulouse which stocked classic styles from England and she had bought the coat for a special occasion. Raoul was fascinated.

As he packed Celestine's luggage into the boot of the car, their heads came close, enveloping him in the aroma of perfume so exotic he fumbled his little speech of welcome. As they settled into their seats Celestine opened her coat and Raoul was confronted by the lowest décolleté he had seen since he had left Paris. He was enraptured.

Celestine allowed him no respite. She half-turned in her seat and gave him a look of unblinking admiration. No one knew better than she that men found it impossible to resist women who gave them their full attention.

'It's very good of you to come for me,' she said huskily, 'I've heard a great deal about you from Anamar. She has been telling me of your expert translation of old manuscripts from the Latin. I find the past irresistible.'

Raoul was captivated. He talked with nervous excitement, answering her questions almost before they had been asked. Celestine encouraged him, appealing to his vanity, flattering his virility. On a sharp corner she allowed herself to be thrown gently against his shoulder and remained in contact beyond the bend. She praised his driving. She invited him to stop on a pass so that they might look at the view together. She told him she could not remember having a more enjoyable drive through the mountains.

Near Mont L'ours she put a hand on his arm.

'You are so strong,' she said, gripping him gently, 'I feel so safe with you at the wheel.'

Over the years and without being aware of it, Anamar had gradually awakened Raoul's feelings for women but now on this single journey Celestine aroused erotic, lustful emotions he had never felt before. When they reached the village he felt confused, embarrassed. He attended Celestine, taking her coat, looking after her luggage. And Anamar made it even more difficult for him. She asked him to take Celestine's bags to her room, which just happened to be next to his.

When he had gone upstairs with her luggage Celestine put an arm around Anamar's shoulders.

'How am I doing, chérie?', she whispered in Anamar's ear, not needing an answer. 'I'm going to enjoy my stay, and to think I only came here to do a favour for a friend!'

Anamar, Celestine and Raoul went walking in the snow. Ramón came too, but at the end of each walk Anamar ensured that Celestine and Raoul were left to return on their own. At dinner each evening she placed Celestine and Raoul together and encouraged Raoul to dominate the conversation in a way she would never have allowed him to do, had Celestine not been there.

Doña Marie was aware that something was happening and took her lead from Anamar. Madam Mons disapproved of Raoul's air of familiarity with her employers and the discourse at dinner confirmed that view. However, she observed with pleasure his infatuation with Celestine. They were well matched, this Parisian who walked like a girl and the painted lady from St-Girons. Neither was a suitable friend for Anamar. If Ramón noticed the burgeoning romance he said nothing.

After dinner on the first evening, and in spite of the cold, Raoul suggested that they go outside to look at the stars. Doña Marie declined. Anamar apologised, saying that there was a household matter she needed to discuss with Ramón. Celestine was already on her way up to her room to dress against the night air. She returned in coat, hat and gloves, pulling her long skirt up on the bottom stair to kick a leg in the air and show she was wearing walking boots.

The arc of dark blue sky caught between the cliffs of the MontL'ours valley glittered with a myriad stars. A comet swooped across the gap between the crags, its tail scattering light like a gigantic firework.

'Is it an omen?' Celestine whispered the question in Raoul's ear, needing no reply. She took his arm and spoke with the urgency of a girl of sixteen, asking the names of the constellations, wondering why the moon was not on show. He put an arm around her and wrapped her in his coat. They returned to the house glowing with pleasure and later, when Celestine retired to bed, Raoul followed at a decent interval.

Next morning, Celestine was up early for breakfast. She felt years younger, happier than she had been since childhood. When they were alone Anamar faced her in mock indignation.

'How dare you, madam! You have stolen the heart of my suitor, in my own house and without the grace to look guilty.'

Celestine hung her head and pretended to be ashamed.

'Forgive me, chérie,' she said penitently, 'I could not help myself. I am overwhelmed with love. This man is a Svengali, he has us both in his power.'

They began to giggle like schoolgirls and had to quickly compose themselves when Ramón and Raoul came down from the study.

Over the next few days they visited the Bear Sanctuary, trekked on skis in the high alp further up the valley and walked the paths around the village. And Anamar managed to make sure that Raoul and Celestine were left on their own as often as possible.

By the third morning Anamar, Doña Marie and Madam Mons had decided, quite independently, that Raoul and Celestine were more than good friends. Anamar guessed that they had been from the first night. Madam Mons had the advantage of supervising the girl who made the beds and tidied the rooms. The signs were obvious. The lovers were sharing Celestine's bed. Doña Marie needed no such evidence. Her instincts told her that the older woman had seduced the younger man and she wished her well.

When Raoul drove Celestine back to St-Girons he stayed the night. Next day their parting was emotional. They agreed to meet as often as possible when he could borrow a car to make the journey.

Two weeks later when she met Celestine for lunch in St-Girons Anamar was concerned that she had selfishly involved her friend in a serious relationship which might collapse and leave her disappointed in love.

'Don't worry, my little Irish friend.' Celestine was at her best. 'This is an affair, chérie. We are sharing the frenzy of passion, not the bliss of true love.'

---

On the afternoon of the first performance of the Christmas Show five stilt walkers, dressed as clowns, paraded around the village square. The snow had been cleared and they were accompanied by Jules in his showman's black suit and black beret. He had a megaphone and invited everyone to come to see the wonders of the Mont L'ours Christmas Show.

That evening the hall was full. When the stage curtains were pulled back Marie Claire's singers and musicians were the first item on the programme. They started with a rousing chorus of the National Anthem and continued with a quiet lullaby. They finished with a song about a farmyard duck which waddled and quacked and tried in vain to fly, the singers performing actions to the words.

There were shouts of 'Encore! Encore!' and Marie Claire insisted that the audience stand up and join in a reprise of the action song. The singers were enjoying themselves so much they were reluctant to leave the stage but with Raoul's help the platform was cleared.

Raoul strode on and announced the jugglers. There were only three, two boys and a girl and they were very nervous. Each dropped a ball and had to begin again. In desperation, Raoul joined them and he missed a ball too. The audience laughed and clapped, thinking this was part of the act. Raoul was mortified.

One of the boys decided to play for laughs and the others had to join him. They let the balls bounce across the stage and scurried after them. They caught the wrong ball. They fumbled the easiest of catches. At the end the four of them stood in a square and juggled together. This time they juggled without mistakes and the audience gave them a loud round of applause.

The boys' tumbling team marched on in brilliant white shorts and vests. They dived through hoops to land on mattresses. They leapfrogged and tumbled around in pairs, holding each others heels to make a wheel. One of the boys walked across the stage on his hands. Most of the rest did the crab's bend.

Their finale was a tableau with Monsieur Decot as the base. One strong youth stood on his shoulders and a younger boy climbed almost to the ceiling of the hall to sit on his shoulders with his arms stretched out to the side. The audience gasped. The other gymnasts took up their poses against the human tower, doing hand stands or head stands. The crowd cheered and clapped as the boys jumped to their feet and ran off the stage.

The girls' gymnastic team danced on to the platform trailing brightly coloured ribbons behind them in swirling patterns. They exercised with bamboo hoops and Indian clubs. They finished with the most intricate skipping routine Anamar had ever seen. Their parents were thrilled. Their children looked so graceful. The mothers remembered the skipping games of their youth and wished they could join in.

The stilt walkers were so tall the people at the front had to lean back to see them properly. Jules had taught them to dance on stilts and they hopped and skipped around the stage. They formed a line, one behind the other, each following the steps of the one in front, kicking a leg to one side in time with the others like trained giraffes in a circus. They made a circle, hands on the shoulders of the person next to them and slowly performed a sideways, galloping step. It was remarkable, the adults said, to see these children do such a dance on stilts.

There was a pause with the stage curtains closed before the last scene. When they were drawn back the children were seated around the sides and back of the stage. There was a drum roll and Deirdre strode on to the middle of the stage as the 'montreur', dressed in a black coat and the large black beret of Ariège, sporting a huge, drooping moustache.

Deirdre thanked the audience for coming to see their show. She told them that every girl and boy in the school had taken part. There was a drum roll and she announced the final act.

The lights over the stage were switched off and Deirdre made her exit stage left. A boy drummer and a girl with a fife entered from stage right, playing softly. As the lights came on Deirdre entered from stage left leading a big brown bear on a chain. Two smaller bears followed, staying close. The big bear's mask and costume worn by Jules were superb but it was the way the big bear moved which made the audience gasp. It was easy to believe this was a bear, not a man in a bear's costume.

Deirdre's voice carried to the back of the hall.

'This is Martin and his cubs, Fi-Fi and Rudi . Martin is the finest dancing bear in France.' She pointed to the audience. 'Tell Martin that he is welcome to our show.'

'Welcome Martin!' the crowd shouted, 'Welcome to Mont L'ours!', a single voice called from the back, 'The village of the bears.'

Martin bowed his head as Deirdre gently pulled the chain. She called for music and Martin began to rock from side to side to the sound of the fife and drum. He turned slowly in a circle, first one way, then the other so that the chain did not become entangled. The twins, playing the cubs, Fi-Fi and Rudi, skipped along behind him.

The audience watched in total silence as the big bear gently hopped and pranced to the 'montreur's' commands. In one swift movement Deirdre removed Martin's chain. There were fearful shouts from some of the crowd. Martin paused for a few moments, as if surprised by his freedom. Deirdre began to clap and the spectators took up the rhythm.

Martin danced where he stood with the grace of a giant dancer and the power of an animal. Fi-Fi and Rudi followed his movements, as did Deirdre but hers was the dance of a human and theirs was the dance of the bears. The effect was mesmeric.

Ramón was sitting near the back. He had seen Jules's performance at their mountain camp but was astonished to find that his children were sharing with him in this act. He remembered reading research documents in Toulouse University. They recorded the finding of fossilised foot prints in Pyrenean caves which had shown that humans and bears had, without doubt, lived together and danced together in prehistoric times. This was history brought to life.

The Dance of the Bears came to an end and the crowd clapped and stood up to cheer. Jules and the twins removed their masks and took their bow. The other children moved in from the back and sides and took theirs too. The producers joined them. The stage was packed. The parents and friends clapped and cheered. It was the best night in the village since the celebrations at the end of the war. And that was before any of these children had been born.

## THE BATTLE OF THE ESERA VALLEY

Ramón and Raoul met to discuss the Manuscript. Although the translation of the second part had not been completed, it was clear that the two parts had been written by the same hand. Together they told the story of the life and times of Ramón's forebear, Alfonso Barriano, formerly Alfonso de Codés, Marqués de Barra.

The document recovered from Decuré's family was by way of a Postscript. It recorded that all the papers had been written by Pierre Ranisolles, the Cathar, and the maps drawn by Lady Margaret. She had initiated the work and decreed that it be kept within the Cult.

Ramón decided that when the translation was finished, they would print sufficient copies to allow him to send one to each member. A special meeting would be called to arrange an expedition to the Cathedral in the mountains. It would involve all the members of the Cult who wished to be included. The Postscript, however, would remain confidential until after the expedition.

By the end of February the printed manuscripts were dispatched to members with notice of the special meeting to be held at the beginning of April.

............THE SECOND PART OF THE MANUSCRIPT CONTINUES

*Alfonso and his men spent five days in Balaceite. Under the direction of Jean de Pires they repaired the house he had found for his sister. Blanche Ranisolles was already sure that she and her children could settle in this village. It was hidden away in the hills, far from trade routes and a long way from their enemies in France.*

*She was disappointed that her son Pierre would not be staying, but her brother Jean was a revered village elder. The priest, Father Hernandez, was a man to be trusted. It would be difficult to farm in this hard land but the villagers, led by Jean, worked together and together they would survive. After years of uncertainty she was sure that she would be happy here.*

*Alfonso and Redcared retrieved the Holy Icon from the church and with the help of Father Hernandez wrapped it in fine leather and stowed it in the satchel.*

*On the fourth day two mounted messengers arrived. They brought an invitation to Alfonso from Comte Roger de Foix. He had been impressed to hear from the merchant Arnaud of the land and sea trading which Alfonso had developed in Navarre. He wanted to discuss an agreement which would create trade links between them. The Count would be pleased to meet Alfonso and was offering him the hospitality of his Chateau at his convenience.*

*Alfonso decided to split his forces. He would take a small party, Hassan, Redcared and three men-at-arms and ride back to Foix in France the way they had come. James Lamont would lead a larger party with Pierre Ranisolles and the remainder of the men-at-arms. They would take the pack horses laden with the precious goods acquired by trading and head back to Navarre. Alfonso's lightly-weighted party would be able to travel quickly and would arrive home a week later.*

*On their last evening Father Sanchez appeared. He had heard that Alfonso was about to leave for France and begged to be allowed to join the party. He had been summoned by the Bishop of Carcassonne, he said, and hinted that he was hoping for news of a senior appointment.*

*The two parties left Balaceite together and camped the first night on the road to Alcañiz. Next morning they parted, James heading North-West for Zaragoza, Logroño and Navarre, and Alfonso travelling North to Baga, Puigcerda and over the Pyrenees to Foix. As before, the Holy Icon would travel in his care.*

*Seven days later Alfonso was back in France, riding down the road from Ax to Foix. They climbed the hill to the magnificent stronghold which was the Castle of Foix. The Count, alerted by his sentries, met him in the castle yard and Alfonso was treated as a guest of honour. In the bustle of their arrival in Foix no one noticed that Father Sanchez had left the party as soon as they had entered the town. And he did so without thanks for having been allowed to travel within the protection of the troop.*

*Next morning Arnaud de Foix, the trader, arrived early. It became obvious that he had been discussing the arrangements with the Count's officials, preparing an agreement which would benefit both Alfonso and the Count. While the details were being explained to Alfonso, the Count burst into the room and took him boar hunting.*

*The following day, when the details of the agreement were becoming tedious, Arnaud produced a map drawn by a scribe. It showed North-West Spain and South-West France and all the lands between. The scribe inked in the overland routes between Foix in Ariège and Alfonso's lands in Navarre. He illustrated the sea routes to the East from the Count's port of Collioure on the Mediterranean and Alfonso's port of Bilbao on the Bay of Biscay.*

*The way was cleared for the agreement. Each party would provide storage and protection for each other's mule trains and cargo ships. They would assist each other with information and in the collection of money owed for goods or services. They would share the costs of joint ventures. Together they would fund the appointment of Arnaud de Foix as their joint agent.*

*A servant went to tell the Count that the papers were ready to be signed. But for all his sporting energy and disdain for trade, the Count was aware of the importance of such an agreement. In their day the Templar Knights had controlled these land and sea routes and had grown rich in property and gold. Now they were gone and this new alliance would link East and West. They would take their places as the trusted merchants of Christendom.*

*A banquet in Alfonso's honour was arranged for the night before he left for home. Preparations began in the morning and by the evening the great hall was filled with music and laughter. There were servants darting between the guests, carrying laden platters and jugs of wine. There must have been twenty musicians and almost as many dancers. Alfonso was seated on the Count's right hand and Hassan, Redcared and Arnaud had places of honour further down the table.*

*With barely a pause, the music and dancing continued throughout the evening. There were jesters and jugglers, tumblers who could somersault through the air, a fire eater breathing flames like a dragon. There was a great shout heralding the appearance of four cooks carrying a huge silver platter with a whole roasted pig and a roasted cockerel on its back. There was green soup with the taste of Oriental spices, dishes of quails, roasted chickens, pies, a whole carp served in jelly, dishes of oysters in onion and cream sauce, whole roasted cygnets, herons and peacocks.*

*Alfonso had never seen such an array of food. The wine flowed and the talk and music were so loud he had to shout to be heard. As dishes were cleared from the table others took their place, galettes and pears in red wine, sugared plums, dishes of cherries and olives, five kinds of bread and an array of sweet biscuits.*

*Alfonso left his seat to talk to Hassan and Redcared. Both were so amazed they could hardly speak. They had eaten little and had drunk no wine. He wanted them to try to remember this banquet, he said. Lady Margaret would want to know every detail, the foods, the musical instruments, the entertainers. Arnaud could help them with the names.*

*Later Count Roger took Alfonso to an ante-room and they sealed their agreement with goblets of fine wine. The Count was especially fond of the music and when they returned he ordered his captain to call for silence. It was his wish that the musicians and singers perform for his honoured guest while the others remained silent. The great tumult of noise was hushed.*

*The first air was sung by two boys whose voices had not yet broken. They were quietly accompanied by the lute, tambourine, drum and fiddle. The bagpipe and hand organ took over for a livelier melody. The Count called for a tune by name and the rebeck with its three strings plucked or bowed and a cittar like a small harp played the Count's favourite air. The singers and the dancers sang and danced on into the night.*

*Before he left next day Alfonso asked Arnaud to speak to the Count's chief cook and find out which spices had been used for the food at the banquet. By noon Arnaud was back with a sack of spices, each in its own bag - cinnamon, saffron, white and green cardoman, mace, white pepper. Margaret would be delighted.*

*She had her own cook who would know how to use these precious condiments.*

*Count Roger de Foix came to see his visitor on his way. He was well pleased to have Alfonso as an ally. It mattered nothing that he suspected that Alfonso had been a Templar. Their trade might even prosper because of his partner's past. He was sure they would become friends. It was a pity they lived so far apart. In time of war he would like to have gone into battle with this man at his side.*

*Over the next few days Alfonso's party travelled quickly through Luchon and camped at the lakes below the Col de Benasque, the pass over the Pyrenees. In the morning they climbed the track, dismounting to lead their horses up the steep slope to the crest. On the other side they remounted and were in good spirits as they walked their steeds around the Peña Blanca, down to the Esera Valley which led to Benasque Town.*

*It was a beautiful early Summer day, perfect for riding in the mountains. Across the valley the huge massif of Maladetta on the sky-line dominated all. This was Redcared's home land and he told Alfonso that these were reputed to be the highest peaks in the Pyrenees.*

*The air was warm, the breeze fresh. They had time to stop and wonder. The head of the valley was to their left. In its upper reaches it split in two, with one arm a narrow canyon and the other a much wider basin but ending in a sheer wall of cliffs. To their right, and still many hours ride ahead, the valley led down to Redcared's home, the Cagot village in the forest above the town of Benasque.*

*Alfonso was talking to Hassan about the banquet, his only regret that Lady Margaret had not been there to enjoy it. He decided that they would have their own banquet to celebrate their return. Redcared joined them and they laughed as they recalled the whole roasted pig and the roasted cockerel on its back.*

*As they came near the forest, there was a great shout from behind a mound of boulders and a fusillade of arrows struck the party from close range. Two of the soldiers were hit in the chest with such force they were knocked from their horses. Hassan took an arrow in the stomach and fell forward. He grasped his horse's neck but its movement drove the arrow further into his body.*

*Alfonso grabbed the reins of Hassan's horse. He yelled to Redcared and the soldier, calling them to follow him. There were upwards of twenty soldiers emerging from the trees and behind them, on a rock, a black robed priest. It was Father Sanchez brandishing a sword, encouraging the strangers to attack.*

*Had his full force been with him, the order from Alfonso would have been to stand and fight. But this was a time to run.*

*As they galloped off a second fusillade fell short but one archer was closer. His arrow hit Alfonso in the back piercing the leather satchel and his light chain mail armour but only just. Later they found that the Icon had taken the force of the arrow and only its tip had come through to nick the skin of his back.*

*By the time the attackers had retrieved their horses and set off on the chase, the remnants of Alfonso's party were ahead. As they rode Redcared shouted to Alfonso that they must head for the canyon. It was too steep and rocky for horses, he said, but there was an escape route from its upper reaches. If they took the other branch of the valley they would be trapped below the wall of cliffs at its head.*

*Above a short steep rise they came to a huge hole. On the upper side a mountain torrent, fed by the snow melt, tumbled down into its depths in a great waterfall. Alfonso's horse was travelling well, as was Hassan's, whose bridle he still held. Hassan was still lying on the horse's neck, arms around it, hanging on. Alfonso was aware that his one surviving soldier was falling behind. He looked around and one of the enemy on a fast horse had ridden ahead of the others and had run the soldier through with his lance.*

*A short time later Alfonso looked around again and the main party of the enemy had stopped. His soldier had fallen from his horse, wounded, perhaps still alive but he was lifted by three men and flung head first into the great hole.*

*They reached the grassy plan below the canyon and Alfonso and Redcared slid down from their horses. They tried to help Hassan but his wound had been mortal, his arms about his steed's neck. He had been the most accomplished horseman of them all and now, in death, still secure in the saddle.*

*The enemy was still some distance away and had slowed to a trot. There was no need for haste. Their adversaries were doomed with only one man and a boy to overcome.*

*But Alfonso could see the priest amongst the men urging them to hurry. These attackers were strangers except for him. At this moment Alfonso remembered seeing Father Sanchez in the church at Balaceite after the pilgrimage. He had been kneeling before the Holy Icon and Alfonso had watched him from the doorway. The priest had not been a penitent seeking grace but a devotee of the Holy Icon, coveting possession. His contacts had enabled him to find a warlord as an ally, no doubt for gold. But it was not the destruction of Alfonso's party which was important to him. It was possession of the Holy Icon.*

*They laid Hassan in a cleft in the rocks and prayed for his soul. They removed the harness and saddles and let their horses loose. Alfonso took his helmet from a saddle bag and clamped it on his head. Redcared had been carrying food for the journey and they took it with them. As the enemy advanced towards the grassy plan they climbed quickly into the mouth of the canyon.*

*A narrow gully was the only way up the gorge. It was a fissure, broad enough for one man to pass at a time. There was a sheer cliff on one side and tall rocks above the river on the other. In one place the path ascended on blocks like stone steps but as steep as a church roof. Near the top of the slope the narrow passage turned sharply to the right. Alfonso decided this was the place to stand and fight. Only one man could attack at a time. From here he could defend the ascent.*

*Redcared could climb like a squirrel and he found a protected position on a ledge above Alfonso. He gathered a pile of stones, from the size of pebbles to rocks as big as his head. Alfonso was wearing his habergeon, the light chain mail tunic he had donned each day of the journey. He held his dagger in one hand and a curved Saracen sword in the other. The Arab sword-makers were the best in the world. They forged swords of the finest hardened steel, light, strong and exceedingly sharp. He had no shield but his conical helmet would protect his head.*

*The sharp turn in the gully would prevent an archer having a clear line of sight. Redcared was the look-out. As well as the pile of rocks he had his own dagger and a shorter version of Alfonso's sword. But his secret weapon was his sling shot. All his life he had used it for hunting but never against another man.*

*Alfonso had chosen this place to make a stand. He took up a firm stance and waited for the attack. The enemy would be in single file trudging up the steep, narrow passage. He could hear the clank of arms against armour and the shouts and curses of the men. They fell silent as the climb steepened but Alfonso could hear the rasp of heavy breathing. He looked up and Redcared nodded. The enemy had arrived. The point of a sword appeared around the corner. It was a broad sword, more useful in open country. Alfonso waited.*

*When the man behind the sword emerged, he was huge, so big he was almost stuck at the corner. His sword, too, was immense, too unwieldy for the narrow confines of the passage. Alfonso lunged at his chest. His sword drove into the man's body as a big boulder fell on his head, driving him to his knees. Alfonso recovered his sword and glanced up. Redcared had another boulder at the ready. Alfonso shook his head. The giant was already dead.*

*The next man had to clamber over the body of his comrade and was mortally wounded before he could find his footing. There was a pause while the enemy pulled back their dead.*

*At that moment Redcared and Alfonso saw an archer scaling the cliff to a vantage point above them. Alfonso gestured towards the man and Redcared slipped away from his look-out position. Moments later Alfonso glanced up again and the archer had reached a narrow ledge. The next soldier appeared in front of him in the passageway and Alfonso parried his first thrust. The man withdrew. His mission had been to see around the corner.*

*There was a wild cry from the cliff above. Before he could loose a shaft the archer had been hit by Redcared's sling-shot. He fell free* of the cliff, tumbling over in the air and disappearing into the gorge below.

Alfonso's new assailant was of a much lighter build. He came forward at speed, behind his shield, taking the fight to Alfonso. They battled, thrust and parry, only able to slash from above. Both sustained cuts to their sword arms. The rock under their feet ran with blood. Their swords locked and they slipped together on the gore. Alfonso reached over his assailant's shield and stabbed him with his dagger, deep into his neck. The dead man fell against Alfonso and knocked him to his knees.

There was barely time for him to rise before the first of three more attackers appeared in quick succession. The first two retired quickly, slightly injured. The third tried to avoid the fight. It was obvious that he had been sent to look and withdraw. As he turned away Redcared, now back on his perch, rained stones down on him.

The enemy pulled their dead comrades back and Alfonso heard an angry shout. Was it Father Sanchez? The response was the voice of a nobleman speaking harshly. He ordered the priest to be silent.

The light was fading quickly and, by his clothes and weapon, the noble was the next man into the fray. He jeered and yelled at Alfonso, knowing that his adversary must be near exhaustion. He slashed downwards with his sword, the blow glancing off Alfonso's helmet and striking him on the shoulder. Alfonso went down on his back and the nobleman bent over him, steadying himself for a lunge to his chest.

Redcared flung his heaviest boulder down with all his might. It struck the nobleman on the back of the neck. He tumbled forward. As he fell on top of him, Alfonso struck upwards with his left hand and his assailant impaled himself on his opponent's dagger.

Redcared skipped down from his perch and together they pushed the corpse back around the corner. There was a silence, broken only by the sound of the man's body being trailed away down the rocks. Darkness came down on the mountain as if the light had been lost forever.

*In Navarre, Lady Margaret was sitting by the fire at dusk, thinking of Alfonso, troubled by a sense of foreboding. Suddenly she felt herself smitten by fear for his life. She screamed. The servants came running. Father Romero came too but no one could help her.*

*Alfonso rose and leaned against the rocks, his energy gone. He gasped for breath, his right arm hung limply at his side. Redcared whispered in his ear. The enemy did not know that Alfonso's sword-arm was injured, he said. The enemy voices were receding. Now was the time to flee. He knew of a hiding place higher up. There was a cave with a hidden entrance.*

*With Redcared's help Alfonso struggled upwards. His young squire gripped him by his waist belt and hauled with all his might. When they reached the top of the narrow gully the moon shone briefly through a break in the clouds. At the top of a scree slope, just below the cliff, there was a huge boulder. Redcared lay down on his back beside it. He wriggled sideways and disappeared under the rock.*

*The moon came out from behind a cloud into a patch of clear sky. Alfonso had often longed for such a Hunter's Moon but not now. To-night he was the quarry. He looked back and saw two soldiers and a dog emerge from behind a buttress. The dog was following their trail by the scent of blood.*

*The soldiers had seen him but Alfonso hoped they did not know that he had seen them. He lay down beside the boulder and painfully wriggled under it. The cave was used by the Cagots as a shepherd's shelter. Redcared had found their flint and tinder and lit a candle. Alfonso told him that he had been seen by the soldiers and Redcared took the candle into the passage at the back of the cave and returned to wait for the enemy.*

*The dog was the first to appear, roughly thrust under the boulder by the boot of one of the men. He squirmed to his feet, twisting around to face them, his eyes already able to see them in the dim light. He bared his teeth and drew back on his haunches, ready for fight or flight. Alfonso leaned forward slowly and blew a gentle breath towards him.*

*The dog was a hound with a rough coat, his head waist-high to Alfonso. He was lean, long limbed. Alfonso blew another breath towards him. The dog moved one step forward and Alfonso breathed again. He held out his gloved left hand and the dog moved closer, no longer stiff with aggression or fear.*

*The top of a helmet appeared below the rock. The first of the soldiers was following the dog inside. Alfonso and Redcared moved silently behind the man as he rose to his knees. There was no sign of welcome from the dog to his master. The soldier called to his companion to follow him. Alfonso stepped forward and hit him on the back of the neck with the bottom edge of his stiff left hand. It was a blow which would have smashed a plank of wood and Alfonso shuddered with the force of it. The man was already dead when he slumped forward to the ground.*

*Alfonso and Redcared, daggers drawn, waited for his companion. The man died as soon as his head appeared from under the stone. Alfonso's legs gave way. Utterly exhausted, he fell against the wall of the cave and slid down to the floor. The dog came to him and sat down at his feet.*

*Redcared pulled the dead soldier inside the cave. He lay full length, his ear to the gap below the stone at the entrance and listened for sounds of the enemy. He slid underneath out on to the mountainside. The moon's light was as bright as their candle inside the cave. There was neither sight nor sound of the enemy. He wriggled back under the stone and helped Alfonso through to the second cave.*

*There was a pool of water, fresh and clear and a smooth stone ledge like a monk's bed. Redcared helped Alfonso onto the ledge and tended his injuries. The chain mail had saved his life. When the nobleman's sword had slashed down on his shoulder it should have killed him. But the chain mail had been fashioned with its heaviest links over the shoulder and chest. The sword had not been able to split the armour. Alfonso had taken an almighty blow but it was not a mortal wound.*

*At the same time, back in Navarre, an exhausted Lady Margaret felt her spirits rise. Later Father Romero would say that it was the power of prayer, but she knew that the shadow of death over Alfonso had passed on to some other poor soul.*

*Redcared told Alfonso that he knew this cave. Shepherds from his village used it but only they knew its whereabouts. He had been here twice before. He fetched a leather water bucket and two wooden cups from a corner. He found a big shepherd's cloak thick enough to keep a man warm on a Winter's night. On a ledge there was a parcel of dried meat and bread, so hard they had to soften it in water. But most important of all, he said, there was another way out.*

*He and Alfonso bedded down with the shepherd's cloak around them. Alfonso called to the dog and he came to lie beside him. He had lost his horse but he had found a dog. His squire was a foundling too, and as true as any man he had ever met.*

*They slept for a long time and when Alfonso awoke he felt his wounds a little easier. Redcared lit a candle and they ate bread and dried meat and drank deeply of the water in the pool. He named the dog 'Valor'. 'With us,' he said, 'Valor will earn a name for courage.'*

*Valor stayed behind Alfonso as he struggled to follow Redcared. They travelled the passageways between small caves and squeezed through a narrow slit to enter a huge cavern, bigger than any church Alfonso had seen since his days in the Holy Land. At that moment he decided that this vast cavern below the mountain, like a great cathedral, should be the resting place for the Holy Icon. It would be safe here. Redcared's people would cherish it. It would be under their protection. They would be honoured to have it here.*

*Redcared used a sharp stone and the blade of his dagger to enlarge a natural ledge on the back wall. He and Alfonso prayed aloud as they lifted the Icon onto its place. The broken arrow was still embedded, its tip protruding from the back. Alfonso winced with pain as he reached upwards. His body shuddered as he laid the Icon on the ledge. A great sigh escaped from his chest. The Icon had been his companion since he had fled from Acre Castle. But now it was time to let it rest and they left its satchel against the cave wall below the ledge.*

*Redcared went to look for their escape route. He scampered up a ramp to a large ledge high up on the wall of the cave. Alfonso watched as his squire disappeared behind a buttress. He stroked Valor's head and talked to him in a whisper as if the dog could understand. He felt his strength return, entering his body through the hand which touched the dog.*

*Redcared found the narrow channel which was the escape route. Outside on the mountainside he could see no sign of the enemy. By the position of the sun, it was afternoon. They should wait until dark, he suggested. He would lead the way up through the canyon and around the northern flank of the massif. They would leave the mountains by a valley on the other side of Maladetta. It would take two days but they would bring the shepherd's cloak and sleep out on the mountain. This route would bring them down to his home village from a different direction.*

*Alfonso smiled. His young squire had taken charge. His left hand still ached from the blow which had killed the soldier but he laid it on Redcared's shoulder as a sign that he trusted him to find the way.*

*They rested and ate. Redcared went again to the way out. Outside, it was dark, and time to go. They brought what was left of the food he had taken from the saddle bag when they had freed the horses. They took the dried meat which had been left by the Cagot shepherds. Redcared rolled the shepherd's cloak and carried it like a pack.*

*The night was cold and clear, the moon almost full. There was still no sign of the enemy. The first slope led to the higher levels of the valley. They reached a long narrow lake, its surface sparkling in the moonlight. Redcared went first and the dog followed Alfonso without a sound. Higher still they came to a long snow slope leading to a narrow col. The men used their daggers to help them climb the steep slope and the dog scrambled upwards in his new master's footsteps.*

*At the pass Redcared pointed to a long rock ridge protruding from the snow, sloping downwards to the left. It looked too steep to climb but half-way up there was a notch in the rocks. Redcared made directly over the snow for this tiny gap. It was the only way across. The men were able to climb the short cliff but Valor found it impossible to spring upwards from the soft snow. Redcared went back down to help him. At one stage the dog had a back paw on each of the boy's shoulders. Just one more jump and he was up.*

*At the crest of the ridge Alfonso felt the power returning to his right arm. There was no sign of pursuers. Across the head of another valley, walking on hard snow, they passed a magnificent lake, its surface frozen. Above it was another col, the highest pass of all.*

*On the other side Alfonso needed a long rest. He collapsed into sleep in a sheltered cleft as soon as they stopped. The boy and the dog curled up beside him beneath the shepherd's cloak. When they awoke it was almost dawn. Descending rapidly, they passed small lakes into a wide deep valley. Redcared called it Vallibierna. They were now on the South side of Maladetta.*

*All day they made a slow descent with frequent rests. By nightfall they had reached the forest which hid the Cagot village amongst its trees.*

*Under cover of darkness Redcared went on alone, following a path through the forest to his home. When he returned he brought good news. Early that morning the enemy soldiers had ridden down the road in disarray. They had been accompanied by an angry priest. The villagers had heard that a nobleman had been killed in battle. Redcared's grandfather had bought a magnificent horse from the soldiers which Redcared recognised at once as Alfonso's half-Arab mare.*

*Alfonso was received as a hero in the village. Redcared's grandfather, Jacobi, was proud that his grandson was squire to the nobleman who had saved the boy's life last time he had been here. But he was horrified to find that his grandson was not wearing the Cagot mark. Alfonso intervened. He had ordered the removal of the crow's foot symbol, he said and Jacobi accepted the decree without question. He saw to it that Alfonso was lodged in a house near his own and had the women bring him food, water and wine.*

*Jacobi examined Alfonso's wounds. There were no broken bones. He rubbed the shoulder with an ointment which smelt of the herbs of the forest. He laid yellow flowers, he called them the Arnica of the mountains, and bound them in place with cloth. Later, Jacobi served him a warm drink made from juniper berries and in the evening brought juniper leaves and branches to burn on the fire.*

*Redcared stayed in his grandfather's house and spent the evening and most of the night telling him of his adventures. The villagers were surprised to see Alfonso allow his dog inside his house and to hear him insist that only he must feed Valor.*

*Jacobi sent a party of Cagot men up the Esera Valley to bury those who had been killed in battle. The enemy soldiers had interred their own but had left the others for the animals and birds. Alfonso and Redcared rode up the valley for the burial of their friend Hassan. They dug his grave a little way from the others, pointing East and carved his name on a smooth black stone from the river.*

*Knowing nothing of the rituals of Islam, they prayed for the repose of his soul. Redcared helped the burial party retrieve the bodies of the two soldiers killed inside the cave and placed a large rock on each mound as his own token of respect.*

*They rested for a week and Alfonso pronounced himself restored to health and ready for the journey home. When Jacobi saw that Redcared wanted to accompany Alfonso, he agreed. To keep our children, he said to Alfonso, we must let them go, to soar like arrows from a bow and fly where ere they will.*

*The whole village came to see them off. Redcared was proudly astride a mountain pony with food in his saddlebags. Alfonso had a leather hat instead of a helmet, his chain mail repaired, his mare prancing to be on the way, his dog, Valor, circling them with his great loping stride. Little boys ran behind, waving their hats, cheering them down the road to Benasque.*

# LADY MARGARET'S PILGRIMAGE

*It was a glorious journey. The weather was good, the local people friendly and hospitable. The roads were in good repair, winding on hard baked earthen tracks through rugged hills and across the plains. Don Alfonso and Redcared were back home in Navarre in less than a week.*

*Lady Margaret had been preparing for her husband's return since James had arrived. His party had travelled quicker than expected and reached Navarre five days before. She was saddened by the death of Hassan. Manuel Diego Bin Rahman tried to hide his tears. He had loved the Saracen as a brother. In the mountains above Codés del Camino he built a column of stones at the crest of a pass, as tall as a man. Lady Margaret decreed that the celebration of the travellers' return would be preceded by Mass for the immortal souls of all those who had died in the battle of the Esera, including the Moslem, Hassan.*

*Alfonso spent a sad, lonely day in the hills, the elation of his home coming dispersed by the toll of dead. Valor followed his master without a sound. He was allowed the run of Alfonso's house and had never been known to bark or howl. Other dogs were kept at bay with a silent baring of the teeth and an almost inaudible growl. And Valor knew what his master was thinking by merely standing at his side.*

*In the afternoon Redcared and Pierre came to look for Alfonso in the hills and made him smile by pretending that the loss of the sack of spices had been a great tragedy. On the way down to the village Pierre explained that Lady Margaret had commissioned him to write the story of her husband's life. But although Pierre knew about the work of the Cult and Alfonso's recent exploits, he needed to hear of his early life as a Knight-at-arms and his sojourn in Scotland.*

*A room had been set aside in the house Alfonso had built within the castle walls. Pierre was excused all other work. He had a table beside the window overlooking the village. He was allocated a young man as a servant and scribe. Felipe, a village boy from Codés del Camino cooked Pierre's meals, prepared his materials and was learning to write in the manner of a scribe. Lady Margaret intended to draw the maps herself with help from Le Poing and Manuel who, between them, were familiar with most of the land and sea routes of Western Europe.*

*Le Poing and Manuel helped Lady Margaret prepare for the celebrations. Father Romero was elated when she told him that they would begin with Mass for the dead. He needed support for the work of the Church and was aware that many noble families resented the power of the Bishops. Lady Margaret was giving the Church its proper place in village life.*

*Two days later the celebrations began with the Mass at noon. In the afternoon Alfonso entertained the members of the Cult to a feast in his house. He announced the trade pact with Count Roger de Foix, and made it clear that everyone would be responsible for making it a success. It was a happy gathering but there was sadness too. Hassan would be missed.*

*For the main celebration Lady Margaret had decided that there would be singers and musicians but neither jesters nor dancers. Her maid, Morag, would tell a story in the Scottish tradition and play the Scottish bag-pipes as the food was produced. There would be Scottish foods like puddings made from sheep's offal and blood, oatmeal and spices, and boiled in a bag made from the animal's stomach. The wines would be red from their own vineyards.*

*Lady Margaret rose to her feet and announced that within a year she would make a pilgrimage to give thanks to God for the deliverance from death of her husband and his squire. She would go to the Pyrenees to pray in the great cave Alfonso called the Cathedral.*

*When she sat down, Alfonso kissed her and swore to help her pilgrimage in any way he could. He would accompany her, he said, and Lady Margaret smiled. She would have expected nothing less.*

*Later that evening Alfonso told his wife about the splendid meal and revelry at Foix Castle. Before the end of the year they would stage a fiesta and banquet for everyone from the three villages of his lands in Navarre.*

*Pierre worked on the Manuscript through the Autumn and Winter. When it was almost finished Lady Margaret revealed her plans for the pilgrimage.*

*They would leave in the Spring and travel on horseback. She and Alfonso would be accompanied by Father Romero as their spiritual advisor, Redcared and Morag, Pierre, who would record the pilgrimage and Le Poing in charge of ten mounted men-at-arms and the pack mules.*

*Each day they would build a cairn of stones to mark their passage. Each morning before they ate or prepared to leave, Father Romero would say Mass. They would ring a hand bell to call the pilgrims together. They would bring two golden candlesticks to place on the ledge beside the Holy Icon in the Cathedral.*

*They would carry Pierre's Manuscript with them and each evening he would read from it before they ate. To make it easier to carry, the Manuscript would be divided into two parts. Redcared asked Alfonso's permission to wear the crow's foot Cagot emblem on his sleeve for the duration of the pilgrimage and his lord agreed.*

*Lady Margaret had already arranged that the twins, Maria and Robert, would be cared for by James's woman, Beatrice. To Alfonso it seemed an admirable arrangement. James would take charge while he was away. Manuel Diego Bin-Rahman could ensure that trade with Arnaud de Foix fulfilled the expectations of Count Roger de Foix and himself.*

*A week before the Pilgrimage set out, two Cagot messengers arrived. They had been sent by Redcared's grandfather, Jacobi, with a message for Alfonso.*

*The same priest who had been seen withdrawing with the enemy soldiers after the battle, had appeared again. He had come up the Esera valley one morning and returned the next afternoon. As the priest had ridden down past the village, Jacobi could see that he had a satchel slung over his shoulder which he had not carried on the way up. He was certain that it was the same satchel that Alfonso had carried when first he had come to their village.*

*Lady Margaret's voice was calm. The purpose of their pilgrimage, she said, was to visit the Cathedral cave to make their devotions to God, the Holy Spirit. It would be a disappointment not to see the Holy Icon again but she was certain that the man who had stolen it would never have a lucky day.*

*Pierre ceased work on the Templar Manuscript to prepare for the pilgrimage and he was directed by Lady Margaret to divide it into two parts. On the pilgrimage he would carry the first part in a leather satchel and Redcared would carry the second in a similar bag.*

### ............A POSTSCRIPT TO THE TEMPLAR MANUSCRIPT

*The rain began to fall heavily and the pilgrims left Codés del Camino in a sombre mood. For two days it continued with hardly a break. The road surfaces turned to mud. The pilgrims were sodden and cold but Lady Margaret insisted that the ritual of the pilgrimage was followed to the letter. Cairns were built, Masses said each morning and readings of the Manuscript made from the shelter of Alfonso's tent every evening.*

*At Mass on the second morning Father Romero addressed the party as they stood in the open, huddling together in the driving rain. He avowed that the inclement weather had been sent to try them. If they rose above such difficulties, he said, they would be rewarded with even greater grace. Some of the soldiers shuffled their feet, clearly unimpressed, but a fierce look from Lady Margaret forestalled any act of levity.*

*On the third morning the dawn broke without a cloud in the sky. The spirits were far more uplifted by the sunshine than Father Romero had been able to manage by his prayers.*

*They built a great cairn in the village of Tiermas beside the River Aragon when Alfonso thought they had reached half-way. It was as tall as a man on horseback. Everyone helped to carry stones,*

*Lady Margaret working like a man and Alfonso smiling encouragingly at Father Romero to show that he was meant to work too.*

*They spent a night at Redcared's village and some of the soldiers were reluctant at first to associate with the Cagots. However, such was the villagers' hospitality and Redcared's reputation as Alfonso's squire, their fears were allayed. Alfonso invited Jacobi, Redcared's grandfather, to join them for the final stage of the Pilgrimage.*

*On this last day, Lady Margaret decided that they would make their pilgrimage on foot, walking their horses up into the mountains. The pilgrims climbed the Valley of the Esera below the great peaks of Maladetta. The narrow gorge at its foot opened out to the summer grazing and Redcared showed them where the battle had been fought. They stopped at the great chasm to see the river fall into the bowels of the earth. The spray flew from the waterfall, gently wetting their faces, as if by tears for their fallen comrades. Father Romero prayed for the soul of the soldier who had been flung into the hole and for all who had been slain in the battle.*

*They camped above the higher gorge where Alfonso and Redcared had stopped to fight in the narrow cleft. They pitched their tents below the big boulder which marked the entrance to the caves. Father Romero, his face pale and drawn as if he had not been able to sleep, said Mass next morning at dawn. He staggered like a man drunk with exhaustion as he led them up the slope. Pierre and Redcared took him by the arms and Cathar heretic and Cagot untouchable led the priest towards the concealed entrance to the cave.*

*It had been Father Romero's intention to insist that he led the pilgrimage into the cave, but hours of darkness spent in prayer had banished personal triumphalism. Before, it had troubled him that his association with Alfonso Barriano, Marqués de Barra and his tribe was a marriage of convenience. But Alfonso had used his wealth and energy to banish poverty and neglect from his lands. He had formed the Cult of the Holy Spirit and used it to transform his domain. He had aided pilgrims on the way to Santiago de*

*Compostela. He had improved the farms and vineyards of the estate to make them the best in Navarre. He had developed trade with the Comte de Foix across the width of France and Spain.*

*Father Romero had found himself unable to disregard these laudable facts, but had he compromised his holy calling by ignoring the heresies before his eyes? The young man, Pierre Ranisolles, was a Cathar, the follower of a faith deemed heretic. The boy, Redcared, was a Cagot, forbidden by his master to wear the Cagot mark on his clothes. Don Alfonso's friend, Hassan, now dead, had been a Moslem. The trader, Manuel Diego Bin-Rahman, was either Catholic or Moslem as suited his purpose.*

*Although Alfonso's wife, Lady Margaret, was devout, she saw her priest as her servant not her master. However, it was she who had paid for repair work to his church and it was she who had mounted this pilgrimage, appointed him its spiritual advisor and insisted on strict adherence to religious observances.*

*But above all, Alfonso the nobleman, was surely a renegade Templar Knight who had escaped arrest and trial by the Inquisition for heresy.*

*As the night had passed, Father Romero had wrestled with his conscience. Before first light, he had come to the conclusion that these were good people, loyal to their friends, implacable in the face of their enemies, helpful to those who lived on their lands. They had made this pilgrimage the most important act of devotion for him since his ordination. He would accept them as they were, he decided, not on sufferance, but with a full heart.*

*Le Poing tolled the bell. Father Romero's legs were weak. He stiffened his body to stand erect. The Cathar and the Cagot held him upright before the hidden entrance to the cave. In a loud voice he invited them to go first and light the candles within the cave. Lady Margaret would follow, he announced, then Alfonso. As their priest, he would enter last.*

*To his amazement everyone, including Lady Margaret, accepted his directions. Redcared and Pierre led the way and the others followed. When it was his turn to wriggle under the stone, Father Romero felt his strength return. He stood up in the half light of the candles and saw that they were all waiting for him. He and Lady Margaret led the procession through the passages and caverns, Redcared beside them, whispering directions.*

*They climbed a ramp of boulders to reach a narrow passageway and squeezed through a slit which brought them into a great cavern. As they entered, one by one, they fell on their knees, their heads bowed in prayer. Time passed and Father Romero rose to his feet. The others followed, gazing upwards in astonishment. This was the Cathedral, vast, magnificent, more awesome by far than Alfonso had described.*

*Father Romero's faith had never been stronger. Such a revelation could only be discovered by the worthy. He organised the men to drag a large rock into position as an altar stone. He saw Alfonso and Redcared staring at a ledge in the rock wall and knew at once that this was where they had placed the Holy Icon. But it was gone. Lady Margaret saw it too and had Morag fetch the gold candlesticks. With her maid's help she placed them, one at each end of the ledge, and lit their candles with a glowing taper. She stepped back. The space where once the Holy Icon had rested glowed with a pale yellow light. It was as if the Icon was still in place. She dropped to her knees and the priest knelt down beside her.*

*For the first time in his life Father Romero doubted that the relic had a power of its own. It was holy only by association.*

*'We do not need the Icon here,' he whispered to Lady Margaret, 'It is enough for us to be where once it stood.' She nodded, for once the priest was right.*

*Father Romero proclaimed an act of sanctification, his voice shaking with wonder. He was a man reborn. Before, he had been a guardian of the rites of the Church. Now he believed what once he had preached for others to obey. The turmoil of his conscience of the previous night was over. The Holy Spirit had set him free to serve his true vocation.*

*As she worshipped, Lady Margaret thanked God for the joys of her life. She prayed for her husband and children, for her family in Scotland, dead or alive, for the soul of Hassan the Saracen, for all her fellow pilgrims.*

*Alfonso stood behind them and marvelled. Nothing he had done in his past life had prepared him for this moment. For the first time he truly felt absolved from his Templar vows. His life in Navarre was his destiny. As she had often done before, his wife had chosen the way to celebrate their fortune. This Pilgrimage would uplift them all.*

*Before they left, Lady Margaret called on Pierre to read from his Manuscript. Twenty candles were lit, flaming steadily on the altar stone. Pierre took the second part from Redcared's satchel and related the story of the Battle of the Esera. His voice quivered as he described the fight in the gorge below their camp where Alfonso and Redcared had held the enemy at bay. He told the story of their escape into the cave and across the mountains to the Cagot village. As he spoke, it had already become their history.*

*It was late afternoon when the pilgrims began to return to the cave entrance and Redcared was last as they filed out. They were talking excitedly, shouting to each other. Suddenly there was a rumbling noise and a shower of debris fell from above. Those at the back surged forwards. Stones and gravel began to tumble down. Above the clamour there was a loud crack as if a massive rock had split and one huge flat slab fell behind them with a roar and a thump.*

*Outside on the open mountain Le Poing checked the party. There was one person missing. It was Redcared.*

*Le Poing and Alfonso went back into the cave with two of the soldiers. It had not been a big stone fall, just enough to block the passage. Only one large rock had fallen. They called for more men and levered the stone onto its side. Below it, Redcared lay dead in a shallow depression not deep enough to let him live. The Cagot boy had died instantly.*

*Ignoring advice, Lady Margaret, Father Romero and Jacobi came back into the cave and the others joined them. When the dust settled, it was Jacobi's suggestion that they should replace the slab of rock and let this be his grandson's tomb. Pierre was anxious to remove Redcared's satchel containing the second part of the Manuscript but he glanced at Lady Margaret and saw her shake her head. The second part of the Manuscript, for which Redcared had been responsible, would be buried with him.*

*Father Romero consigned Redcared's mortal remains to his tomb by the rites of his Church, but his grief was no ritual response to the death of a fellow Christian. He had forgotten the taste of tears and now he knew his were real. Lady Margaret threw a handful of dust on the body as they began to lower the stone and Alfonso turned his back. His grief was the anguish of a father for his son. Jacobi's sorrow was the most profound of all. He stood erect, his body shaking with each sob. He was proud of his grandson. The boy had been squire to the first nobleman he had felt was worthy of the title. He turned to Alfonso and grasped him by the hands.*

*'He saved my life.' Alfonso said quietly, 'Not once, but twice and I will never forget him.'*

*On the way down the valley to the Cagot village they stopped at a little group of stone buildings with slate roofs, on the track which led across the mountains to France. Alfonso knew that this had been a Commanderie of the Knights Templar at the time of the suppression of the Order. He had thought it was now derelict but Jacobi insisted that he should meet the old monk who had been sent there as caretaker and was now virtually a recluse.*

*The monk was a member of the Order of St John, the Hospitallers, to whom the Templar properties in Aragon had been ceded. Jacobi knew the monk but when he tried to introduce Alfonso to him, the Hospitaller held up a hand to stop him. He already knew Alfonso's name. He was aware that Don Alfonso had been a Templar Knight. He understood why this band of pilgrims from Navarre were in his valley high in the Pyrenees.*

*Two young novices brought wine, bread and water for the party and the Hospitaller took Alfonso and Jacobi into a quiet corner. He told them that after the battle in the Esera, the soldiers who had attacked Alfonso's party had called with him on their way out of the mountains. There had been a priest with them who argued continually with the men. Months later, the priest had returned by himself and had tried to make an ally of the Hospitaller.*

*One evening, when he had drunk too much red wine, they had talked far into the night. The priest had spoken of Alfonso and his past as a Templar. In hushed tones he had described the magnificent Icon which Alfonso carried in a leather satchel wherever he travelled. He told the Hospitaller that, after the battle, he had hidden on the mountainside, watching and waiting for a sight of Alfonso and the Cagot boy. Eventually they had emerged from the cave where they had been hiding. They had been accompanied by a dog which had belonged to one of the soldiers who was missing after the battle. Don Alfonso had not been carrying the satchel. He must have left it in the cave.*

*The priest had been too weak to follow them over the mountains and had no wish to share the value of the Icon with the soldiers, now their captain was dead. It would be easier to leave the Icon in the cave and return for it later. Now he was back on his way to the cave. The Icon would be his to find and keep. He would take it back to Morella and present it to the Bishop for the glory of God. He promised he would call to show it to the Hospitaller on his way down.*

*Next day, while the Hospitaller watched from the doorway of the Commanderie, the priest had returned, but in spite of his promise he had not called to show him the Icon. And now, across his shoulder, the priest had a leather satchel slung from a stout leather strap.*

*Before he left, Alfonso made a donation in gold coin to aid the repair of the Commanderie. The Hospitaller was deeply grateful but wondered why Don Alfonso smiled as he passed over the money. He was not to know that this was a sum similar to that given to Alfonso when Acre Castle had fallen to the Saracens. The money had been to pay the expenses of returning to France with the Holy Icon but he had worked his passage and it had never been used. Now, a proper settlement had been made.*

*When they reached the Cagot village where they would stay for the night, Alfonso asked Le Poing to prepare a burial feast to honour his faithful squire, Redcared. As they sat at tables in the open air, Don Alfonso made an offer to Jacobi. Should this Cagot community ever find themselves persecuted, or aggrieved or harmed in any serious way, they could migrate to his lands in Navarre. There, they would be welcomed. They would be given land and helped to settle. They would have an honourable place amongst his people.*

*At the end of the feast Lady Margaret rose to her feet. She spoke with her hand on her husband's shoulder. The Icon had been their Holy Relic, she said. It had carried Don Alfonso from the killing grounds of the Holy Land, across the Mediterranean Sea. It had saved his life when Philip the Fair had killed his comrades. It had brought him to her home in Scotland and back to the lands of his father in Navarre.*

*It had brought her a husband and two fine children. He who had the Holy Icon now, would find it was a scourge, not a talisman. But now she was certain. No more lives must be lost in its pursuit. It had guided their pilgrimage to the great Cathedral under the mountain and, even though the shelf was empty when they came, its power was with them even more surely without its presence. It was time to leave it be.*

*Don Alfonso smiled. He lifted her on to the table and raised a great hurrah. She was right, he said, still laughing. His wife was always right.*

*In the morning Alfonso set off again from the Cagot village for Navarre. His new squire, Redcared's brother Peyrolet, led the company. His master followed on his half-Arab mare, prancing now she was on the way. Lady Margaret was flanked by Father Romero and Pierre. At the back Morag rode with Le Poing, the men at arms and the pack mules.*

*And circling the party, loping between the horses like a young wolf, Valor kept his vigil. He ranged back behind the mules, keeping them up to the mark without a sound and finally settled at his master's stirrup thong.*

## THE TEMPLAR TREASURE

Ramón always enjoyed Winter at home in Mont L'ours-les Cascades, but in this particular year he was glad to feel the early approach of Spring. He decided to send out the printed text of the Manuscript before the Cult met in April and was confident that it would ensure a full attendance.

He rang Don Carlos Conde Parrado, the most senior member of the Cult and asked him to come to Mont L'ours to stay for a few days. At dinner on the first night, they discussed the planning of the Cult's expedition to the Cathedral cave with Anamar and Raoul.

It was clear that the great cave to which Anamar's explorations had led, was the same cavern where Alfonso and Redcared had hidden after the battle in the Esera valley. The location of the Cathedral of the Cult, the first mystery of the Cult, had been solved. The Manuscript had also shown that the skeleton under the stone had indeed been Redcared and they had rescued the second part of the Manuscript which had been in his keeping.

But they were no closer to finding the Holy Icon. In the morning Ramón gave Don Carlos a copy of the Postscript to the Manuscript. Anamar and Raoul were familiar with this text, but none of the other members had seen it since it had been recovered from the Decuré family.

By the time they met for dinner on the second evening Don Carlos had read the Postscript twice and when Ramón proposed that they should form a search party to look for the Holy Icon, he smiled. He had already guessed that this was why he had been invited to Mont L'ours.

'When do you propose we go on this quest, Don Ramón?' he said quietly, 'I could be ready to leave in the morning.' They all laughed. Don Carlos was retired and had been a widower for ten years. One telephone call to his housekeeper was all that was required.

To the surprise of the others, Raoul asked to be excused. Later he told Anamar that he thought the quest might take weeks not days, and it would be unfair of him to be away from his beloved Celestine for too long.

Two days later their quest was underway. They would drive South, following, where possible, le Chemin des Bonshommes, the traditional Cathar escape route from the Inquisition. It would take them across the

Pyrenees and through Catalunya to Morella in the heart of the hills of El Maestrazgo.

They would travel by car, in Ramón's Citroen saloon. He and Anamar would share the driving, but she had insisted on taking the first stage over the Pyrenees. The front-wheel drive and the clever engineering of the suspension were ideal for the tight bends in the mountains.

Beyond the Spanish frontier town of Puigcerda, they took the motor road to LLeida and stopped for the night at an inn in Valderrobres. In the morning they continued towards Morella and were captivated by the town when it appeared ahead of them. It was on a huge rocky knoll, a thousand metres above sea-level. It totally dominated the wild and rugged hill country of El Maestrazgo.

This medieval fortress city was enclosed by a formidable wall around the base of the knoll. At the summit was the bastion of a well-nigh impregnable castle. Below, and between it and the walls, the town was packed around the hill in tiers.

They drove through the gates of the wall, parked the car and booked rooms in a small hotel. After lunch it was good exercise to climb the steep steps between the tiers of transverse streets to a level just below the castle.

At the church of Santa Maria la Mayor, Don Carlos spoke to a cleric to enquire about early records. The young novice was delighted to have an excuse to break with routine and insisted on taking them on a tour of the church. This was the famous 'arch-priest's church' and a most inspiring visit. Anamar was fascinated by the stuccoed alabaster of the Old Testament figures on the spiral staircase leading to the choir. Don Carlos was intrigued by a huge flattened arch below the choir, which had almost no curve at all. But Ramón rushed them through the visit and encouraged the young novice to take them through dark corridors to the scriptorium. There he decided to be frank.

'We seek information about a priest who served here in the early part of the 14th century,' he said, 'He was called Father Sanchez de Pallaresa and he is mentioned in an ancient family manuscript.'

The novice was intrigued. He conferred with an older colleague whose black, low-crowned, broad-brimmed hat seemed to indicate a position of authority. Together they consulted huge, dusty volumes of hand-written lists. Ramón, Anamar and Carlos watched and waited. The records seemed complete but the earliest related to the latter part of the 14th century, fifty years after Father Sanchez would have served here.

Another conference between the two clerics revived their hopes. There was a museum at the Monastery of San Francisco. They should try there. The young novice set off at speed. He marched out of Santa Maria and up the hill to San Francisco. The others trotted after him. Most of the monastery buildings were in ruins but a museum had been created in a group of rooms to one side. A small man in a monk's habit and sandals welcomed the visitors. When the young cleric explained the nature of their quest and mentioned the name of Father Sanchez de Pallaresa, he smiled broadly and beckoned them to follow. He led the way into an inner sanctum.

Using a rickety ladder he retrieved a book from the top-most shelf and placed it on a table.

'One hundred and fifty years ago,' he said conspiratorially, 'A Franciscan compiled this book.' He winked. 'It is probably the most intriguing volume in our library. It tells the stories of some of our most interesting, some might say scandalous, predecessors.'

He beckoned to Ramón and his friends to come closer and began to whisper.

'Let us say, it chronicles the lives of the most notorious clerics of Morella in medieval times and I can tell you that your Father Sanchez merited inclusion.'

The two clerics looked surprised and the one in the black hat moved closer so that he could read from the book. The monk raised a hand to stop him and insisted that the priests join Ramón and his friends at the other side of the table. He was enjoying himself.

'My problem is that this book is for the eyes of members of my order only. However, I am familiar with the story of Father Sanchez and you may ask me any questions you wish. I will answer if a reply is appropriate.'

The novice brought chairs and they all sat down. The monk opened the book and found the right page. Ramón spoke first.

'Father Sanchez is mentioned in a family manuscript. We would like to know something of his life here in Morella.'

The monk looked up from the book, his face serene.

'He was a senior priest here, a man of great ability, but infamously known as "Padre Sanchez el Marido, Father Sanchez, the Husband". He was born in the Pallaresa valley of the Pyrenees and served as a priest there. In those remote mountains the priests sometimes followed civil law when it suited and ignored the rules of the Church. Father Sanchez married a local woman by a civil ceremony and when he came to Morella she came with him.' The monk paused and consulted the book.

'During his time here did he present the Church with a holy picture?' Anamar was surprised that she was asking the question. The monk inclined his head to indicate that this was a question worth asking.

'Yes he did. It was a magnificent Holy Icon, slightly damaged but a wonderful acquisition. There was a great ceremony and the Bishop dedicated it to the glory of God. But his Grace died soon after and the new man disapproved of Father Sanchez's marital arrangements. He decreed that Padre Sanchez el Marido be sent back in disgrace to the wilds of the Pyrenees. When Father Sanchez left Morella, his "wife" went with him, and the Holy Icon disappeared, never to be seen again.'

It was disappointing but, at least, they had another lead. The monk politely refused Ramón's invitation to dinner that evening, but the priest in the black hat and the young novice accepted gratefully. It was a simple meal but the clerics were good company and talked exuberantly about Morella and its history.

The priest in the black hat explained that the construction of the 'arch-priest's church', Santa Maria La Mayor, had been started in the middle of the 13th century but had proved to be difficult on such a steep slope. Levelling work had been necessary to a depth of sixty-five metres, with a retaining wall two metres thick, and, although building work was not completed for another thirty years, the church had been opened in 1311. Ramón was engrossed. This was precisely the time of Father Sanchez's service here as a priest. The priest in the black hat continued.

At the end of the 13th century the people of the town had undertaken to build the San Francisco Monastery at their own expense and had agreed on an annual subsidy to the monks to buy clothing, food and wine. For their part, the monks were obliged to take confession, to preach to the people and to fulfil all their religious duties.

The young novice's eyes twinkled. He looked at the priest in the black hat, wondering if he dare tell the tale of the miracle performed by San Vincente Ferrer. The priest smiled and nodded as if he could read his colleague's mind. Every tourist deserved to hear the story of San Vincente's miraculous powers. The young novice lowered his voice.

'San Vincente visited Morella,' he said quietly, 'He was to be fed at a house on the Calle de la Virgin de Villavana but the woman chosen to entertain him had nothing suitable for him to eat. She decided to chop up her child to make a stew and serve it to the Saint. To her amazement, San Vincente not only refused the meal but performed a phenomenal miracle by restoring the child to life.'

The young novice glanced nervously at the priest in the black hat. Having said his piece, he was suddenly uncertain of the moral of the story. The miracle was a wonderful illustration of the power of the famous saint but what did it say about the humanity of the devout people of Morella?

But his superior smiled reassuringly. He had enjoyed the meal and the wine and this was the best company he had shared for years. He wished Ramón and his friends success on their quest and secretly wished that he could have gone with them.

When they left Morella next morning, Anamar wanted to see the Cathar village, mentioned in the Manuscript, which had become the home of the Ranisolles family. They turned off into mountain terrain, wild, barren, inhospitable. The road was poor, unsurfaced, badly in need of repairs. Ramón drove slowly up into the desolate hills. The village marked the end of the road and, although there were ruins of twenty or thirty homes, only three families remained.

The men were away and none of the women had ever heard of the Cathars or the family name of Ranisolles. There was neither shop nor bar. The school was closed and boarded up. The church was in ruins, its roof caved in, its bell tower fallen. The ground which once had been tilled by the hand of man was being eroded by the blazing sun and the wind, taken back into a hard land where only thorns and rock would survive.

When they left, the road skirted around a ravine about twelve or fifteen kilometres from the village. Anamar was driving and suddenly stopped the car. Could this be the place mentioned in the Manuscript where Redcared saved Alfonso's life? And there it was, perched on a rise, an untidy pile of pale yellow stones, the washed-out colour of the earth. This was the cairn which still marked the start of the Pilgrimage of the Cathars at the end of their journey.

They rebuilt the cairn to waist height and paid their respects to Don Alfonso's party and the Ranisolles family, far more profoundly than ever they could have managed in the village.

It was late in the afternoon of the next day when they arrived in the Pyrenees, where Father Sanchez had been born and to where he had been sent in disgrace at the end of his ministry.

They stopped in the town of Sort at the foot of the Pallaresa. This was once one of the great valleys on the Spanish side of the mountains which had a measure of independence. Each was governed by a seigneurial family. Some had a form of currency of their own, others issued their own stamps, all had their own civil laws. Now, only Andorra retained its freedom.

While Don Carlos went to find the priest, Ramón and Anamar explored a small privately-owned museum which was also a book shop. The priest was not able to help, there were no Church records available before the 19th century. However, Ramón was able to buy maps of a scale which showed Father Sanchez's home village and the hamlets nearby.

Anamar found a booklet on a shelf at the back of the shop, listing all the Romanesque churches of the area. The proprietor smiled when she wanted to buy. He was the author, he said modestly, and had plenty of spare copies. He laughed aloud and explained that he had sold only five copies in the past five years.

After a night in the village of Llavorsi it was uphill again in the morning. They left the main valley and climbed to the North-East on a poor gravel road. The banks rose steeply on either side. The fields were carefully cultivated and every few kilometres there was another village, all with similar sounding names, Arlan, Acrós, Asing. The road was poor now, rising towards the Pica d'Estats, the highest peak in Catalunya.

A battered sign by the roadside announced their arrival in Father Sanchez's home village, Alvertos, at the head of the road. To the East, two rock peaks dominated the village which was perched on a ledge below the scree and above the fields and grazing. The church was 19th century and it was dedicated to Sant Andrue, while the name listed in the book of churches, which Anamar had bought in Sort, was Sant Vicenç.

An old man appeared from behind a wall as if he had been watching and awaiting their arrival. He shook his head when they asked for the church of Sant Vicenç and then he began to laugh. He beckoned them to follow and led the way past the church of Sant Andrue, through the village to the only copse of trees in this high valley. He leapt over the wall like a mountain goat and burrowed his way through the bushes.

The ruins of a Romanesque church stood in what had once been a clearing, now being rapidly reclaimed by the vegetation.

'Sant Vicenç!' the old man waved his hand dramatically and made the sign of the cross.

The bell tower had collapsed. Part of the roof had fallen in. The walls were breached. A spindly tree grew up through the slabs in front of the door. Creepers festooned the walls and what was left of the roof.

They scrambled inside over piles of cut stones. It was dark, damp and cold. The wooden steps leading up to the pulpit were rotted away. The baptismal font was intact but filled to the brim with dirty water. The stations of the cross were only just identifiable by location.

Anamar, Ramón and Carlos all saw it at the same time. It hung on what remained of a wall, between two stations of the cross and directly under a part of the roof which was still intact. It was a picture draped with cobwebs, dust lying on dust, stained by water trickles. Its silver and gold inlays were as dull as pewter, neglected for centuries. Still embedded in one corner of the wooden base was a broken arrow shaft.

It was the Holy Icon. No one could speak. Carlos's face was pinched and pale. Ramón felt sick with excitement. They had found the Templar's Treasure. The second secret of the Cult had been revealed. The old man watched in awe as these strangers stared in amazement at what was just a miserable old picture, dirty, damaged, worthless.

Anamar alone knew what to do. She lifted the Icon down, rested it on a rock and used a handkerchief to lift the cobwebs and brush away the dust as gently as she could manage.

The local priest appeared behind them. The old man's wife had seen him return and told him that there were three strangers in the ruins of the old church with her man. Ramón recovered his composure and told him about the mention of the Icon in his family papers. He offered to buy it. The padre could name his price.

The priest was young, very recently ordained. He laughed.

'Take it,' he said grandly, 'An old and dirty picture like this could never have a place in our new church. Your family was once entrusted with its keeping and we have ruined it by neglect. Had it depicted the Madonna, or a Saint, or Christ himself, it would have been transferred to Sant Andrue when the new church was built. It's yours again. Treat it well.'

Later, Ramón would sell some of the valuables in the archive trunk and return here to arrange the funding of a project with the priest. It would be designed to help the whole village. But, for now, it was a joy to wrap the Holy Icon in one of his shirts and take it home to Mont L'ours.

Raoul wept when he saw the Holy Icon. His tears were not only for the state of this priceless treasure but for his own absence when it was found. He set to work with the skill of an expert restorer and allowed no one else to see it for the three days it took him to finish the job.

Ramón had the Icon hung on the wall of his study. Doña Marie, Madame Mons and Jules were invited to a private viewing. Ramón had already decided that it would not be mentioned to any of the other members of the Cult, for the present.

The meeting of the Cult was held in early April in Aulus-les-Bains at Monsieur Paul Huguet's hotel. There was a full attendance and only two items of business - a reading of the Postscript to the Manuscript and the arrangements for the Cult's Expedition to the Cathedral.

Raoul read the Postscript aloud and there were attentive nods as the members followed Lady Margaret's Pilgrimage and heard of the death of Redcared and the fate of the Holy Icon. The Postscript made sense of the Templar Manuscript and brought to a close the story of these years of Don Alfonso's life.

When the reading ended, Raoul was commended for his good work on the translation. Ramón presented him with a silver Templar cross from the archive trunk. He saw a tear in the corner of the young man's eye as he hung the cross around his neck. He presented two more crosses to Paul Huguet and Raymond Bodelot, who had retrieved the Postscript document stolen by Marc Decuré.

Don Carlos proposed that the Cult should have, as its posthumous patron, Don Alfonso Barriano, Marqués de Barra and it was passed by acclamation.

It was agreed that the Cult's expedition to the Cathedral cavern would take place at the end of June. They would meet on the last Sunday in that month at an hotel in the town of Benasque, spend the night there and go up to the caves in the morning. Everyone wanted to go. Monsieur Paul would contact the hotel to book rooms. Alfonso would arrange for the hire of horses, so that they could ride up the valley from the bridge above Benasque.

The meeting ended just after noon and the excitement at lunch might have been that of a school group, planning an adventure in the great outdoors.

They assembled on the appointed Sunday, all wearing their medallions of the soaring dove. Monsieur Paul had arrived early to check the rooms. Ramón and Anamar shared a double, and there were twin-bedded rooms for the rest of the party.

Early next morning they drove the fifteen kilometres to the bridge above the town, where the unsurfaced road continued as a mountain track. Two grooms, sworn to secrecy, were waiting with the horses and in half an hour they were mounted and on their way. Some were inexperienced riders and the pace was slow. Ramón asked Anamar and Jules to ride ahead with one of the grooms to check that the entrance to the caves was still passable and he gave a large rucksack to Jules before they rode on.

On the way up, Ramón pointed out the landmarks mentioned in the Manuscript to the members who had not been on the previous expedition. Above them was Maladetta, the Evil One. They stopped at the Trou de Toro, the Cavern of the Bull, where the river fell in a great waterfall into the bowels of the earth and where one of Don Alfonso's soldiers had been thrown to his death during the battle of the Esera.

Towards the head of the Esera valley they left their horses with the grooms and climbed into the ravine above. They followed the single file path up through the rocks, where Don Alfonso and Redcared had made a stand to fight the unknown enemy.

Above the narrow part of the gorge Anamar and Jules were waiting below the snow-line, at the site of the camp on the previous expedition. The water was boiling on an open fire and coffee was ready. Lunch was taken early, but although no one was hungry, they needed to eat. They might be underground for hours.

Up at the big boulder Ramón recited the final clues discovered by Anamar,

**'And at our hallowed sanctuary's door,**
**It is not enough to kneel and pray.**
**To lie and writhe is the only way.'**

He invited those who had not yet been inside the cave to take their torches and go first. Monsieur Paul led the way. As instructed, he knelt beside the rock, lay flat on his back and wriggled sideways under the stone. Father Brian followed, finding it something of a tight squeeze, Monsieur Jean-Pierre was next and finally Doctor Vincente.

The others waited for a few minutes to let the vanguard get their bearings and then took their turn. Their torches threw shadows on the walls of the first cave. Ramón led the way and they followed in single file. In the second chamber he filled the pewter tankard at the well and took a little drink. It was passed back down the line to let everyone sip the clear cold water. At the back, Don Carlos replaced the tankard on its ledge before he moved on.

They filed through the cavern of the stalactites without a word and climbed into the small cave with its inscriptions and symbols. At the top of the steep ramp of boulders, Ramón stopped at the narrow cleft through which they must all pass.

'We will take it in turn to squeeze through this slit,' he said, his light illuminating the fissure and his voice echoing back down the ramp.

He led the way between the rocks, pulling a small sack after him. Father Brian was next. As he saw Ramón's bag disappearing into the crack he felt as if he might never see his friend again. He entered the fissure side-ways on, as Ramón had done, but his girth jammed in the crack.

'I'm stuck!' he yelled to Jules, 'I can neither go forward nor back.' Only his left arm was visible. He dropped his priest's bag and his fingers wiggled and strained for a hand to grasp.

'For the love of God, Jules, pull me back!' The muffled roar of his disembodied voice was panic-stricken.

Jules gripped a rock on either side of the crack, reached into it with one leg until his foot rested on Father Brian's hip. With one violent thrust he pushed with all his strength and the priest shot through the hole into the unknown beyond. Father Brian stumbled, fell and rolled over. He sat up and rubbed his chest and abdomen, scraped by the rocks. Ramón helped him to his feet and he found himself in the faint light of a vast cavern.

'Holy Mother of God,' was all he could manage to say and it was a prayer, not an exclamation.

The others followed, the next man bringing the priest's bag with him. Jules waited until the end in case someone else might find it difficult. Later, those who had not been in the caves before would admit that Father Brian's experience had been most encouraging. If he could make it, anyone could.

When Jules emerged from the crack, they were all through and those who had come first had adapted to the dim light. There were two lighted candles on a large rock in the middle of the cavern. There were two more, set in golden candlesticks at the ends of a natural shelf on the cave wall behind. Between them, perched on the rocky ledge, was a religious picture. It glowed as bright as candlelight. A golden bird soared above a golden chalice on a background of blue. The picture was inlaid with images in silver filigree, a Cathar cross, two knights on a single horse, the Templar symbol of poverty, a knight in a white cloak with a red cross, standing erect in battle armour with his sword at rest.

Precious stones decorated the images. The gold of the soaring bird and the chalice was real metal, not gilding paint. Near the bottom of the picture a broken arrow remained impaled in the wood of the base. It was the shaft meant to kill Don Alfonso.

In a top corner was a picture of a saint. It had been hidden under a layer of grime but, as Raoul had cleaned the dirt away, he had recognised it as an image of St. Euphemia, martyred by pagans at the beginning of the 4th century. He and Ramón had checked the reference books and found that the saint's relics were reputed to have been possessed by the Templars at Acre Castle just before its fall.

This was the Templar Treasure, the Holy Icon.

Ramón smiled. Some of the members must have wondered why he had given the extra rucksack to Jules when he and Anamar had gone on ahead. They had made good use of their time and ensured that the Icon was in place before the rest arrived.

The members moved towards the great stone led by Father Brian, anxious now to say Mass. Don Carlos, Messieurs Raymond and Jean-Pierre followed him and knelt down before the altar. Doctor Vincente and

Monsieur Paul had long since allowed their faith in the Church to lapse and, although for them this was not the sublime religious moment it might be for others, they were both aware of a strange mystical connection with this place.

Raoul kept to himself. He went down on his knees. Tears came easily and he cried for joy. It had been his skill which had restored this beautiful Icon from a stained and filthy fate.

Jules, perhaps the only one whose faith was unreasoned, unquestioning and almost forgotten, its rituals easily avoidable but never ignored, followed Don Carlos and knelt behind him.

For Ramón it was as if his whole life had come together in one sublime moment.

Anamar found herself wondering if any of the members who had been here before were thinking of the cave lined with fragments of coloured glass, pieces of mirror, semi-precious stones, where she had moved a single candle in a circle and made it seem as if the cave was spinning around their heads.

Had it been here before Don Alfonso came? Was it a secret Cagot shrine?

But that was for another time.

Her childhood on her knees was tugging at the sleeve of her shirt, bringing her closer to the altar stone. She let herself slip down to the cold rocks of the floor, her hands together before her face. She thanked God, smiled to herself and took Ramón's hand. Next time I come here, she promised herself, I'll bring the children and Ramón too, of course, and we'll take them to see the cave of a thousand twinkling, spinning lights.